Swept Away

Other books in the Quilts of Love Series

Beyond the Storm
Carolyn Zane

A Wild Goose Chase Christmas
Jennifer AlLee

Path of Freedom
Jennifer Hudson Taylor

For Love of Eli
Loree Lough

Threads of Hope
Christa Allan

A Healing Heart
Angela Breidenbach

A Heartbeat Away
S. Dionne Moore

Pieces of the Heart
Bonnie S. Calhoun

Pattern for Romance
Carla Olson Gade

Raw Edges
Sandra D. Bricker

The Christmas Quilt
Vannetta Chapman

Aloha Rose
Lisa Carter

Tempest's Course
Lynette Sowell

Scraps of Evidence
Barbara Cameron

A Sky Without Stars
Linda S. Clare

Maybelle in Stitches
Joyce Magnin

A Stitch and a Prayer
Eva Gibson

A Promise in Pieces
Emily Wierenga

Rival Hearts
Tara Randel

A Grand Design
Amber Stockton

Hidden in the Stars
Robin Caroll

Masterpiece Marriage
Gina Welborn

Quilted by Christmas
Jodie Bailey

A Stitch in Crime
Cathy Elliott

SWEPT AWAY

Quilts of Love Series

Laura V. Hilton and Cindy Loven

Nashville

Swept Away

ISBN-13: 978-1-4267-7362-4

Published by Abingdon Press, P.O. Box 801, Nashville, TN 37202
www.abingdonpress.com

Published in association with the Steve Laube Literary Agency

Quilts of Love Macro Editor: Teri Wilhelms

Library of Congress Cataloging-in-Publication Data

Hilton, Laura V., 1963-
Swept away / Laura Hilton and Cindy Loven.
pages ; cm. — (Quilts of love series)
ISBN 978-1-4267-7362-4 (softcoverr)
1. Quilting—Fiction. I. Loven, Cindy. II. Title.
PS3608.I4665S94 2014
813'.6—dc23

2014027913

Printed in the United States of America

1 2 3 4 5 6 7 8 9 10 / 19 18 17 16 15 14

1

Sara Jane Morgan gasped for breath, scanning the crowded pathways. Everyone showed up for the Heritage Festival, which was good for the artists and vendors, but bad for her. Especially considering . . .

No. She couldn't voice her concerns. At least not yet. But losing a loved one in this mob would cause anyone to panic. This was why mothers kept their toddlers locked securely in strollers and older children attached to harnesses with straps.

But one couldn't exactly fasten a grandmother to a leash. And Sara Jane, being a grown woman, shouldn't be having a panic attack.

She pulled in a shaking breath and forced herself to calm down. She could handle this. Stepping to the side of the paved walkway, she let a woman pushing a double stroller pass, then a man driving a motorized wheelchair. She feigned interest in the open-air tent beside her. A display of corncob dolls. People still made them?

Well, this was the Appalachians. There were tourists here from all over the country who expected to find mountain handcrafts for sale.

She merged into the crowd and peeked into the next tent, making sure to get a look at the people inside. This one showcased CDs and DVDs by Appalachian musicians—or rather, one particular group. Pretending to shop while scanning the customers, she lifted a case off the rack by the entrance and looked at the picture. Banjos, played by guys in overalls. She put it back.

Another booth held pocketknives and hunting, fishing, and utility knives. Grandma wouldn't be here. Mostly men anyway. She moved on.

The tent next to it held screen-printed t-shirts . . .

Panic filled her again. Grandma had wandered further than she expected. How long had she been missing before Sara Jane realized she'd disappeared? She pushed her way past a few people holding a conversation in the middle of the sidewalk. She caught a glimpse of a uniformed Boy Scout. Weren't they supposed to help people? He disappeared into the throng before she caught up to him.

Sara Jane went on to the next display. Oh. Wow. Brightly colored quilts. This was where she would have expected to find Grandma. She loved to quilt and belonged to the Christian Women's group at church. But Grandma wasn't with the women oohing and ahhing over the quilts.

Maybe. A gray-haired woman stood off to the back, head bowed as she studied the stitching. No, she wasn't Grandma. Her hair was a different cut, and she wore a green t-shirt and a blue jean skirt. Sara Jane would come back and check this tent again later, in case Grandma made her way here.

The next tent was completely enclosed, the canvas doors tied open with twine. Sara Jane poked her head in, ready to rush on. The tent was void of people except for two, a man and Grandma.

Expelling a breath she hadn't realized she held, Sara Jane grasped the edge of the tent door and forced herself to look around.

Grandma was in here. With brooms. Whoever knew there were so many ways to make a broom?

The man behind the table looked as bushy as his wares. His shaggy brown beard hung down to his collar, and a rumpled button-up shirt draped over his blue jeans. His hair was almost as long as his beard. He looked up as she entered. His eyes reminded her of dark chocolate.

Grandma stood beside the scruffy-looking man, holding a piece of paper, saying words Sara Jane couldn't catch due to the sudden rush of blood in her ears. She turned. "Oh, there you are, Sara Jane. I hired Andrew to do some odd jobs around my house since I'm thinking of selling. Doesn't he have the cutest business card?" She held out the cardstock.

Sara Jane took it and gave it a cursory glance. *Starving artist/pay the bills handyman* in bold, colorful print topped the card. Andrew Stevenson. Followed by a phone number, and a picture of a bright-red tool box. She handed it back to Grandma. "Adorable."

The adjective didn't apply to the owner of the card.

"Grandma, don't you think you'd rather hire someone we actually know to do the repairs?"

"Sara Jane! I raised you to treat people better."

Drew Stevenson tried to control his grin as the older woman tore into the younger one.

Rude or not, he couldn't tear his gaze away from Sara Jane. She was . . . stunning. But so not his type. A woman like her would never look twice at a man like him. Not as if he'd want her to.

She had long, dark hair, the color of espresso coffee. He couldn't see her eyes, hidden behind sunglasses, but he imagined they'd be brown, like her hair. Or maybe hazel. She wore tailored jeans, undoubtedly designer, the type with a permanent crease up the front middle of the leg. A fitted blouse in a shade of a pinkish-orange reminded him of peaches. The top two or three buttons were unhooked, giving a tantalizing glimpse of . . .

He glanced away. He had no right to look. Her husband . . . he scanned her hand. Not married. Her boyfriend wouldn't appreciate another man ogling his girl.

Her gaze skittered over his brooms with a dismissive look, the same one she'd bestowed upon him. As if he weren't worthy of consideration—either as a broom maker or a man. His passion and art deserved some appreciation. Irritation ate at him. His hand tightened around the handle of the broom closest to him.

"Sorry, Grandma, and you too, Mr. uh . . . sir, but I don't think . . ."

He ranked so low on her importance scale she didn't remember his name. Oh. That hurt. He clenched his jaw. He refused to think of the time he asked a woman out and she laughed in his face, as if he'd been telling a joke.

The older woman stiffened. "I don't care what you think. It's my decision, Sara Jane. My house. And my right to . . ."

Drew straightened his spine and turned away from them, rearranging a display as he tried not to listen to the animated conversation. It wasn't too hard when other people drifted into the tent.

"Oooh, look at these brooms! Isn't this a cute little one? What's it used for?"

He looked at the middle-aged woman in front of him. "It's called a turkey wing broom. It's used for brushing off countertops and tables, or other surfaces."

"It's so cute. How much do you charge for it? Do you do custom orders? I like pink, and try to keep everything as pink as possible around my house."

He worked his mouth a second before he found his voice. "Pink. Yes, ma'am, I do custom orders." But pink? "It'd be slightly more expensive, though."

"Oh, it's okay." The woman whipped a pink cell phone out of her pocket. "Let me take a picture of you with this broom. You look like a real mountain man."

Sara Jane's mouth dried even as tears burned her eyes. Grandma intended to sell her house? Since when? She'd never mentioned it in all the conversations they'd had recently.

Putting the Appalachian-style log cabin Grandpa had built Grandma as a new bride aside, how could Grandma think of hiring someone who looked like this man? Didn't he own a razor? He looked as if he came straight out of the wilderness, like a John the Baptist wannabe. Maybe he ate locusts and honey.

Her stomach clenched. By the looks of him, he could be a mass murderer, with the beard to keep people from recognizing his picture on the most wanted list. She peered at him again. He looked familiar. He'd probably been on a recent episode of *America's Most Wanted*.

He did make nice-looking brooms, assuming he'd actually done the work, but it didn't matter in the least. She couldn't allow Grandma to hire him.

Besides, Grandma kept hiring incompetent people, like the last one Sara Jane discovered stuffing sterling silver candleholders in his toolbox.

Maybe if she changed the subject. . . . Sara Jane gently took her grandmother by the elbow and steered her farther away from the table. "You scared me out of my skin, taking off like that. What were you thinking?"

Grandma frowned and shook her head. "I didn't take off. You were the one who wasn't paying attention. You obviously didn't hear me when I said I wanted to see what else was out there. Not everyone is interested in looking at books about Daniel Boone and forts and what types of Indians were native to these hills."

Okay, that'd been about the time Grandma had gone missing.

"I didn't know you were thinking of selling your house. We'll discuss it later. If you need a handyman, why don't you hire your nice neighbor, Charlie Jones, to work on the house for you? We don't know this man."

Grandma made an unfeminine snort and rolled her eyes. "I don't need a babysitter. Have you ever considered you're smothering me?"

Sara Jane gasped. Smothering? How could Grandma think she was smothering her?

"Besides, Charlie Jones can't work on my house. He died a year ago." Grandma folded her arms and stared Sara Jane down.

Sara Jane tried hard not to sigh. Her handy excuse to get Grandma away from the John the Baptist impersonator disappeared and made her look foolish in the process. And since when did Grandma get so argumentative? It had to be something to do with old age. She'd read something about it in a magazine article somewhere.

"Grandma . . ."

"Sara Jane, I like this young man and I intend to hire him. It's my house and my decision. And that's final." Grandma punctuated it with a decisive nod. "He'll be there Monday at eight."

2

Monday morning, Drew held his buzzing electric razor and stared at his reflection in the mirror. Should he—or shouldn't he?

He scowled at his image. It shouldn't matter what Sara Jane Morgan thought. Her grandmother hired him. And he wasn't attracted to the uptight, modern type. So why was he suddenly obsessing over his looks?

Drew unplugged the razor, turned the bathroom light off, and headed for the kitchen in his small rental house to find something for breakfast. He might have one toaster pastry left. His coffeemaker was preprogrammed to turn on automatically.

After feeding his dog and letting her out, he poured a cup of java and opened his cupboard door, reaching for the discounted brand of toaster pastries he'd bought. The package lifted light in his hand. He peeked in. Empty. He tossed the box in the trashcan and frowned at the bare shelf. He'd have to go grocery shopping on the way home tonight. He'd go through a drive-through on the way to Mrs. Morgan's house this morning. No, on second thought, he'd go in and order the big breakfast—pancakes, scrambled eggs, and whatever else came with it. No telling what kind of handyman chores she'd have him do and he'd need his strength.

He raked his fingers through his long, tangled hair.

Especially if her granddaughter was there.

Sari scratched her head. There'd been something she planned to do today. Something to keep Sara Jane present, yet away from her new handyman. She wanted them to get acquainted, but didn't want her granddaughter harassing him to the point where he'd quit, like the last man she'd hired.

But it didn't matter. Nor did the fact Sara Jane had done such an amateurish job painting the bathroom that Sari needed to find someone else to redo the task. What mattered was the chore she'd had in mind. . . . If only she could remember what it'd been. She should've written it down the moment she'd thought of it, especially since lately, she'd been forgetting more things than she remembered.

She whispered a prayer God would help her remember, and started walking around inside her house. It might help. Maybe a hot shower would jar her memory. She headed for the bathroom, when something clicked, like a door latching shut. She stopped and listened. If it was Sara Jane, she'd call out. If it wasn't . . . Sari would need to call the police.

A phone. Now, where'd she leave it?

"Grandma, where are you?"

Sari sagged in relief. It was Sara Jane. "Just fixin' to take my shower, dear. Have you had breakfast?" No point in worrying her granddaughter with her bad memory.

"No. I'll go ahead and make some coffee and oatmeal. Then we can start our search in the sewing room."

Ah, that's what she'd forgotten. She'd planned to clean and search the sewing room for the ballad quilt blocks she'd started years ago. It was something her grandmother told her about. For centuries, Appalachian women created quilts depicting the many folk songs popular in their area. Sari had picked *The Ballad of Pretty Saro* for her quilt, since Saro, Sarah, Sari, and Sara were all names in the family for generations. She'd been thrilled when her son and daughter-in-law decided to name their baby girl Sara Jane, keeping the tradition alive.

Sari finished her shower, then went out to the kitchen as Sara Jane placed buttered toast on a small plate next to her bowl of steaming oatmeal. Sari noted Sara Jane skipped oatmeal for herself, and had only taken two slices of toast, with peanut butter.

Sara Jane glanced at her as she entered the room. Her mouth was set in a firm line, the way it always was when she got perturbed. Sari should apologize for fussing in front of Andrew, but she wanted Sara Jane to stew. Grandchildren weren't the keepers of their grandparents, and Sara Jane needed to understand, even if it had been the two of them for the past twelve years.

Sara Jane had taken one bite of her breakfast when a loud knock came from the back door. Before she could put the peanut butter toast down and get to her feet, Grandma hustled over and swung the door open.

The handyman Grandma had hired stood on the porch in all his bearded glory. He nodded briefly in Sara Jane's direction without meeting her eyes. His hair was unkempt, as if he'd finger-combed it. She shook her head, her gaze skimming down his paint-covered jeans and ragged t-shirt. Ugh. What could Grandma possibly be thinking?

"Come on in." Grandma went toward the cupboard for another mug and poured coffee in it without asking if he wanted any. She put the carton of half-and-half and the sugar bowl on the table. "Come on now, don't be shy."

"I already had my coffee, and have a thermos full in the truck." The John the Baptist look-alike raked his fingers through his hair, messing it up further.

Sara Jane looked away and tried to control a grimace.

"Have some oatmeal. It'll stick to your ribs and fatten you up. You need to add some meat to your bones." Grandma spooned some into a bowl and set it next to the coffee. "Doesn't your mama take care of you?" She swung around and grabbed his left hand, making a point of peering at it. "Haven't you got a woman? No matter, Sara Jane here is looking too."

"Grandma, I am not!" Sara Jane sputtered. Thankfully, she hadn't spewed coffee across the table.

"Well, you should be." Grandma set her mouth in a narrow line. "Andrew, have a seat and eat up. I won't take no for an answer."

"Yes, ma'am." Drew nodded, his beard and long hair bouncing with the movement. "My friends call me Drew."

Grandma studied him. "I prefer Andrew."

Drew nodded and sat in the chair she indicated. "Looks good, ma'am."

"It is. My granddaughter made it. She's a good cook."

Drew turned his head in her direction and nodded again. Probably acknowledging Grandma's comment. He took a bite of his oatmeal.

Grandma finally rose from the table and turned to Sara Jane. "Go to the sewing room and see if you can find the quilt I started. I'll be there in a few minutes."

"Actually, I thought I'd go around with you and Mr . . ." She glanced at the business card lying on the table. "Mr. Stevenson and see what all you have in mind for him to do. Maybe I could do some of the work and save you some money."

Grandma's spine stiffened like it did when she got aggravated. "Sara Jane." Her voice sounded stern. "You git back there and do what I told you. I'll show Andrew what I want him to do. Do you hear me?"

Sara Jane frowned, suddenly feeling as if she were twelve again. With Grandma's current mood swings, it was easier to go along with her than to try to reason. "Yes, ma'am. Sorry, Mr. Stevenson."

He nodded.

Could this get any more humiliating?

"And you will leave Andrew alone and let him work."

"Grandma—"

"Yes, ma'am." Grandma lowered her chin and set her jaw.

Sara Jane rolled her eyes. "Yes, ma'am." She carried her plate over to the dishwasher, loaded it, and headed to the sewing room.

Seriously, she could think of better things to do with her time than digging through boxes of fabric. How many years had Grandma collected this stuff? It wasn't a few boxes either. They were stacked to the ceiling all across one wall of the room. Sara Jane surveyed the scene and shook her head. How would she recognize the pieces if she did find them?

Nothing to do but dig in.

She sorted through three or four boxes of fabric and found all the white background quilt blocks Grandma mentioned, but she hadn't found any of the pieces she'd talked about appliquéing on. Maybe they hadn't been cut out yet.

Grandma certainly did have a lot of material, though—an overwhelming amount, in bright colors: reds, blues, yellows, greens, and others. She was sure there was more than enough cloth to finish the quilt, possibly a dozen more, without a problem. Why had Grandma bought so much fabric anyway?

Sara Jane laid out all the quilt blocks on the sewing table but didn't know what to do next.

Grandma strode into the room as Sara Jane opened yet another box, looking for something that might go on a quilt. Somewhere in the background, a lawnmower roared to life. "Okay, I have him set. I showed him the back porch steps to be replaced, and when he finishes, he can fix the broken pane in the kitchen window."

Sara Jane bit her tongue to keep from questioning her grandma's judgment again. Last thing she needed was another tongue-lashing. Especially when arguing reminded her of . . .

She swallowed hard. Blinked, to hold back the stubborn moisture threatening to spill over.

She'd had enough scoldings in front of that irritating mountain man Grandma insisted on hiring. Why did he bug her so much anyway? She was used to different types of individuals, unique personalities. She dealt with the students in her history classes and the other teachers at the high school on a daily basis. But for some reason, Andrew Stevenson got on her last nerve. She'd never reacted this strongly to a person in her life. Why now?

3

Drew knocked on the back door. He'd mowed and weed-whacked the yard and now needed to run to the store for a few supplies for the home repair jobs Mrs. Morgan had given him. He surveyed the quiet neighborhood while he waited for someone to answer. After a while, he knocked again. Nothing. He cringed, but opened the door a crack. "Mrs. Morgan?"

No answer.

He called out again, a little louder.

"We're back here, Andrew."

Not sure where "back here" would be, and not wanting to go tramping through someone else's home, Drew shut the door and waited. A few minutes later, it opened.

"You should have come in. Do you need something?" Mrs. Morgan left the door standing wide open, turned, and walked off without waiting for an answer. She was a trusting woman, leaving her door open like that. A bit strange too, but he needed the money for the trip to Arkansas he wanted to take.

Not knowing what else to do, Drew entered, shut the door, and followed her through the kitchen and living room, and down a hallway lined with pictures.

At the end of the hall, Mrs. Morgan went into a bedroom on the left.

Drew hesitated in the doorway, raking his hand through his hair, unhappy Mrs. Morgan had made him walk all the way back there.

And not only that, but now she ignored him as she lifted a bolt of colorful red fabric to a table.

Material was piled on the floor, in open boxes spilling over, stacked on the table, even lined up in a sea of blue on yet another table. Every color under the sun seemed to be in the room. Beautiful.

His gaze rested on Sara Jane. She sat in the midst of a pile of fabric. She had a book open on her lap and didn't look up to acknowledge his presence, though he thought he saw her posture stiffen. Probably resented his presence in the room.

He forced his attention to the older woman, cleared his throat, and raked his fingers though his hair again. "Mrs. Morgan."

"Call me Grandma. Everyone does."

"The steps will take more than simply *fixing* with a few nails because of the rotting. I need to go into town for some pretreated lumber. I'm afraid if they aren't rebuilt, you might accidentally fall through them, or they might collapse."

Grandma picked up a pair of orange-handled scissors. Wielding them like a weapon, she swung around to face her granddaughter. "See there, Sara Jane, I told you those steps were shaky, but you didn't listen to me."

Sara Jane didn't look away from the book, and other than tightening her lips, she didn't acknowledge her grandmother either. Whatever the book was, it held her attention—or at least she pretended it did. And since she'd made her dislike of him obvious, he suspected the latter.

"Nice collection of material, Mrs. Mor . . . Grandma."

Grandma laughed as she turned back to face him. "You're looking at fifty years of a bad habit. I've always wanted to make a song quilt, so every time I saw pretty fabric, I bought it. No telling how much money I spent over the years." She glanced around the room. "I'm pretty sure I have enough here to make forty or fifty quilts. And here I just wanted to finish the one I started when I was a teenager."

Drew blinked. "Oh, you're making a ballad quilt? My granny made one when she first married. Mom made one too. I think my brother has them." He frowned. He hadn't thought of those quilts in years. He wasn't even sure what songs they'd represented. Of course, he hadn't seen his brother in years either. Not since . . .

"Maybe your wife will make you one someday." Grandma raised her chin and glanced at Sara Jane.

Mrs. Morgan really pushed this matchmaking thing. She must not catch on that the vibes between Sara Jane and him weren't attraction. More like . . . God only knew what. Drew certainly didn't.

Sara Jane stared at the page, but she couldn't tell what was on it. All her senses were focused on the grizzly man filling the doorway. She didn't like him, so it didn't make any sense why he registered on her internal radar. He'd filled her thoughts while she attempted to listen to Grandma rattle on about ballad quilts. She hoped she'd made the appropriate sounds, because she couldn't remember a word Grandma said.

He cleared his throat again, and it took all her effort to keep from looking up at him. She pressed her lips together and furrowed her brow, staring at the blurry page in front of her.

"Anyway, the steps," he said. "I'll go to the lumber yard and get the wood. To save a trip, I'll measure the broken window in the kitchen and get the glass."

"Okay." Grandma's voice was bright. "You know, Andrew, I think I want handrails on those steps, and maybe a railing around the porch, in case I wobble. I'm not getting any steadier, and it'd be nice not to have to worry about falling off when I'm out there."

"Yes, ma'am. Then I'll need to measure the porch before I go."

How many times had Sara Jane suggested the same thing? Grandma had scolded her for the suggestions.

"Oh, you might want to take Sara Jane with you. She'll know what kind of spindles I want."

She would? Sara Jane gave up all pretense of reading the book and looked up to see his gaze locked on her. A strange flutter made her stomach clench.

He looked away first. "Mrs. Mor . . . Grandma, it's not necessary. Describe the style you want and I'll get them. Do you want plain or a design?"

"I want the ones that go around and around with narrow parts in between the wide. I don't know what they're called. I'll send Sara Jane along. She'll know them."

He glanced at his watch. "I'd thought I'd get my lunch while I'm out."

Grandma's scissors rose and she pointed them at the man in the doorway. "You'll do no such thing, Andrew Stevenson. You will come right back here and eat lunch with us." She gave a decisive nod. "Sara Jane will pick up the fried chicken I like and some mashed potatoes and coleslaw. Get a big bucket, Sara Jane. We'll need it since we're feeding a *man*."

Sara Jane swallowed a huge lump in her throat. She was sure she sported a serious deer-in-the-headlights look, probably similar to the one the John the Baptist impersonator wore.

"Grandma, I think . . . Mr. Stevenson . . . Andrew . . . knows what he's doing. He'd probably enjoy having lunch away from us." She'd enjoy eating without being aware of his every move.

"Well, I need some time alone to think about what I want to do on this quilt." Grandma's eyes flashed.

And that settled that. No point wasting her breath arguing further. With a sigh, Sara Jane forced a smile and looked at Andrew . . . Drew . . . *him*. "I'm ready when you are."

Drew somehow managed to get the measurements he needed for the expanded porch project and the kitchen window, then strode from the house to his pickup without expiring from the impending doom. He wasn't quite sure how it'd work having Miss Morgan's pristine white pants in his dirty truck, but maybe he had an old blanket stuffed behind the seat. Although it wouldn't be much cleaner than the seats. He had straw and wood shavings from his brooms everywhere. If he'd known he'd be hauling a woman with him on his errands, he would have taken the time to vacuum the interior.

Or not. Maybe Miss Priss needed to know how the common man lived. Dirt and all. He doubted a dust bunny would find a safe environment in her home, while they lived and thrived in his. Her grandma's house appeared spick-and-span. No dust bunnies in sight.

Sara Jane marched along at his right, as if she were headed for execution. She'd probably never darkened the doorway of a home improvement store in her life, whereas they were his second home.

He walked to the passenger side door and opened it with a flourish he considered worthy of any game show host. "Your chariot awaits, milady."

"Thank you, kind sir. . . ." She stumbled as she caught sight of the interior of his truck.

He reached out and grabbed her elbow to steady her.

Unexpected sparks shot up his arm. It took an effort not to jerk away and leave her off-balance.

Instead, she was the one who pulled away, staring at him as if he'd suddenly grown two heads.

4

Sara Jane tried to ignore the tingles racing up her arm from his touch. She hoped Mr. Stevenson . . . Drew . . . wouldn't notice the distaste washing through her as she stared at the interior of his truck. Didn't he own a vacuum? She glanced at the remnants of . . . straw. Wood chips. A bit or two of twine. None of it appeared to be dirty-dirt. Just . . . craftsman discards, similar to what Grandma's spare room looked like after she went on a sewing spree, with scraps of fabric and thread scattered everywhere. Nothing a good cleaning wouldn't take care of.

She forced a smile and turned to face him. "Mr. Stevenson? Maybe it'd be better to take my car. Then you won't have to worry about . . ." What? Making room for her? There was room. Paying for a dry cleaning bill for her white pants? Wouldn't Grandma have a conniption if she heard her? Besides, it wasn't so filthy.

No, the truth was, she wanted to irritate the man. Make him quit, like the last one. So she could hire someone who looked more civilized. Someone who looked like Robert Downey, Jr.

She closed her eyes for a second. She was so shallow. His personal care wouldn't reflect on his work ethic, would it? She needed to move beyond the first impression. Then the second. And the third.

She opened her eyes and looked at him again. The grizzly mountain man didn't vanish. But she did see a touch of humor in those chocolate-brown eyes. A hint of intelligence. And something else she couldn't quite put her finger on.

He arched a brow and looked at her four-door Toyota Prius. Then back at his several-years-old, and so-not-"green," red pickup. "I don't think your vehicle would be big enough for the supplies needed, Miss Pri . . . uh, Morgan. But if you prefer to drive separately, then I could meet you at Lowe's."

Miss Pri . . .? What had he been fixing to call her? Maybe he knew someone named Priscilla. But never mind that. He'd offered her an out. She opened her mouth to accept, but a movement caught her attention. Grandma stood in the doorway, holding a mug and making wild hand motions as if she were shooing a fly away, and mouthing, "Get in the truck, now!"

When did Grandma get so overly . . . feisty? Sara Jane didn't want another argument with Grandma today. Not to mention in front of this man—again. Best to give in.

Sara Jane took a deep breath, brushed off the seat, then climbed in and sat.

He looked at her doubtfully. "I might have a blanket you could sit on, or a tarp, if you're afraid of getting your clothes dirty."

Her turn to raise a brow. "They clean, Mr. Stevenson."

He nodded, his gaze moving from her white pants to her face. "I answer to Drew, ma'am. Or Andrew. Just about anything, except Andy."

She couldn't control a smirk. "Andy, then. If you insist. And I answer to Miss Morgan." He could call her what her students did. It might keep the man in his place. Despite Grandma.

He grimaced, but without comment closed the door.

Drew fumed as he strode around the front of the truck. This woman tried his patience, no doubt about it. No one had the right to call him Andy. No one except . . .

He blinked hard to keep the moisture burning his eyes at bay. He'd dealt with this already. He wouldn't be plunged back into the depths by this . . . this woman.

As he opened the driver's side door, he noticed her reach for her smartphone. She could be checking messages, but he doubted it. Judging by the set of her chin, it would be more. Something he probably wouldn't appreciate. Like posting pictures of the interior of his truck on Facebook along with the caption "Can you believe I have to ride in this?"

He hoped she didn't get it in her head to plan out the shopping trip. It would be the last straw. He climbed in, buckled the seat belt, and inserted the key into the ignition.

She typed something into the phone.

He reached over and flipped the radio on to his favorite station. Miss Morgan probably preferred classical or opera. Right now, he didn't particularly care what she liked. Not as if he dated the woman.

Miss Morgan, indeed. He shook his head.

The engine roared to life, and he backed out on the street.

Lord, I need help. She is getting on my last nerve. I need this job. Please give me the ability to not respond in anger.

The beat of the music annoyed him. Might be better to put on something calming, so his blood pressure didn't go through the roof. Not something he normally worried about.

He thumbed through his music collection and pulled out a praise and worship disc. He slid it in and adjusted the volume so it was at a quiet level. Hopefully, it'd relax him.

He glanced over at Miss Priss. "Buckle up."

She gave him what he could only call a baleful glare, but reached for the stained seat belt, gingerly pulled it across, and snapped it in place.

He turned his attention back to the road but couldn't help noticing her frustrated growling sounds when he drove out of town. He hid a grin. She should know better than to try to get good coverage in these mountains. She put the phone back into her purse and pulled out a notepad and a pen.

Yep, she'd drive him insane. Why had Mrs. Morgan sent her along? If only she'd agreed to drive separately. She could've ordered what her grandmother wanted for lunch, and he could've gotten the supplies needed to do his job.

He sighed. He should've been man enough to insist. This is what he got for operating his business out of his back pocket. A beautiful but high-maintenance power queen. And he had to play nice.

The trip into Morgantown passed in silence, other than the soft music in the background and the scratching of her pen on the paper. And the occasional taps of the bottom of the pen against the notebook as she must've thought about whatever she wrote.

Whatever it was, he didn't want to know.

He pulled into the parking lot at Lowe's and cut the engine. He got out and started around the truck. He'd at least be polite and open the door.

She didn't wait. She climbed out and brandished her notebook. "I made notes of what you need." She ripped out the page.

Drew's eyebrows shot up. He took the list and gave it a cursory glance. Glass, wood screws, boards. . . . She wouldn't get too far if she handed it to an employee. He refrained from laughing. "Thanks. This'll go a lot faster if you go pick out those posts your grandma wanted. I'll meet you there." He pocketed her list. He had no intention of looking like an idiot in the place where he did a lot of business. Especially since he'd already ordered all the items needed, except the balusters, on his smartphone before they left her grandmother's house.

She huffed.

No matter. He had no intention of waiting to see if she followed his directions. Drew headed for the store. He'd tell an employee he was there since most of his order would be ready for pickup, and then find Miss Morgan and see what she chose.

Once inside, he dared to glance back. She brushed off her pants and followed him into the store. The next moment, she had her smartphone out, typing something in. She didn't seem to pay any attention to where he was at all.

Good.

Now maybe he could do his job.

Still, he couldn't keep from watching her as she walked past him as if he didn't exist. She didn't look up from her phone. Her attention appeared to be captivated with what she saw on the screen.

She really was beautiful.

But oh, so not his type.

Sara Jane accessed the web to search for the posts Grandma needed but had a failed map issue. It would be so helpful to be able to enter what she needed and let the phone tell her what aisle it would be on. Maybe she could put it in the store's suggestion box. It'd be so much easier and less humiliating than asking for help or wandering the store. Neither option appealed to her.

Admittedly, she had a control issue, but she had to give grudging respect to the man for one-upping her. Despite his rugged mountain man appearance, he knew his business. Maybe. She wasn't ready to back down yet. Grandma should've asked her opinion before she hired anyone for the job. Especially a John the Baptist wannabe.

She grinned. Maybe she should let him collect grasshoppers in the backyard for his lunch. She could set out a jar of honey to go with it.

A male clerk approached her, pushing one of their mobile ladders. She waved in his direction. "Sir? Can you tell me where the deck posts are?"

He gave her a blank stare. "Deck posts?"

She inwardly fumed. "The posts used for deck railings."

He nodded. "Yes, ma'am." He turned in the direction he'd come. "Aisle 10. And to the left."

She nodded. She found them with no problem, but after she arrived, she stood there in indecision. Who knew there were so many different types? Grandma had said twisty ones with narrow . . . She heard a shuffling sound and turned.

Drew stepped into the aisle. "Find what you need?"

She glared. "Finish the rest of the shopping already, Andy?"

A flicker of hurt flashed in his eyes. He looked away, his gaze flickering to the post display. "They're wheeling it out." He stepped closer. She breathed in the aroma of pine-scented soap and man. "Which one do you think your grandma would like?"

Sara Jane turned back to the selection. She wouldn't be made to look like an idiot. Again. She studied them, then picked one and handed it to him.

He examined it then returned it to her. "She has a pretty rustic cabin, Miss Morgan. Perhaps she'd like something not so frilly." He reached for another post. One with some twists, but not as many. "Do you think she'd like this one? It sounds like what she described."

Yes. It did. On second thought, it looked more like it than the one she'd picked up.

She nodded, her respect for Drew going up another notch. She returned the one she held to its slot, and stepped back.

"I'll add this to my cart." He slid a glance in her direction, then strode away.

Maybe Grandma had known what she was doing, hiring this man.

And she succeeded in looking like an idiot. Again. Tears burned her eyes.

5

Drew backed his truck into Mrs. Morgan's driveway. Miss Priss unhooked her seat belt and slid out, then grasped the white handles of the fast food carryout bag. Their lunch and his. He'd bought his own meal. It wasn't ethical to expect his temporary employer to feed him. His stomach rumbled again. Smelling the scent of hot fried chicken all the way from Morgantown to Bruceton Mills was a long time for a man to suffer.

Miss Morgan started toward the house without looking in his direction, her posture ramrod straight.

He shrugged. She'd gotten more miffed when she'd learned he'd ordered most of the supplies before they left. He would've asked for delivery, if it weren't for not knowing for sure which balusters she'd want. He hoped he made the right decision. He sure hadn't expected the queen of control to give in so easily. He'd expected her to fight for the one she chose.

He moved toward the back of his pickup, then hesitated. "Miss Pri . . . uh, Morgan?" He really needed to watch what he called her in his thoughts. If it slipped out . . . Besides, God knew. *Lord, help me.*

She stopped and pivoted.

He took a deep breath and stepped closer in her direction. "Look, can we start over? I'm sorry for whatever I did to upset you."

She looked away.

Okay. She wanted to hold a grudge. He turned.

"You don't look like Josh Duhamel or Robert Downey, Jr."

He hesitated. Her response came completely out of left field. Good thing he wasn't vain about his looks. Or lack thereof. He glanced over his shoulder and chuckled. "No, I don't suppose I do. But impersonating actors isn't in my job description."

She smiled. Giggled. A light musical sound. And walked in his direction.

Drew's stomach clenched.

"I suppose I can start over. I'm sorry I judged you based on your appearance. It was wrong of me. I'm Sara Jane. I teach history at the high school in Morgantown." She extended her hand.

He cringed. He was guilty of judging her by appearances too. For a moment, he stared at her manicured nails and the soft-looking skin, then he looked at his callused, work-roughened fingers. He frowned, then hesitantly took her hand in his. "Andrew Stevenson. Broom maker and handyman, at your service."

She was as soft as she looked. Sparks shot up his arm. His heart pounded into overdrive. He released her and backed away.

"I'll get the supplies unloaded."

"They'll wait until after lunch. The food will get cold."

As if it wasn't already, after a half-hour drive?

But he nodded and followed her toward the house.

Sara Jane knocked, then opened the front door. "Grandma?" A rustling sound came from her right and she turned. Grandma backed out of the heavy folds of the curtains.

"What were you doing?" Spying on her and Drew?

Grandma looked down, color filling her cheeks.

Yep, she'd been spying.

Sara Jane went into the kitchen, set the bag on the counter, then got out Grandma's dishes. It would be easier to use paper plates, but

Grandma was more frugal than that. She didn't even use paper towels or napkins. When Sara Jane mentioned something about buying paper products, Grandma would invariably say something about how her family went through the Great Depression and how Sara Jane lived in a throwaway generation.

Grandma was right. She did.

Apparently, catalogs didn't count as throwaway. Then again, Grandma did have a box full of them back in the spare room. Maybe more than one.

If Grandma was serious about selling her house, she'd have to get rid of a lot of junk.

"Let me get it for you, Mrs. Mor . . . Grandma."

Sara Jane turned to see Grandma on tiptoes reaching for a serving platter. Drew reached from behind her, lifting the platter down with ease.

"Thank you, Andrew." Grandma beamed at him, then turned and busied herself pulling the chicken pieces out of the bucket and arranging them on the platter.

Sara Jane opened her mouth to object, but then shut it again. It wouldn't do any good to discuss this. It would only invite a scolding. Besides, Grandma seemed to want to treat Drew like an honored guest.

And maybe he was. He'd somehow managed to work around Sara Jane's defenses to become someone she respected, at least, if not liked. He deserved some recognition for it.

After lunch, Drew went out to get the glass for the kitchen window, and the other supplies he needed. He'd do the window repair first, then work on the steps and deck railings. When he returned, Sara Jane was alone in the kitchen.

"Grandma wanted a little nap." Her voice was hushed. "She gave me orders to finish sorting through her fabric, but I have no idea what she has in mind. Ballad quilts can be so different. There isn't a set pattern."

He nodded, trying to think back to the ones his mom and grandmother had made. He couldn't remember much. Quilts didn't rank high in importance, except on cold nights.

"There was an exhibit at the university, maybe a month or so ago, about ballad quilts. I took Grandma since she loves quilting. I think it's what put the idea in her head about wanting to finish hers. But some of the quilts were one big picture, a scene. And on some of the series were little scenes that told a story."

Her voice took on a lecturing tone, as though she spoke to a classroom of students, and not one man trying to concentrate on something else. He smiled.

"Grandma says she started one about the song 'Pretty Saro'. Have you ever heard it? It's a sad song about a man who came to America, and he met this girl named Saro, and fell in love with her, but she rejected him to marry a landowner. He ended up living as a drifter."

Drew made a grunting sound he hoped she took as acknowledgment.

"Have you ever heard it? Wait a minute. There's a version I found on YouTube when Grandma started talking about it. Let me find it."

He darted a quick glance in her direction. She looked at her smartphone, typing something in. A few minutes later, the slow, twangy tones of a female singer accompanied by a guitar or banjo broke the silence. Maybe it was an autoharp or dulcimer. Not seeing the video clip, he couldn't tell.

Drew finished the window while he tried to understand the singer's words. He didn't succeed very well but couldn't say he was interested enough to look up the lyrics. He'd cleaned up the mess and put the violets that'd been on the sill back in place by the end of the ballad. As he gathered his supplies, he turned to look at her.

Sara Jane glanced up. "We have some relative somewhere back in the family tree named Saro. I think it was Grandma's grandma. Or maybe her great-grandma. I'm not positive. I have it written down somewhere. I'm sure it's in Grandma's family Bible. I'll go check." She straightened.

He didn't need to know who Saro was in her family tree. "I'll take these out to the truck and get started on the steps, Miss Morgan. Unless you think the noise will disturb your grandmother. The cordless tools make a buzzing sound."

"Call me Sara Jane, please. Don't worry about Grandma. She takes her hearing aids out when she naps and can't hear anything."

"Sara Jane." He tried the name out. Heat rose in his cheeks. He hoped she didn't notice.

It'd never do for her to know he was infatuated with this kinder, more talkative version. He didn't know if he could bear another woman laughing in his face, like . . .

He frowned. He wouldn't—couldn't—think about that.

After he finished this job, he'd never see Sara Jane Morgan again.

6

Sari opened her eyes, blinking in the dimness of the bedroom. She must've napped longer than she intended. She listened, but couldn't hear a sound. Nothing. Seemed she should hear pounding out on the porch. Or a power tool of some sort even without her hearing aids.

But no. Absolute silence.

She got out of bed, reached for her "ears," as Sara Jane called the hearing aids, and slid her glasses on, then wiggled her feet into her slippers. Then she listened again. Still not hearing anything, she shuffled out to the hall and peeked in her sewing room. Sara Jane should be in there, working on the quilt, as she'd directed.

The room was empty. Silence prevailed. She reached up to check her "ears" to make sure they were turned on. She heard the shuffle of her slippers on the carpet, but nothing to indicate anyone else was there.

Had Sara Jane run this handyman off too? Would she spout some nonsense about him trying to steal her wedding candleholders? She hadn't believed Sara Jane the first time, nor would she now. Did Sara Jane think her grandma was senile? Why would anyone want to steal from her?

She hurried down the hall and into the kitchen. The window glass shone with newness. She looked through the screen door at the porch, and it was completely finished. The steps repaired, the railings installed, handrails going down the stairs. Andrew Stevenson was a stellar craftsman. It was beautiful as well as functional. It hasn't looked this good since Cade initially built it. She couldn't remember asking Drew to fix the handrail, but he seemed to be an intelligent young man. And considerate.

He reminded her of Cade, God rest his soul, back years ago when they first met. A bit rugged and rough around the edges, but nothing a woman couldn't polish. And so kind . . . just the type of man she'd like to see Sara Jane settle down with someday.

She went through the living room and peeked out the front window. Andrew's truck was gone. Sara Jane's small car was still in the driveway, so she must be around here somewhere. She went back through the house, peeking in each room, but didn't see her.

Finally, Sari checked the backyard. She went outside this time, put her hands on Drew's new railings, and looked down. Sara Jane knelt in the dirt, in front of the porch, pulling weeds. She'd been at it a while too, judging by the big pile.

Sara Jane must have heard her, because she looked up with a smile. "Have a good nap, Grandma?"

"I slept too long. Where's Andrew?"

Sara Jane shrugged. "He finished up and left. Don't worry, I paid him. I thought he did a good job."

A good job? This was huge, coming from Sara Jane. Sari blinked and looked around again. The finished porch was much nicer than she'd imagined. Nicer than it looked peering at it through the door. But . . . "I had other jobs for him to do."

Sara Jane straightened. "You didn't mention them to me, so I didn't know. You still have his business card, don't you? It was on the table at breakfast, but I didn't see it there at lunch."

Sari stiffened. "Of course, I still have it." Maybe. If she could find it. "You think I'd throw it away?"

Though she'd been losing more things than she liked to recently.

Drew pulled into his driveway after church Wednesday night. With a weary sigh, he shut the truck door and headed for the house he rented in Morgantown. He unlocked the door, then opened the mailbox bolted to the brick facade and pulled out his mail. He thumbed through it. Electric bill. Cell phone bill. And a postcard from his brother and his wife, forwarded from his post office box in a different town. *Wish you were here. Joey and Carly.* A picture of a beach and palm tree was on the front. They must've gone to Florida on their vacation. Nice.

Maybe he needed to take a few days off. Not to go to Florida. Maybe a day hike. Or canoeing. Either one sounded fun, and would give him a much-needed break from his current schedule. Maybe this weekend. He'd contracted to work at a local church for the remainder of this week and into next, helping them install a storage shed for their lawn tools, construct a playground for the kids, and then doing some work inside their daycare.

He opened the door and was greeted by his dog, a Siberian Husky. Wynter danced at his feet, tail wagging, then dashed outside.

His phone vibrated. He dropped his mail on the coffee table and pulled his phone out of his pocket, glancing at the number. He didn't recognize it. But . . . "Drew." He stepped over to the door to keep an eye on Wynter.

"Is this Andrew Stevenson? The handyman?" An elderly voice quaked. It sounded vaguely familiar.

"Yes, ma'am. May I help you?"

"This is Grandma. Uh, Sari Morgan. You did some work for me on Monday." The voice cleared a little, as well as his memory. She was the woman with the beautiful granddaughter—and not so beautiful personality. At least, not at first.

"Was there a problem?" Had he left something undone? Or not done the job to her specifications?

"Oh, no. I thought I'd never find your card. I hunted and hunted. You'll never guess where I found it. I'd put it in the freezer. I found it when I got some stew meat out to thaw for tomorrow, and thought I'd give you a call."

He grunted in acknowledgment. Why did women think they needed to use one hundred fifty words when five would do? He half-listened to her while he kept an eye on Wynter. She sniffed at the lilac bushes.

"My granddaughter, Sara Jane, let you go without checking with me about other jobs. I need a new roof. Well, not all the way new, just reshingled. And there was something else I needed you to do. It . . . oh bother . . . I should've written it down."

His heart rate increased, thinking of seeing Sara Jane again. She'd filled his dreams for the past several nights. Maybe he could go . . . No. He had to do the work at the church first.

"Mrs. Morgan." He reached for his calendar. "I am busy for the next week and a half. It'll be, say, Thursday of next week before I can come to look at your roof. Will then be okay?" He was thankful for the work to fill up the empty days looming after the church job.

"Maybe by then, I'll remember the other job. Well, you will eat your meals with us, right? I won't take no for an answer. The sun will be hot and you'll need a break in the air conditioning."

Drew chuckled. He had no intention of letting her provide his meals, but it was sweet of her to offer. "I'll see you a week from tomorrow."

Something thumped on the other end of the phone. Silence followed.

"Mrs. Morgan?"

"Yes?" There was another long pause. "I'm sorry. Who is this again?"

He frowned. "Andrew Stevenson, ma'am. You called me." His brow wrinkled in concern. She'd stored his business card in the freezer . . . Had she fallen and hit her head? Was it the thump he heard?

"Andrew Stevenson?" She sounded confused. A crash sounded somewhere in the background. "Are you the police? I think something is outside my house. There's . . . there's a shadow. I see someone." A note of panic crept into her voice. "Send an officer right away."

"Ma'am?"

A click followed.

Should he call the police? Or check this out himself? His next-door neighbor had recently walked in on a burglary. He'd call the police. On the other hand, his grandmother had fallen downstairs and it'd been three days before someone found her.

He'd swing by.

Sara Jane maneuvered her car down the road in front of Grandma's house. Vehicles lined both sides of the road, and the scent of a barbecue filled the air. Someone must've had a birthday or a block party. It could explain why Grandma hadn't answered her phone all afternoon—and why she hadn't shown up for the prayer and Bible study at church. Grandma never missed, unless she was sick. And the only reason Sara Jane went was to appease Grandma.

She pulled into the driveway and climbed out, scanning the dark house. She didn't see the blue flicker of the television.

Had Grandma gone to the neighbor's for the celebration?

She'd check the house first. Too bad Grandma didn't carry a cell phone. And too bad she no longer owned a car.

Sara Jane went up on the porch, knocked once, and then tried the door. Locked. Odd. Grandma never locked her door. She didn't bring her set of keys to get in. Perhaps the back door would be unlocked.

She went around the house. A light shone in the kitchen window. Sara Jane knocked once on the back door, then opened it. Grandma sat at the kitchen table, across from Drew, and they both were drinking coffee. A platter of store-bought chocolate chip cookies sat in the middle of the table. Cookies and coffee at this hour? She shook her head. What was he doing there?

Sara Jane blinked and looked at Grandma.

"What are you doing here, Sara Jane?" Grandma stood. "You want a cup of decaf?"

"You weren't in church. I was worried. And then you didn't answer the phone when I called."

Grandma frowned. "Church?"

"It's Wednesday, Grandma. You always go, unless you're sick."

Grandma looked at Drew. He nodded.

"I must've gotten my days mixed up. Don't worry. I stepped over to the Browns' for supper. They invited the whole neighborhood because old Mr. Wilson celebrated his ninetieth birthday today. When I came home I got stew meat out of the freezer for dinner tomorrow and I heard a noise. Andrew was nice enough to come check it out for me."

Sara Jane glanced at Drew. "A noise?"

A smile flickered across his lips. "It was a raccoon in the trash can. Or a cat. I couldn't tell in the dark, but it knocked the lid off and tipped it over."

Wow. He drove out from—wherever he lived—to check on a noise?

She grinned.

Red stained his cheeks. He drained his coffee and stood. "Best get on the road, Mrs. Mor . . . Grandma. Goodnight." He nodded at Sara Jane, then looked back at Grandma. "I'll see you a week from tomorrow to get started on the roof."

His gaze flickered toward Sara Jane and his eyes briefly met hers. He looked away, his color deepening as he hurried out the door.

Sara Jane watched him go and glanced at Grandma.

She nodded. "He's a good man, Sara Jane. A good man."

7

Saturday promised to be hot and sunny. Drew pulled the truck into a parking space at Fort Necessity and glanced around. His best friend and hiking buddy, Wesley King, was already there. Wes leaned against his truck while he talked on his phone. Probably to his girlfriend. The two were inseparable.

A pang of jealousy shot through Drew. He squelched it as best he could. No point in longing for something he wouldn't have.

Wes slid his phone into his pocket as Drew approached. "Hey, Broom-man! 'Bout time you got here. I'm ready and waiting. Time's a-wasting."

"Hey, Lion King. Where's Chris?" Drew looked around for their other friend who'd planned to join them—the only reason he and Lion King came to Fort Necessity instead of driving further to hike a portion of the Appalachian Trail.

"He went in to pay and start looking around. He didn't know this was the actual site of a French and Indian War battle George Washington fought in."

"How can someone grow up around here and not know?" Though, admittedly, Drew didn't focus much on the area's bygone days. Only when he had to, while working on a historical site. Then he had to focus on preserving the integrity of the past.

Sara Jane would be someone who would study the ancient times. As a history teacher, she had probably soaked up all the yesteryears' sites in this part of the country. He looked around, almost expecting to see her small car in the lot.

It wasn't, of course. A pang of disappointment shot through him. He couldn't have explained why. Half the time, he didn't like the woman. *Rude, bossy, prissy, a high-maintenance drama queen, control freak. . . .* But the more recent Sara Jane, the friendlier, more talkative one—yeah, he could go for her.

Not that he would.

She wouldn't look twice at him.

And he didn't want to face rejection.

Again.

Lion King laughed. "Yeah. Lots of history in them thar hills. Have you been here before?"

Drew shrugged. "Once or twice, on a field trip, as a kid."

"You should take the time to look around in addition to hiking the trail. I was here, oh, maybe two weeks ago with Alana. We spent hours. Brought a picnic lunch along and hiked out to eat it on the picnic loop." Lion King looked around. "Come on. Let's get started. I promised Alana I'd take her out for dinner and a movie tonight, if we get back in time."

Drew and Lion King entered the building and approached the admissions desk and the small gift shop surrounding it. Drew looked around at the information about the French and Indian War and the history books for sale, picking up some of them, before he pulled out his wallet to pay for his admission.

"This is the prelude to the Revolutionary War. George Washington was a young soldier in this war. Beginning of his military career." The man behind the desk accepted their money.

Drew nodded, but he couldn't recall ever learning it. If he had, he'd forgotten.

Chris had already disappeared into the museum part of the building. When Drew and Lion King caught up with him, they went out a side door.

Lion King pointed. "We'll start out over there. The trail will lead by the fort. Imagine this place teeming with French soldiers, Indians, and Washington's men." He shook his head. "It can feel spooky."

"You gotta be kidding. Ninety minutes to hike this?" Chris shook his head. "I thought you said it'd be an easy walk. Compared to what?"

Drew looked away to hide his smirk. "The Appalachian Trail."

"Yeah, well, not all of us want to be close to nature. I'd rather watch my favorite cooking shows."

"And scarf down pizza and chips?" Lion King nudged him. "Time to walk off some of those calories you intake, Doughboy."

"Hey, some of us have body mass. Drew would blow away if it weren't for his mane of hair weighing him down." Chris poked him in the side. "Not an ounce of fat on the man."

Drew chuckled. "It's all muscle."

"And hair."

"Now, shhhh," Lion King directed. "Listen to the sounds of the forest. Pretend you're an Indian scout or one of Washington's men, watching for the first signs of the enemy."

Leaves crunched in the woods. A shiver worked its way up Drew's spine, though the sounds probably came from squirrels bounding through the undergrowth. It was easy to imagine scouts hiding in the woods. Or warriors with weapons drawn, waiting to see if they were friend or foe.

As much as he loved the forest, it was a relief to reach the meadow, and the relative safety of the fort.

Tourists, and maybe a few locals, milled around the building. Drew gave them a cursory glance, then hesitated as his gaze rested on someone who resembled Sara Jane.

Long brown hair, pulled back in a ponytail. Slim jeans. A sheer shirt over a purple tank top revealing a tantalizing glimpse of . . .

Oh, yeah.

His stomach clenched, and his heart pounded into overdrive.

He needed to say hi. No, he couldn't. She was with a friend. She'd prefer to pretend she didn't know him.

He wouldn't subject himself to being ridiculed in front of his friends.

Chris dug his elbow into Drew's ribs. "Hey, check out the hot babe to your right."

Sara Jane's friend, Marci, aimed the camera, taking shot after shot of the fort George Washington had been in. It was so amazing to stand in a place where the father of their country had once stood. Seeing something similar to what he saw. Breathing the same scents. It almost made Sara Jane want to twirl like a little girl. If it weren't for the embarrassment factor, she would've.

If only she could make her students so excited about history. Such wonder in the experience.

A tickle of pine soap reached her. It reminded her of Drew. He wouldn't be here though. She couldn't imagine him visiting a battlefield. He'd be the type who frequented more rugged hiking grounds.

Still, she couldn't keep from looking over her shoulder. A man with thick, tawny hair and beard walked behind her, headed in the direction of the hill on the other side of the meadow. Two other men were with him. One was a bit stocky, the other was as tall and thin as Drew. The tavern—closed now—where George Washington allegedly ate and drank was up there. The first man looked like Drew. But if it was, he must not have noticed her.

She watched him a second more, but the sense of familiarity didn't cease. After all, she'd seen his backside when he worked on the kitchen window at Grandma's house.

She took a couple of steps toward him.

The stocky man turned to look at her. He stopped, then walked in her direction. "Hi. I'm Chris." He held out his hand.

At least he didn't use a cheesy pickup line. She could appreciate that. She shook his hand, then pulled back. "Nice to meet you, Chris. I'm Sara Jane. I thought I recognized your friend." She gazed over his shoulder at the man stalking away. "Is that Andrew Stevenson?"

"You know him?" Chris's eyebrows shot up. "Hey, Drew. She says she knows you. Get back here."

Both men stopped and came back. Red stained Drew's face as he approached. "Miss Morgan." He nodded at her. "Didn't expect to see you here." He glanced at his friends. "I did some work for her grandmother."

"I told you to call me Sara Jane." She tilted her head and smiled.

His face turned brighter. "Yes, ma'am. Sara Jane." He looked at the ground.

He must be shy. She couldn't think of any other reason for his reaction. Sweet.

His friend, the one who wasn't Chris, stared at Drew, then looked at Sara Jane, his eyebrows shooting up.

Marci's camera brushed against Sara Jane's left arm. She glanced her way. "This is my friend, Marci."

The unnamed man's glance slid toward Marci, then to Sara Jane, and to Drew, before returning to rest on Sara Jane.

"I'm Wes. Did you ladies bring your lunch, or would you want to join us? There's a pizza place in Farmington."

Drew made a funny choking sound, solidifying her impression he was shy. His friend slapped him on the back.

"Pizza sounds good," Marci said. "It's been ages."

Ages? Two weeks. They'd had pizza while watching a romantic comedy at Sara Jane's apartment. But she wouldn't remind her. It did sound good. She nodded. "I like pepperoni." But then, who didn't?

"Great. It's a date." Wes grinned at her, then smirked at Drew. "We're going to hike to the tavern, then look around the museum awhile." He glanced at his watch. "So an hour?"

"I think I'll stay here with Sara Jane and Marci," Chris said. "They need protecting from the enemy soldiers lurking in these woods. I'll catch up with you guys at the museum."

"My hero." Marci linked her arm with his. "See you guys later."

"And who's going to protect them from you?" Wes raised a brow. He winked at Sara Jane. "Don't worry. Doughboy's harmless.

Broom-man here, you have to look out for. He'll sweep you right off your feet."

Something she couldn't identify flickered in Drew's eyes, before they slid over her. Tingles worked through her, reminding her of when he'd caught her the other day.

"Later." He turned away, glowering at his friend.

Was it wrong she wanted his expression to be longing?

Drew tried to will his heart rate back under control as he strode away. Lion King marched beside him, silent now the damage had been done. He should be grateful Sara Jane hadn't laughed at the offhand comment. Even more thankful she hadn't ignored him and turned the other direction, pretending she didn't know him.

No. He'd been the one who'd done that. Rejecting her before she could reject him.

Shame washed over him. *Forgive me, Lord.*

If only he could take back the lunch invitation Lion King had offered. She'd probably only accepted because Wes and Chris would be there, and she wouldn't be alone with him. She'd be disappointed to learn Wes was taken. Of course, Chris was available.

Not for long. Because either Sara Jane or Marci would snatch him up.

Leaving Drew.

His eyes burned as he looked toward the tavern. It blurred.

How many times had he told himself he wasn't the marrying type?

Not the marrying type. Not the dating type. Not the relationship of any sort type.

Unless it was with his dog. He'd wanted—planned—to bring Wynter with him today. She'd enjoy the hike—needed the activity, actually. But he wasn't sure what the park rules would be concerning domestic animals.

Tonight he'd go home, with a butcher's bone, in apology for leaving her behind, and then take her for a run. She was easy to please and a female he understood, unlike the two-legged variety.

Wynter was enough.

If only his heart believed it.

8

Sara Jane watched Drew and Wes walk away. Beside her, Marci and Chris flirted, but nothing they said or did registered. Maybe she should run after Drew and Wes and join them as they peeked into the tavern. It wasn't open to the public—at least not today—though it was on special occasions, such as reenactments. She'd been in it once. Another bit of history.

She'd have to come back the next time they had a reenactment.

Marci handed her camera to another tourist and grabbed Sara Jane, pulling her back into the moment. "Stand here. Chris, put your arm around her. Good. And I'll stand on your other side. Put your arm around me." She giggled, as Chris must've tickled her a little. Marci's flirting annoyed her. She picked up a guy every time they went out to do something together. It kind of made her wish Drew was still there. Maybe reaching to tickle her. She glanced at them—still headed away from her. "Hold still. I want a picture."

This was more than awkward, having her picture taken with a complete stranger. What could Marci possibly be thinking? Sara Jane forced a smile.

The stranger snapped a couple of pictures, then gave the camera back to Marci.

"I'll have to post this to my Facebook page when I get home. I'll tag you both. You'll have to tell me your last name, Chris."

"Stewart," he said. "But I haven't set up a page yet. Probably won't. I don't get online much."

"Oh? What do you do?"

"Barber." Chris glanced after his friends. "Not that you could tell by my current companions." He chuckled. "I'm waiting for the day Drew walks into my shop."

Sara Jane looked toward Drew again. She did want to peek inside the building while she was here. She looked at Marci. "I'm going to catch up with them. I want to see inside the tavern."

"Okay." Marci kept her attention on Chris. "I'm a business education instructor. I work at the same school as Sara Jane. We're both first-year teachers. We graduated together from . . ."

Sara Jane hurried off, breaking into a jog as she left the tourists milling around the fort. She hoped Drew and Wes wouldn't mind her joining them.

Drew marched on, keeping his focus on the tavern ahead of him. Somewhere, he'd read in George Washington's day there was a tavern every mile on this road, offering rest, food, and drink for travelers. He tried to imagine himself as a soldier under General Washington, as per Wes's previous instructions, but the pounding of feet coming from behind him broke into his thoughts.

He glanced over his shoulder, half-expecting to see a scout running up behind him, but to his surprise, it was Sara Jane. His steps faltered.

Lion King recovered first. But then, he'd always had the gift of conversation with the ladies. Chris, too. But Drew followed another rule. Just the facts. Short, unsweetened, and to the point.

If only he could tell her she looked beautiful. Mention her high ponytail bouncing behind her as if she were a little girl. Compliment her on her color choice or wardrobe. Maybe suggest they could get together sometime on a not-accidental, not-work-related basis.

But. . . . It'd never happen.

He'd never ask.

He sighed.

Sara Jane slowed to a walk between them. "I thought I'd join you. I'd already looked around down there and taken some pictures, and I wanted to peek in the windows at the tavern before I go to the grave site of General Braddock."

Lion King glanced toward him as if he expected him to answer. But Drew couldn't formulate any response other than a grunt.

The look Wes gave him could be translated only one way. *Pathetic.*

Yeah, he agreed.

He scratched his neck.

"Nice you decided to join us, Sara Jane." Wes smiled. "You're sure to brighten this trek. Don't you agree, Broom-man?"

"Yep." He winced. *Brilliant conversation.*

Sara Jane breathed a little hard, as if she wasn't used to the exercise.

Drew struggled to find something to say. Something beyond the inane "Beautiful weather we're having." Too wordy. Too obvious.

Nothing else came to mind.

"So where'd you come up with these nicknames? Doughboy, Broom-man. Do you have one?" Sara Jane glanced at Wes.

"Appalachian Trail. No one walks it using their real name. Trail logs, fellow hikers, everyone knows you by your nickname. Mine is Lion King." He winked. "Cuz I'm the boss."

"So all three of you hiked the trail?"

"No, Doughboy sat at home and munched. Didn't you notice his spare tire?"

"It's not so bad." Sara Jane shook her head. "I can figure out where you got your name. Broom-man." She gazed at Drew. "It's when I met you. Selling your brooms. I don't think I made a very good first impression."

Other than her looks, no. But he'd never admit that. He slid a sideways glance over her again. *Wow.* His heart rate kicked up another notch. "Neither did I, Miss Mor . . . Sara Jane." And he still didn't make a good impression. Not the first time, not the second, and not the tenth. Sometimes, he wished he could change it. If only he could go back to the beginning, and meet Sara Jane as a man she might've been attracted to.

Too late now.

They reached the tavern.

He peered in the surprisingly clean window but wasn't too interested in the discovery. A set table, a fireplace on the side of the room. An old chair resembled one his grandparents stored in the attic.

Sara Jane rested her hand lightly on his arm. His breath hitched. He hoped no one noticed.

"You were kind. Considerate. And you impressed me more with your professional knowledge. You know what you're doing."

He looked down. His face heated.

Wes slapped him on the back. "Might want to pay a visit to Doughboy to get your mane trimmed before you ask her out."

Sara Jane laughed and pulled away.

He'd known it would be her reaction. So why did it hurt so much?

"Not asking." Drew turned and stalked off.

Marci parked in the lot, and Sara Jane gave a quick look around. There it was. Drew's big red pickup. She smiled, relief filling her. Though he clearly wasn't interested. If only . . .

Chris's little black car was parked across the lot from Drew's.

"Did I tell you Chris and I talked about renting a movie tonight and having popcorn at my apartment? Some of his friends might join us. Who did you have your eye on?" Marci dropped her keys in her big baggy purse. "Probably Wes, right? He's kinda cute. The other guy looks like he got lost in some reality survivor show and hasn't found his way out yet."

Sara Jane opened the car door. For some reason, it bothered her to hear Marci speak that way about Drew, though her initial impression was close to the same. It felt wrong hearing someone else say what she'd thought. The real man was so much more, and she'd barely scratched the surface in her acquaintance with him.

Even though their relationship would never go beyond superficial.

Broom-maker. Handyman. Kind. Considerate. Polite. Respectful.

"Don't tell me you like the caveman look." Marci turned to look at her. "You're a fashion plate."

Sara Jane laughed. "Hardly a fashion plate." But she had to admit, buying ready-to-wear clothes beat wearing the homemade outfits Grandma had made. She might've been a great quilter, but Grandma didn't have an eye for style. And Sara Jane had always been laughed at as a teenager for having homemade jeans and button-up shirts in weird patterns. Years when conformity was the name of the game. Both still hurt. They made fun of Grandma's efforts, and she'd been the subject of ridicule.

Of course, Grandma's homemade clothes were better than the third- or fourth-hand-me-down rags she'd worn when she was in foster care right after her parents' deaths. During the horrific months when they worked through all the red tape the government had to go through to have her placed with her family.

The relative whose only child she'd accidentally killed.

She didn't want to talk about it either.

Tears burned her eyes. If only she hadn't . . .

She violently shook her head.

Temptation washed over her to throw the topic back on Drew's shortcomings to get away from her bad memories. It'd be better to make fun of him than to—.

No. It wouldn't.

She wanted to boldly say, "There is nothing about Drew Stevenson I don't like." But the words didn't come. They lodged in her throat.

She couldn't open herself up for ridicule.

Instead, she forced a smile. Aimed it at Marci. "Let's go eat. I hope they thought to order the salad bar." Although they could add it to the order if they hadn't.

The three men sat at a round table in one corner of the restaurant. Plastic bowls full of breadsticks already sat on the table, and the men didn't appear to have waited for Sara Jane and Marci. Chris had a sauce-covered piece halfway up to his mouth when they approached.

A smile played on the edge of Sara Jane's lips as Wes and Drew both rose to their feet. A moment later, Chris made the belated move to stand.

Drew was a much better catch than Chris. Marci was welcome to him.

Wes pulled the chair out between him and Chris.

The other empty chair was on the other side of the table between Wes and Drew. Since Marci had indicated she and Chris were at the beginning of a dating relationship, Sara Jane walked around the table to the chair Drew pulled out. She smiled at him. "Thank you."

He nodded.

"Chris was telling us he and Marci are going to rent a movie and go to her apartment. I called Alana and she thought it sounded fun. You two in?" Wes looked at her and then Drew.

"I promised to spend time with Wynter," Drew muttered. "She's expecting me."

He had a girlfriend? Wife? Figured. Everyone seemed to be a part of a couple.

She didn't want to be the odd one out. She shook her head. "I need to check on Grandma. Maybe I'll stop by later."

But probably not.

She glanced at Drew out of the corner of her eye. Who was Wynter?

And more important, why was she a bit jealous of this unknown woman?

9

When lunch was finished, Drew headed out to his pickup. First stop would be the butcher shop for a nice juicy bone for Wynter and a steak for him. He might have a shriveled potato left. And maybe some wilted lettuce for a salad. He'd stop at the store for groceries later. In the meantime, he'd eat the veggies before any of the good stuff from the store. "Waste not, want not," as Mom always said.

Wes already drove out of the parking lot, and Chris and Marci hung out by Marci's car, talking. Sara Jane sat in the passenger seat, her phone to her ear.

Drew slid into his truck, inserted a key into the ignition, and turned it. His phone rang, startling him. He pulled it out of his pocket and glanced at it. Unknown number.

"Drew."

"Andrew? This is Grandma." For a moment, panic filled him. Grandma had tracked him down? The voice sounded familiar but not like he remembered his grandmother's voice.

But who else would identify herself as Grandma? Oh, Sara Jane's grandmother. Mrs. Morgan. He glanced toward the other car but couldn't see the woman who'd filled too many of his thoughts. Chris and Marci still talked. Drew turned his ignition off.

"I have your business card in my purse, and I can't think of what Sara Jane's number is. This kind young man here dialed your number for me. I can't figure out these touch phones. My fingers are too clumsy."

"Sara Jane is here, Mrs. Mor . . . Grandma. Just a second while I get her." He slid out of the truck and hurried toward the other car.

"Good. I was so worried. I borrowed her car to go to quilting at church today, since we had it piled full of fabric I wanted to donate. I decided to stop at the grocery store on the way home, and I think someone stole Sara Jane's car. I can't find it anywhere." Her voice filled with panic.

Alarm bells rang. The last time she'd called, she'd found his business card in the freezer. Then she couldn't remember she'd called him and thought he was the police. It was possible she'd forgotten where she parked. "Have you looked around? I think those cars like to hide from us sometimes."

"Of course I have! I looked everywhere. It's not here. What am I going to do?"

He pursed his lips. If the car was really stolen, not good. Sara Jane would stop being the nice, friendly woman he'd been around today and become the high-maintenance drama queen. He pulled in a breath, wishing he didn't have to be the bearer of bad news. "Just a second. Let me give the phone to your granddaughter." Drew knocked on the window, and then opened the car door.

Sara Jane stared at him. He shoved the phone in her direction. "It's your grandmother."

She hesitated, looking at his phone with orange ribbons embossed on the white protective cover. Her finger traced over one of the ribbons. She glanced up at him, a clear question in her eyes, before she slid her basic black phone back into her purse and raised his to her ear. "Hello? Grandma?"

Drew stepped around the car to give her maximum privacy. Though he could imagine what her reactions might be to hearing her car was stolen.

A few minutes later, she followed him around the car. Her lips were set in a tight line and her eyes flashed. He winced, hoping he didn't get rewarded with the sharp end of her tongue. He'd already experienced enough of that. She looked at Marci as she handed him back his phone. "I let Grandma borrow my car and she thinks someone stole it. We need to go now."

Marci shot an irritated gaze toward her.

Drew pocketed his phone. Pulled in a deep breath and hopefully some courage along with it. "You can ride with me, Miss Mor . . . Sara Jane, if you'd like. I'll be going right through Bruceton Mills on my way home."

She swung around to face him. "That'd be great. Thank you, so much." Her expression relaxed into a smile.

He nodded, but as he turned toward his truck, he cringed. What had he been thinking? The cab was still a wreck.

Sara Jane grabbed her purse off the floorboard of Marci's car, then hurried over to Drew's truck. It was so nice of him to step in like this. He'd be the strong shoulder to lean on if Grandma had lost her car or if it was some of the troubling forgetfulness Sara Jane was getting concerned about.

Drew opened the passenger side door and used a cute little broom to sweep off the seat. He left the broom there while he shook out a blanket.

She started to get into the cab, not hesitating as she had the first time, when he came up behind her. "Just a second. Hop down a minute."

She did as he asked, and he spread the blanket out on the seat.

"This should be a bit cleaner."

It wasn't necessary—but then, remembering her first reaction to his truck, maybe it was. Her face heated. She'd been rude. No wonder he had no interest in her.

Well, there was also the Wynter woman . . .

She frowned. "Thank you."

He nodded.

She climbed in and sat, arranging her purse beside her, then reached for the seat belt. He stood there, in the open doorway, watching her. It made her feel cared for. And insanely jealous of the Wynter woman for getting to him first. When she finally was settled, he shut the door and jogged around the front of the truck.

"Do you know where your grandma is?"

Sara Jane nodded. "At the grocery store. It's strange someone would steal my car in Bruceton Mills. It's a small town. Everyone knows everyone, and it seems people would know it was mine. I never locked it before. I guess I'll need to start." She twisted the handle of her purse. "After it's found, of course. I told Grandma to call the police. She hadn't yet." She exhaled, loudly. "My car! I bought it when I graduated from college in June last year. It was used, but barely."

Drew nodded. He secured his own seat belt, then started the engine. He pulled out on the road. Silent. Did he worry she'd give him the lecture the thief deserved? Was he afraid to say something to set her off?

Probably so. She needed to change the subject, and fast.

"It's nice of you to do this. I hate to keep you from . . . Wynter." It hurt to say the other woman's name. Strange. She glanced at his hand. No ring, but he did work construction. Maybe he didn't wear one.

He shrugged. "Like I said, I'm going through town anyway. And it's not like she's keeping track of time."

"Does she work on weekends?" She twisted in the seat to face him. "Is she your wife or girlfriend?" She needed to clarify and make it official he was off limits before her heart got too committed.

A corner of his mouth lifted, then fell. "My dog."

A wave of relief washed over her. Strange she wanted him to be as unattached as she was. Selfish of her too.

But then, just because Wynter was a dog didn't mean he was available.

She had to know.

"So you aren't going to Marci's to watch movies with your friends because you promised your dog you'd spend time with her?" Did he hear her pathetic attempt to add a flirty note in her voice?

She wanted to ask why he'd walked away from her at the tavern. Why he'd said asking her out wouldn't happen. Why wasn't he interested in her?

She'd seen his gaze slide over her. Seen the heated look in his eyes. The way his gaze lingered on her mouth.

Her pulse warmed.

His dark gaze rested on her a brief moment before he turned his attention back to the road.

Her heart pounded.

He opened his mouth and shut it, twice, before he shook his head. "I . . . she needs to go on a run."

"And your girlfriend? What does she do?" She hated herself for asking. For needing to know.

His gaze slid back to her, then away. "Careful, Miss Mor . . . Sara Jane. I might get the impression you're fishing."

"Maybe I am." She kept her eyes on him. *Please, say you're available . . .*

He frowned, his brow furrowed. His thumb slid over the steering wheel curve.

She held her breath.

"I'm . . . your grandmother's handyman. It's all that matters."

Which didn't answer her question, but it effectively communicated, "Back off."

Drew pulled in a shaky breath and set his mouth. He didn't dare look at her. He was aware of the almost palpable tension radiating in the cab of his truck. She had to be as well. But he didn't understand it.

Not at all.

Seemed their whole interaction today, from the time they met by the fort, had been filled with him being physically aware of her. Imagining what it might be like to have the right to touch her. To kiss those soft-looking lips. To run his fingers through her glorious hair.

She had to be aware of his emotions. Otherwise, she wouldn't be teasing him as she did. Flirting. Almost . . . encouraging him.

Just so she could laugh in his face when she rejected him.

Not happening.

Ever.

He pulled into the parking lot of the grocery store. A police car, lights flashing, idled outside the store, and Grandma stood there with the uniformed officer. Another man, possibly the store manager, waited beside her. He drove up beside the cruiser.

Sara Jane was out of the truck before Drew came to a complete stop.

He parked at the end of the lot, pocketing his keys as he exited the vehicle. He walked toward the group, standing around the police car, but then hesitated as he noticed a silver four-door Toyota Prius.

It looked like her car. It didn't mean it was, of course, but. . . . He frowned, noted the license plate numbers, then went to join the Morgan ladies.

Sara Jane talked to the officer when Drew arrived. She waved her arms around as she spoke as if to illustrate points. As he came up behind her, she described her vehicle, and recited her license plate's first three digits.

The same three as on the vehicle Drew had seen. He reached out and touched her shoulder. "Sara Jane."

She turned to look at him.

He pointed, wordless, out into the lot. Her gaze followed his finger. Her eyes widened, and she started across the parking lot. "My car! Grandma, it's right there!"

Grandma blinked. "When did you get this car, Sara Jane? I thought you owned a blue car." She trailed after Sara Jane, but then hesitated when her granddaughter turned around with a frown and wrinkled brow. "I meant, I parked the car somewhere else. I know I did. Not there. Someone stole it and brought it back and parked it wrong."

Excuses, excuses. To him, Grandma seemed to try to cover up her mental mix-ups. He was surprised she hadn't done so after the police/crashing raccoon phone call. Concern ate at him. He probably shouldn't have brushed aside the earlier episode and warned Sara Jane. But . . . she'd seen it now. No need for him to get involved in something that was none of his concern.

The police officer shut his notebook and slid it into his pocket. "Happens all the time, ma'am." He looked at Drew and shook his head. "I'll wait to verify it is her car."

Drew and the officer followed the women.

"It is my car, Grandma. Sorry for bothering you, Officer." She turned away, taking the keys from her grandma. "What do you mean, when did I get this car? You went with me when I started shopping for a more dependable one. Grandma, I think we need to get you in to see a doctor."

"You'll do no such thing, Sara Jane. How dare you suggest I might be losing my mind? I know exactly where I parked your car and it wasn't there."

Drew shook his head as he headed toward his truck. The Morgan women would be having a loud conversation before too long.

But as he glanced back at the Prius, he noticed what appeared to be a fresh scratch on the rear door.

10

Thursday morning, Sari sorted through the fabric looking for the quilt pieces she'd already finished. She set aside a stack of quilting books for Sara Jane to look through when she arrived. Of course, she might take them home with her. The girl probably needed something to keep her busy during the summer. She might as well learn the stitches for appliqué.

She wished Sara Jane would show more interest in quilting. It involved needles, thread, and sewing, but they had never caught her attention. She seemed more interested in history books and the History Channel on TV. Maybe if Sari focused on the historical aspects Sara Jane would then be interested. Participate. Daniel Boone's mama and wife made quilts. Sara Jane seemed especially fascinated with him right now, rambling on about planning a series of lessons about him for her classes in school.

She bet Sara Jane's ears would perk up if she mentioned Daniel Boone was in the Morgan family tree. Her mother-in-law had traced the family tree back past him. She'd have to drop the tidbit into a discussion when Sara Jane arrived. Mention how they'd probably made a ballad quilt. It should catch her attention.

She sighed and rested her fists on her hips as she surveyed her sewing room. Where were those three quilt blocks she'd finished?

They should be somewhere. Surely she hadn't thrown them out. She opened the lid of the last box. There they were. Right on top.

She'd made the heart one first. One she'd made when she'd first fell in love with Cade, all those years ago. Two hearts in different shades of red. They overlapped like regular hearts found on a Valentine's Day card. Probably where she'd gotten the idea for it in the first place. It'd been a card from Cade.

She picked up the heart quilt block and ran her fingertip over the white background. As a young girl, she'd thought white would be best. It would go with everything. Now, she wondered if it shouldn't have been blue, for the sky in some of the backgrounds. Of course, no one ever decreed all quilt blocks had to have the same background color. If they had, it'd be a rule needing to be broken.

She laid the block on the table and reached for the next one. She was surprised the white background wasn't stained with tears. She'd made this second one when she and Cade had had a nasty fight and broke up. It was the same as the first, but one of the hearts had been cut in half with a zigzag pattern to portray a broken heart. Her heart broke anew, looking at it. A tear made its way down her cheek. She brushed it away.

The quilt. It was about the quilt. One of the hearts had been broken in the song "Pretty Saro." At the time, she'd imagined the song portrayed her own life. In reverse. According to the song, the girl dumped her beau to marry a landowner. In real life, Cade had dropped her to go seek his fortune. He'd settled down quick enough, giving up his California dreams, and came back to marry her and work in the coal mines.

The third quilt block she'd made after their marriage, before their son was born. It was a dove. She'd used a white patterned fabric to make the body of the dove, then a light gray-patterned fabric for the wing. The bird had been appliquéd on a blue cloud, so it didn't get lost in the background of the white block. The whole effect was striking. She'd imagined it portrayed her and Cade setting off on the wings of love. But in the ballad, it symbolized wanting to fly to where the loved one lodged so they could be together. It was still applicable. Cade lived in eternity now. Another tear wandered down her cheek. Some days she couldn't wait until she could join him. She'd never tell Sara Jane though. Death was a taboo subject between them.

She'd also never admit the episode with the car had shaken her up quite a bit. It was by the grace of God Andrew had noticed the scratch on Sara Jane's car. It'd given validity to her false claim someone had moved the car. She cringed as she remembered the scrape of metal against metal. What exactly had she hit?

She shook her head. Her memory came up blank.

Sara Jane would make noises about taking away her license if she confessed.

She heard a car door slam and put down the third block with the others. With a sigh, she went to the front of the house and looked out. Sara Jane had arrived. And so had Andrew.

She'd forgotten he'd planned to come out today.

She watched as Sara Jane turned toward Andrew with a bright smile.

Wouldn't it be wonderful if Sara Jane found love this summer?

Though, watching Andrew stiffen with Sara Jane's approach, it probably wouldn't be with him. Pity. He was such a nice young man.

Unless she could somehow intervene.

Sara Jane's smile faltered as she neared Drew. Why did he seem so unhappy to see her? She'd thought they'd formed a tentative friendship on Saturday, but it seemed she was wrong.

Of course, he'd made his disinterest clear.

His lips curved up, but the smile looked forced. No light appeared in his eyes. And he kept his gaze on her face, though she'd been careful to dress in something he might find attractive. Sexy.

It'd been a wasted effort.

She stopped. He came a couple steps nearer. "Good morning."

"Good morning. What'd Grandma hire you to do today?"

He glanced around. "Yard upkeep and a new roof. I brought shingle samples so she can pick out what she wants. Probably won't get to the shingles today though." His gaze rested in the vicinity of her sandals, then slowly . . . ever so slowly . . . traveled up. They lingered a moment on her lips. He pulled in a breath and averted his eyes. Not quite meeting hers. "Looks like it wants to rain."

Maybe it hadn't been a wasted effort. A tinge of victory. She fought a smile and shrugged. "I doubt it will. It is the end of June."

One corner of his mouth lifted. "This is West Virginia, not the desert. It rains in June."

She cringed. She had to go make herself look like an idiot. Again. "Yes, but generally, the summer drought starts near the end of June." Maybe it would salvage her earlier comment.

He shifted the book in his arms. "The year I hiked the Appalachian Trail it rained a lot. I thought I'd never dry out."

"You thru-hiked the trail?" She remembered the conversation at the fort but hoped he'd elaborate.

He nodded.

Sara Jane leaned toward him. "Does it have anything to do with the orange leukemia ribbons embossed on your phone's cover?" She'd heard some men were driven to the Appalachian Trail by a personal tragedy.

His eyes widened and he coughed.

She rested her hand on his arm. Long enough to feel his muscles contract. His breath caught. Then she pulled away. "Come on in. I'll get you a cup of coffee. While Grandma looks over the shingles, you can tell us about the Appalachian Trail."

He shrugged, but had a wary look in his eyes. "Not much to tell."

She didn't believe it.

Grandma threw open the front door. "Come in. Sara Jane, did you bring doughnuts?"

Sara Jane faltered. "Doughnuts?"

Grandma's hands flew to her hips. "Don't play dumb with me, young lady. I distinctly remember telling you to bring doughnuts."

She did? Sara Jane scrolled back through her memory bank. She definitely didn't remember any conversation involving pastries. "What kind of doughnuts did you ask me to bring?"

Grandma rolled her eyes. "An assortment. Maybe you're the one who needs to see the doctor. Not me."

Sara Jane caught her breath. Tears burned her eyes. She took a step backward. "I'll get the doughnuts now. Sorry I forgot." Except she hadn't.

And if it weren't for Drew being there to witness an argument . . .

She swallowed. Hard. Another argument fought its way through her memory. The tears leaked out, running down her cheek. She wouldn't go there. She wouldn't.

Arguments killed.

She swiped a hand over her face. Turned on her heel and headed back to her car.

Saved by doughnuts. Drew let out a sigh of relief as he followed Mrs. Morgan into the kitchen. He should've known those orange ribbons embossed on the phone cover would come up. And Sara Jane would know they were leukemia ribbons.

He wasn't ready to talk about it.

Never would be.

Wes didn't even know the level of the pain, though they'd met at the trailhead, formed an instant friendship, and remained best friends afterward. Drew didn't know what pulled Wes to the trail—and he never shared his story.

Though he'd seen Sara Jane wipe the tears from her face before she turned and left. Was it from embarrassment or some other reason?

He wouldn't ask, because pushing her to talk about her concerns and problems would open the door to talk about his.

Not happening.

Maybe, with any luck, Mrs. Morgan would pick out the new shingles she wanted and he'd be deep in yard work before Sara Jane returned.

Or—he glanced out the window—the threatening rain would arrive, sooner rather than later, and he'd be long gone.

Drew opened the shingle sample book on the table while Grandma went to pour two cups of coffee, grumbling half under her breath the whole time about Sara Jane not bringing doughnuts. He suspected it was more likely she'd forgotten to tell her granddaughter to get some, but he wouldn't risk his hide bringing it up. Grandma seemed in rare form and upset about something other than doughnuts.

Judging by the moisture lingering on her cheeks, she'd done some crying too. But he didn't know how to ask. Besides, it also fell under the "none of his business" category.

Grandma set the cups of coffee on the table then turned to the refrigerator. "Sara Jane bought me some flavored creamer at the grocery store. It's not too bad." She opened the door and pulled out a bottle of hazelnut creamer. "Would you like some? Or do you drink it black? My husband, Cade, always used to say 'real men drink their coffee so strong they could eat it with a fork.'"

Drew chuckled, then couldn't control the belly laugh that slipped out. "He'd be about right. But I wouldn't mind a taste."

She handed him the bottle and waited while he put a couple drops in his, then poured a liberal amount into hers. She returned the cream to the refrigerator, then pulled out a chair and sat next to him.

He slid the book closer to her. "Let's take a look and see what you want. I can get them ordered from the store and pick them up tomorrow on my way back out, weather permitting." He lifted the cup to his mouth.

Grandma looked at him over the top of her glasses. "I want you."

Coffee spewed across the table. Grandma grabbed a couple cloth napkins and shoved them in his direction then slapped him across the back as he coughed. He mopped his face, then cleaned up the table. "I beg your pardon—"

"Not for me. For Sara Jane."

Oh. This was going from bad to . . . well, not exactly worse. Because truthfully, he wouldn't mind at all, as long as it was the nice Sara Jane. The drama queen, high-maintenance, control freak on the other hand. . . . She'd shake his life up quite a bit either way. His face heated.

"Now, I need to know, young man, if you're seeing someone else."

A flashback of the one time he'd dared ask a woman out. He could almost hear her laughing in his face and calling him uncomplimentary names. He swallowed the bile rising in his throat. Time to take control of this conversation, and fast. "I need to know if you hired me so you could match up your granddaughter, or whether you needed me to work. Because I have no intentions of marrying her or anyone, and it'll be a waste of time for me and money for you if it's your intention." He took a breath.

"Hmmmph. We'll see."

A car door slammed out front. Grandma rose from the seat, grabbed the napkins, and opened a cabinet door, revealing a washer and dryer. She tossed the napkins in the laundry basket sitting on top of the washing machine, before walking away.

"Sara Jane is here. You'll say nothing to her about this conversation."

"I wouldn't dream of it."

"But it's good to know you're available. I've made up my mind, son. No point in fighting it."

Had he said he was available? Or had she drawn correct conclusions from his avoidance of the question?

She left the room. Drew stared at the book of shingle samples. Run—from a job he needed and a challenge? Or stay, knowing he was in the clutches of a die-hard matchmaker?

11

Sara Jane carried the package of doughnuts into the kitchen and set it on the table, glancing at Drew as he flipped through shingle samples. He didn't look up at her, but red crept up his neck. Since it seemed to be his typical reaction to being around her, he had to be aware of her presence. Grandma hurried ahead of her, got out a cup, and filled it with coffee. She set it on the table before grabbing the creamer.

"Did you pick out the shingles you want?" Sara Jane sat in the chair next to Drew and reached across him for the book, but Grandma pulled it away.

Grandma pursed her lips. "Not yet. We were getting ready to discuss what we want." She jabbed her finger down on a sample similar to what was currently on the roof, a brownish color a little darker than the logs. "I like this one better than that one." She pointed at another piece.

Drew lifted a brow. "They'd make a good choice. The specs are—"

"I don't care what the specs are. They mean nothing to me. It says here they'll last twenty years. They'll outlast me. All that matters."

Wow. Grandma was cantankerous. Though she spoke the truth. A pang of sadness hit Sara Jane. While she and Grandma didn't always see eye to eye, they were each other's only family.

Drew nodded. "Yes, ma'am. If it's your final choice, I'll go—"

"Before you do, sit down and enjoy a doughnut and finish your coffee."

Sara Jane nodded. "Yes, please. Especially since I went to get them. It's raining now anyway. You won't get any yard work done." She reached for the sample book again, this time brushing against his arm on purpose. Sparks shot through her.

He glanced at her, his gaze not quite meeting hers, then abruptly stood and walked to the window. "It's sprinkling. I'll measure the roof and figure the area before I call to order the shingles. I'll plan another day to come back to do the work."

"You said you'd pick them up on your way out tomorrow. Do you live in Morgantown?" Sara Jane added creamer to her coffee, then took a sip. Perfect.

"Yes'm." He went out the back door.

Drew seemed so skittish. Had she done something to offend him? Maybe touching his arm bothered him? He was so shy. . . . Or perhaps asking those questions about the orange ribbons embossed on his phone cover had upset him. Her questions were kind of invasive, considering they barely knew each other and hadn't scratched the surface of friendship.

She lowered her eyes, swallowed the lump in her throat, and set her coffee cup down on the table. Maybe she should go and apologize.

"I found the quilt squares this morning." Grandma reached for a chocolate-covered doughnut. "Figured we'd plan out the next few."

Sara Jane tried to rouse a measure of interest. If only she was as creative as Grandma. But she wasn't. "That's nice. I'm glad you found them." Her gaze went to the window as a ladder passed by. The lowest part of the roof was by the kitchen on the attached shed. She started to rise so she could watch Drew but forced herself to stay in the seat. She might be too obvious.

"Daniel Boone's mama made quilts, you know." Grandma sounded almost defensive.

"Huh?" Sara Jane looked at Grandma, trying to ignore the thump of the ladder against the house and the following footfalls crossing the roof.

"I said, Daniel Boone. . . . Oh, you heard me. He's in the family tree, you know. Daniel Boone is. Not a direct line, but he's there. His middle name was Morgan. Did you know that?"

"No." Interest in seeing proof pushed Sara Jane out of the chair. "Do you have a copy of the family tree?"

Grandma blinked. "The point is he used homemade quilts. Probably took one out in the wilderness to sleep under."

"Grandma, you don't drop the bombshell someone famous is in the family tree, and then go on and talk about quilts. It's a given they used homemade quilts back then."

"At least not when the person they're talking to is only interested in history." Grandma made a frustrated sound. "Try to wrap your mind around this. Someone had to make the quilts. It's in your history. And if you pay attention, when we finish our ballad quilt, I'll show you a quilt I have made by Daniel Boone's mama—your grandma several times removed. Do you know what her name was?" Grandma pinned her with a glare.

Sara Jane frowned, her mind scrambling through all the historical facts she had stored somewhere in her jumbled brain. "Her name was—"

"Sarah Morgan." Grandma thumped the table. Doughnut crumbles scattered.

"Right. Sarah . . . Sarah Jarman Morgan. I was named after her?" Sara Jane's eyes brimmed. She dropped back into the chair. "You have a quilt made by Daniel Boone's mama in this house?"

Drew slid his smartphone into his pocket after making the needed measurements on the roof, figuring the area, and making a note. He made his way over to the ladder and climbed down. He'd collect his sample book and call in the order for the shingles.

He collapsed his ladder, placed it in the bed of the truck, and then went to the house and knocked on the door. He tried to mentally prepare himself for Sara Jane. Moments later, the door opened. Grandma stood aside. "Ready for your doughnut?" He resisted looking past her.

"No, thanks. I need the sample book. I'll place the order for the shingles, and then start pruning the low branches on the tree out front."

Grandma peeked outside. "It's still sprinkling."

"Yes'm. But I'm not sugar. I don't melt." He smiled, glad Sara Jane wasn't in sight.

Grandma made a "hmmmph" sound but handed him the sample book. "When you finish, we'll be in the sewing room. I have a few more chores for you. Don't bother to knock, I know you're here and we're family." She adjusted her glasses.

Hardly family and not likely to be. But wouldn't it be wonderful if. . . . Not going that dangerous direction. He managed a nod.

He carried the sample book to the truck, and sat in the driver's seat a moment as he used the phone to place the order for the shingles. Then he grabbed the pruning shears and went to trim the trees.

It seemed wrong to open the door and enter the house, but those were the directions he'd been given. Drew knocked once, then opened the door. "It's Drew."

"Come on in." The voice came from the back bedroom—the sewing room, as Grandma had called it.

He walked down the hall and stood in the doorway. Again, the colorful array of fabric was almost overwhelming. He tried not to notice Sara Jane, as he dared to walk into the room and run the tips of his fingers over a piece of grass-green fabric. The fabric had kind of a nubby feel—or maybe his calluses snagged it. He frowned and pulled his hand back.

"It's supposed to be grass," Grandma said. "We're. . . . Make it, I'm—" she glared toward Sara Jane. "planning a couple quilt squares. One with a log cabin on it and one a mountain scene. Both will have grass on them."

Drew glanced over at Sara Jane. She scowled as she maneuvered a brown square of fabric around on blue background material. "It isn't sitting right."

Drew ran a hand over his whiskered chin. "Possibly because cabins aren't plain squares." He held out his hand. "May I?"

Sara Jane hesitated a moment, then handed the square to him. Thankfully, his fingers didn't brush hers. He took it, reached for another brown piece of fabric, and then the scissors. Laying the two pieces beside each other on the table, he did a little trimming off the bottom and top of one to make it look like the building had a distinct corner.

"Wow." Sara Jane studied it. "You have an artistic mind, don't you? I was doing what Grandma said and laying it out."

"I said, 'Design it,'" Grandma snapped. "You were *not* doing what I said."

Hurt shone in Sara Jane's eyes, then she looked down. "I was trying."

Grandma went from sweet to snarky without warning. Drew frowned. He wanted to jump to Sara Jane's defense. Not everyone was artistically inclined. But it seemed Grandma should be kinder to her granddaughter. Instead, she was kinder to him.

"Unless you have exactly zero aptitude for this, you were not trying." Grandma didn't soften her voice at all. "If you want to see the quilt designed by Sarah Morgan, maybe you'd better start."

Drew blinked. "Sarah Morgan?"

"Daniel Boone's mama." Sara Jane glanced up, briefly. Tears glittered on the edges of her lashes.

He wanted to help. Even if it meant being close to her. He reached for a scrap of light yellow fabric. It had a bit of a tiny pattern on it, but he figured it'd work. He laid it on one side of the brown fabric and glanced at her. "This could be the window. And if you have darker brown fabric, it'd work for the door. If you know how to do embroidery, you could make a doorknob with a couple stitches." His grandma had taught him how to embroider one summer when he'd had a broken leg. It'd helped pass the time, and he enjoyed creating lasting pieces of art.

Grandma pulled him into her arms and gave him a hug. Her head only reached the center of his chest. If only it'd been Sara Jane hugging him. Though he'd probably melt into a puddle on the floor if she did.

"You are a man after my heart. See, Sara Jane, Andrew is trying." Grandma released him and studied his cabin.

"Or maybe it comes natural for an artist," Sara Jane muttered.

Grandma didn't respond. Maybe she hadn't heard. Instead, she busied herself with a piece of dark green material, draping it over the cabin to make a roof. She slid a piece of the nubby light green fabric under the bottom of the cabin for the grass.

"You could appliqué, Sara Jane. It shouldn't be too hard for you. If it is, baste this together with a long running stitch, and I'll show you how to appliqué later," Grandma said. "Now, Andrew . . ." She turned toward him, holding out some purplish-gray material.

He raised his hands. "Oh, no. I finished the trimming and it's raining too hard right now for further outside work. You had some interior jobs?"

"I did?" Grandma stared at him blankly.

"Yes, ma'am." He didn't glance toward Sara Jane, but wondered if she realized . . .

Grandma frowned. "I guess you could help me put these quilt blocks together since you have an aptitude for it. Unless you have something else you need to do, then I'll call you when I think of what it was."

"I wouldn't feel right getting paid for quilting." Drew backed toward the door.

"Of course not. I wouldn't dream of paying you for it. It's pleasure, not work."

Sara Jane made an unladylike snort.

Drew pulled in a breath, his gaze drawn toward the beautiful woman on the other side of the table. Compassion stirred him. Almost without thought, he took the purple material and walked around the table to Sara Jane. He stood beside her, and breathed in the scent of her. It reminded him of the lilac bush outside his front door. *Focus.* "It's not hard. It's a matter of imagination. This purple is supposed to be a . . ." He looked across the table at Grandma and raised a brow.

"A mountain."

He nodded. "What will you need to do to make it into a mountain?" He handed Sara Jane the fabric. His hand trembled. Maybe she wouldn't notice.

She held it, turned it side to side, then folded it. "Maybe cut it into a triangle?" She looked up at him.

He smiled. "Not too many mountains are shaped like a triangle, but for the quilt, I think it'd be fine." He reached for a piece of dusty blue fabric. "This one could be another slightly smaller triangle placed beside or a bit in front of the larger one."

Grandma handed him some white material. "What mountaintop is complete without snow?"

He could think of several, but he nodded. "And what would you do to give the illusion of distance?"

Sara Jane shifted, her arm brushing his. "We could add some trees in front of it?"

"I knew you could do it, if you tried." Grandma smiled. "I want a pond down by the trees too."

"So what is the point of the cabin and the mountains? I get the hearts, and the dove makes sense, since you explained them." Sara Jane reached for a fabric marker, brushing against Drew again.

Sparks flickered up his arm and into his heart. He could stay there all day, even if his friends teased him.

She sketched out a triangle, then started to cut it out.

He moved a step away. His brain would soon be reduced to mush this way.

"In the song, the cabin scene symbolizes the home he hopes to build for her where he can provide for her with silver and gold . . . but in my life, I imagine it meaning the home Cade built for me. This one." Grandma looked around the room. "Filled with all the love we had for each other."

"And you want to sell it." Sara Jane had a defensive note in her voice.

Drew didn't want to be present for another discussion not involving him. He pointed to the purple material Sara Jane held. "And the mountains?"

Grandma frowned. "A line in the ballad mentions a mountain's sad brow. I think it indicates the distance separating him from his love. He still misses her, thinks of her, and wants to be with her."

She didn't mention the application of this one to her life, but judging by the sadness filling her face, he could guess the directions her thoughts had gone. For a second, he wanted to ask where her children were. Why Sara Jane was the only relative who seemed to come by. But then, he wasn't around often. Maybe they did come by. And it really didn't concern him. *Just the handyman.*

He looked at Grandma. "You wanted a body of water by the trees? What about some sort of wildlife? Like a bear or a deer?" It'd be harder, but he could cut something out to resemble them.

"No wildlife."

He nodded. "I need to go, but trees are easy." He glanced at Sara Jane. "Just brown and green. There's an arts and crafts festival this coming weekend. I need to work on my brooms, get a few more finished up to sell. There's also a convention in Arkansas I'm planning to go to in November."

"Let me get my purse so I can pay you." Grandma followed him to the door.

He glanced back at Sara Jane and caught a glimpse of what appeared to be open admiration. He dared a wink. "You can do it."

She blushed.

He hadn't meant to embarrass her.

Grandma pushed past him. "I want to go to your arts and crafts festival. I'll send Sara Jane out with you to get directions, if it's not too far away."

"About an hour, give or take."

"Go grab a doughnut. I'll meet you in the kitchen and give you the money. Sara Jane, pour the man a cup of coffee."

Sara Jane followed Drew down the hall and into the kitchen. But when she headed for the coffeepot, he shook his head. "I don't want one, but thanks anyway. I'll take a glass of ice water though."

"Sure. So where is this arts and craft festival? And is it okay if I take Grandma since she wants to go?"

"Sure. Grandma can go." It'd mean Sara Jane would be there. He could feed his crush. He pulled a folded piece of paper out of his pocket and laid it on the table. "This is about the festival." He'd planned to hang it on the community bulletin board at the grocery store, but he could bring another one by sometime. He might have another in the truck, actually. He'd have to check.

He swallowed his feelings of trepidation about the festival. Chances of his family showing up? The odds weren't good.

Grandma bustled into the room as Drew swallowed a sip of water. Cold and refreshing. He swallowed the rest in a long gulp, then set the empty cup on the counter.

"How much do I owe you for today?"

He hadn't done much. Measured the roof, ordered the shingles, and trimmed the trees. He'd have to come back out and finish all the jobs later. Another opportunity to see Sara Jane. He shook his head. "Don't worry about it. I'll figure it up and since I have to come back out for the yard work and to do the roof, you can pay me then."

"Okay. I wish I could remember what jobs I wanted you to do." Grandma scratched her head.

"The closet door. Remember, we accidentally bumped the door when we got the boxes out of the closet." Sara Jane opened the refrigerator, took out a can of soda, and popped the top open.

Grandma frowned at her. "You're still drinking them? Don't you know they're unhealthy? In fact, I heard on the news some mayor somewhere is campaigning to make them illegal."

"No one is going to tell me what I can or can't drink, Grandma." Sara Jane rolled her eyes.

"Anyway. It ripped the hinges right off the closet door. Almost as bad as the lock you broke the other day, Sara Jane. When I locked myself out of the bathroom and couldn't find the key and you took a hammer to the knob?"

Drew smothered a laugh. He glanced at Sara Jane's manicure. Surprisingly, she hadn't broken a nail.

Sara Jane took a hammer to a doorknob?

Sara Jane's face heated. Looking like an idiot in front of Drew again. She refused to look at him, didn't want to see if derision was on his face. "Well, we found the key. But I still think the medicine cabinet is a silly place to keep it. You can't lock yourself *in* the bathroom."

"It's the other job." Grandma beamed. "Andrew, I need you to fix the closet and the bathroom knob. I knew I'd remember."

"Yes'm." Drew reached for the doughnut box, then apparently changed his mind and pulled his hand back. "I'll take a look at the closet, but the knob will have to wait until I pick up a new one. Where is it?"

"Sewing room."

Sara Jane cringed. It'd take her right back into the fray. She picked up the flyer Drew left on the table and pretended to study it while Grandma showed him the closet. Then she put it down, wandered over to the window, and looked out at the pouring rain as she took a sip of her soda.

Sewing had actually seemed fun when Drew had stood beside her, showing her how to do things. If only she had the talent to see things artistically. Grandma was getting so frustrated with her attempts with the cabin, but she couldn't seem to make it work. Drew had it together in no time.

Not fair.

But he'd come over to stand beside her, to talk her through seeing things to go on the quilt. She could smell the pine scent of his soap as well as a hint of coffee.

For a moment, she'd thought he'd put his arms around her, standing behind her while looking over her shoulder. But Drew wasn't forward. He'd moved away when she touched him.

Just as well. He still looked like a John the Baptist wannabe. She'd be subjected to ridicule by her peers for being seen with him. She cringed as she remembered Marci calling it the "caveman look."

Then again, she didn't care what her friends thought—but she did try to keep everyone on her friendly side.

It was amazing how one unkempt man could interest her so much. The bits of information she learned about him were so intriguing she wanted to know more.

Then again, she wasn't willing to reciprocate and expose her pain. He might have some good reasons for keeping his secrets.

Still, someday, she wanted to learn the story behind those embossed orange ribbons and hear the details of his Appalachian Trail hike.

Though . . . if he hiked through using the name Broom-man, she should be able to find his trail journal—if it was online.

She'd have to check.

Drew came back into the room. "Ripped the facing right off the wall. I'm going out to the truck to see if I have a few things I need to fix it."

She'd be waiting.

12

On Saturday, Drew greeted the people entering his open-air tent. Festivals were a step out of his comfort zone, but a man could use only so many brooms, and he loved to make them. God blessed him with an abundance of sticks from the nearby woods and mountains. His hobby was a side benefit to hiking—for broom handles, if anyone asked.

He'd just closed a sale when he glanced up to see his brother, Joey, and his sister-in-law, Carly, step into the tent.

He'd been found. . . . One of his big concerns about coming to this area. His family lived here and chances were good someone would recognize him. He'd hoped he could avoid family. A pang of longing hit him as he looked in his brother's eyes. It'd been awhile. Four years. Maybe it was time.

"I thought you might be here." Joey gave him a bear hug. "Haven't seen you in a long time, Bro."

Unspoken, but heard loud and clear, "Not since Annie died."

He savored the contact a moment. Then the memories came flooding back. Pain knifed through Drew's heart.

"Everyone misses you. Mom hardly leaves the house, hoping you'll call."

Drew set his lips, looked at the brooms, then picked up one and handed it to Carly. "Give this to Mom. Tell her I love her. I'll call."

Sometime. When he worked up the courage. Tears burned his eyes and he glanced away.

"Tried to talk her into coming to the festival today, but she wasn't convinced you'd be here."

Guilt ate at him. He'd been a terrible son. Walking away from his family in his grief. At least he hadn't walked away from his faith—for long. Struggling his way through the rough terrain of the Appalachian Trail had pulled him back into the fold. Securely. Intimately.

He didn't struggle with anger at God. It was more of disbelief God thought Drew was good enough to be called to serve. He wasn't. Not by a long shot. He didn't understand why he'd been spared—and she hadn't.

Whosoever means me. The mantra raced through his head. His family loved him, wanted him to be in touch. And God loved him. Sometimes, he couldn't exactly picture God welcoming him with open arms. Maybe saying, "Hey. We have a room on the back forty for you."

Though it was where he'd want to be. On the back forty. Rural. Space. Freedom. Hiking.

Drew smiled. Pulled his brother back into his arms for another bear hug. "I missed you too. I'm sorry. I'll try to do better. It's just . . ." He shook his head.

Carly rubbed her stomach. "Joey and I are going to have a baby. It'll be due around Thanksgiving."

His smile widened. "Great! Do you know what you're having?"

"No." Joey laughed. "Only we want his uncle to be in his life."

"Her uncle, you mean." Carly grinned at her husband.

"Whatever." Joey wrapped an arm around Carly. "I'll tell Mom you're here. She may drive up to see you. Even if she doesn't, please join us for dinner tonight. We've missed you. Remember, family is important."

Drew nodded. "I'll be there. Around six?"

"Come by when you close up here. I assume you have a room in town, or will you be displaying your brooms tomorrow?"

"Yes, I'll be here tomorrow."

He hadn't known his brother kept up to date with the arts and crafts scenes, but maybe it was only in an attempt to track him down.

He'd try to do better.

He needed his family.

Carly handed him back the broom. "You give this to your mom yourself. She'll be at dinner tonight too."

Sara Jane sat in front of her notebook computer browsing through trail journals, looking for Broom-man. She'd promised to pick Grandma up in an hour, and they'd eat lunch at the festival. Grandma loved the homemade strawberry ice cream they sold at these events. She'd started talking about ice cream when she found out Drew's festival was close enough she could go.

After some searching, Sara Jane found a trail journal for Broom-man. There were several before and several after, giving her the choice of "following" his journey. If he were currently walking, she would. She bookmarked the page so she could read all his entries when she had more time.

Still, she couldn't resist taking a moment to glance at a couple.

Woke up to sunshine. It felt great as Lion King and I continued our descent. At the bottom was "trail magic." We sat on lawn chairs and enjoyed the sunshine, fruit, candy bars, pop, orange juice, cookies, and other treats. The people who brought the "magic" were nice. We left with two days of snacks. After we walked down the rest of the mountain, we crossed a river. About a mile later we came to a hostel. It was a deep, southern Appalachian mountain place. They had frozen pizzas and a little oven. Lots of hikers spent the night.

Someday, she'd like to go on a hike like this with Drew.

The next one was posted three days later. *I woke to screaming, pounding wind against my hammock, but no rain . . .*

The phone rang, jarring Sara Jane away from the trail journals. She glanced at the caller ID. Grandma. Must be anxious. She smiled.

"Hi. I was just leaving." At least she would've been as soon as she finished reading a few of his entries.

"Good. I'm anxious to see what they got up there. But I won't buy anything. Planning on contacting the real estate agent on Monday. I want ice cream as soon as we get there. Maybe we could pick some up for Andrew too. I bet he'd like it."

"I'm sure he would." Sara Jane glanced back at the screen, then reluctantly closed the notebook computer.

Drew hadn't said anything in the posts she'd read about what had dragged him out there, but it'd been fascinating getting a peek into his life. He was wordier on screen than in person too. A plus.

She stood, slid her phone into her pocket, and headed toward the door. As she did, she glanced around at the apartment she rented. It was small, one bedroom, with a walk-in closet and a bathroom. The living room and kitchen was one long area. Perfect for one person. She'd hate to give up her freedom, but maybe Grandma would forget the foolishness about selling if Sara Jane moved in with her.

On the other hand, she might go berserk if she had to put up with Grandma pushing quilting and sewing every spare moment and grumbling when Sara Jane wanted to sit and watch the History Channel, read a book, plan lessons, or grade papers. Besides, what was the old saying? Familiarity breeds contempt?

And if, on the off-chance she and Drew got together. . . .

She'd do better to keep her space.

But preparing her house to sell? After Grandpa built it for her when they were first married? Daddy was born and raised there, though there weren't any signs left of him. Not even a picture of him and Mama on the fireplace mantel.

Grandma had packed the framed pictures and photo albums away somewhere. "No point living in the past," she'd muttered when she'd caught Sara Jane crying over the pictures soon after their deaths. It was the last Sara Jane had seen of the photos.

Some days she wished she could find them. To see their faces one more time.

She looked away. No point in getting melodramatic now. She had to pick up Grandma. Someday, when she had time, she'd go to the cemetery, take flowers, and tell Mama and Daddy how much she missed them. And how sorry she was.

Several hours later, Drew's brother and Carly were leaving the tent when Sara Jane and Grandma strolled in. Sara Jane carried a bag from one of the food stands and had three large drink cups. He wasn't sure how she carried it all without dumping something. Must have spent some time as a waitress. Grandma held three ice cream cups with little spoons stuck in them. Drew chuckled.

"We've brought sustenance." Sara Jane carried the food over to the table.

"Just call it what it is, Sara Jane. Food." Grandma handed him an ice cream cup. "Eat this first, before it melts."

Out on the sidewalk, Joey and Carly hesitated, glancing at him, before turning and coming back in. His brother looked at him, as if he expected an introduction. And clearly communicating if he didn't get one, pronto, he'd do the introducing himself.

Drew forced a smile. "Joey, this is Mrs. Morgan and her granddaughter, Sara Jane." He glanced at Sara Jane, then Grandma. "My brother, Joey, and his wife, Carly."

"Nice to meet you!" Grandma put the other two ice cream bowls down and turned to give them both hugs. "I didn't know Andrew had family other than us. I'm his grandma-to-be."

Sara Jane fumbled the drinks she held. Drew reached out and took them before they tumbled to the grass.

"Really. Grandma-to-be?" Joey's eyebrows shot up. "Then you will have to join us for the family dinner at our house tonight. An . . . Drew knows the way."

Carly squealed. "When is the big day? And are we getting an invitation in the mail?"

Sara Jane's mouth hung open and she made a funny choking sound as if she tried to suck in air.

She didn't need to take it so hard. But maybe it wasn't dismay. It could be shock. Should he pound her back or correct the misunderstanding first? "We, uh, she—"

"We'd love to join you for dinner. And don't worry, honey. I'm sure you'll be invited to the wedding. It'll be next year sometime. They haven't exactly made the save-the-date announcements yet." Grandma took a bite of ice cream, then set the bowl down.

They *hadn't exactly* started dating and were unlikely to. Drew opened his mouth again, feeling the same choky-ness Sara Jane must be suffering from. He couldn't quite pull in enough air to breathe, let alone form words.

Besides, what could he say? He and Sara Jane didn't even like each other—much—well, maybe he liked her, but it was as far as it went. He was the handyman. They weren't dating and—

"Aren't they the cutest couple? I couldn't be happier." Grandma beamed.

"Adorable." Joey stared at Drew. His brows furrowed into the look he always got when something confused him.

Carly seemed to take it at face value. She crossed the tent, wrapped her arms around Sara Jane and hugged her. "Welcome to the family. I know we're going to be the best of friends." She pulled back. "Come on, Joey. I've got grocery shopping to do. I need to plan a menu. This is sooo exciting!" She took his arm and dragged him off.

Drew still struggled to breathe. Sara Jane turned an alarming shade of red.

Grandma didn't seem fazed at all. She calmly took a bite of her ice cream, then looked up. "You should've told your brother, Andrew. Family likes to know these things. They kind of like to meet the woman you're dating before the marriage is announced too. You should've known this." She shook her head.

Yes, well . . . it might've happened, assuming he actually dated someone. He nodded, not quite able to form words yet. Maybe ice cream would help. Or whatever was in the cups. He picked one up and took a long swig of lemonade.

Sara Jane gave him a look he couldn't quite understand—panic, maybe, or dismay—and turned and disappeared into the crowd, not saying a word. It might have been pure horror Grandma had made the announcement. But it hadn't looked like horror. Perhaps the unspoken communication had been to keep an eye on Grandma, who clearly had something wrong with her mental capacities. Maybe he needed to gently suggest Sara Jane take her to see a doctor sometime, since she hadn't seemed to catch any of the other obvious hints something might be wrong.

He pulled out a lawn chair, indicated Grandma have a seat, then turned his attention to some potential customers who came in.

Drew managed a smile, and prayed the words would come if they had any questions.

At least he'd have a couple allies when he went home for dinner. Except his past would be exposed to Grandma and Sara Jane, and he wasn't ready.

If only he could sweep away the past few minutes and start over. Escape back to the Appalachian Trail where things were simpler.

13

Sara Jane didn't know how long she wandered before she finally calmed enough to realize where she was. At an arts and crafts festival Grandma wanted to go to so she could eat ice cream. Where on earth did Grandma come up with the idea she and Drew were getting married? And why hadn't Drew vehemently denied it? Maybe he'd been as stunned as she.

She wanted to marry someday. But . . . Drew? Okay, he was intriguing. He'd earned her respect. He made her heart race. She wanted to know more about him and understand him, but . . . love?

She didn't even want to date him.

Well, maybe she did.

But not where anyone would see them together.

Unless he shaved and looked anything like his brother. Joey was cute enough to be acceptable. Not exactly handsome, but cute.

She was so shallow. Telling her students they shouldn't judge anything by appearances and she did it herself.

If Drew asked. . . . He wouldn't ask.

Disappointment ate at her.

They still had this confusion created by Grandma to work through.

Sara Jane blew out a frustrated breath. She needed to take control of this circumstance. Grandma would probably insist on going to Joey's house for dinner, but Sara Jane would have the unpleasant task of straightening things out. Maybe she could drive home and not show up. Drew would have to explain things to his brother. It would be rude. Plans had already been made. This virtually unknown person had pulled her into her arms, declared they'd be best friends—a balm to her battered heart—and left to buy groceries.

Well, maybe it'd be nice to have a best friend. She and Marci were friends, but Marci didn't know all her secrets. She'd never understand. She hadn't understood Sara Jane's infatuation with Drew. Though, to be honest, Sara Jane hadn't spelled it out. She'd denied it.

What made her think Carly would be a best friend she could share her deepest secrets with? Was it because she obviously cared for Drew and so had to be able to see below the surface? Besides, this best friend thing was dependent on Drew and her having a relationship.

Which they didn't. His family needed to know. Somehow. It wasn't as if it mattered much what was said. She'd never see these people again. She and Drew . . .

A strange fluttery sensation filled her stomach. Probably hunger. After all, she'd abandoned her gyro at Drew's tent. And she wasn't quite sure where it was. How many miles of tents had she passed?

Her stomach rumbled for real. Making a loud noise complete strangers standing nearby noticed. Drew had probably eaten her gyro by now. Grandma had told her to get him two, but she hadn't listened.

She found a hot dog and funnel cake booth and went to stand in line. It would fill her stomach. She hadn't had a funnel cake in ages. She paid, took her food, and went to find someplace to sit. Her mind still whirled in an alarming way. She quickly ate her lunch, then threw her trash away.

It was high time she went to relieve Drew from keeping an eye on Grandma. She hadn't asked. Just ran off. Hopefully, he'd kept Grandma there with him.

Sara Jane turned in the direction she'd come from. Then turned again. Nothing looked familiar. The tents stretched endlessly in both directions. Well, someone would know where Drew's brooms would be. Panic, similar to the time she'd lost Grandma at one of these events, filled her. Didn't they make maps? She peered into a display.

Piles of books about the Revolutionary War filled the table. Along with some information about the battle at Fort Necessity where she'd spent time with Drew. Maybe it wouldn't hurt to look at a few books before she asked. . . .

Drew glanced at his watch. Where had Sara Jane gone? Grandma was getting restless, and it took all he could think of to keep her there. They'd already eaten lunch. He placed Sara Jane's sandwich and drink in his cooler, but Grandma ate the extra ice cream. First. Before she took her sandwich. She apparently believed dessert was the most important part of the meal.

"I have to go to the ladies' room," Grandma proclaimed, despite the people inside the tent browsing through his collection of brooms. She hadn't hurt his sales any, telling everyone who came within hearing distance he was a great craftsman and his brooms would outlast a discount store's, which was true. But he was a no-pressure salesman. Either people bought or they didn't. Grandma was high-pressure. She talked just about everyone into buying something. His sales today were higher than everything he made last year at these events.

But the ladies' room? Could he trust her to go off, find the bathroom, and then find her way back? He didn't think so. Then he'd have a lost Grandma and a distraught Sara Jane to deal with.

He looked down the sidewalk in both directions, hoping to see Sara Jane coming, but she wasn't anywhere in sight. And he couldn't close down and take her. . . .

Well, maybe he could. The lady in the tent next to his might be willing to keep an eye on his things. He started to call out to her, but then noticed a familiar redhead coming through the crowd toward his tent. He couldn't keep from grinning as Ansley Hunt came into the tent and gave him a hug.

"Hey, Drew! Long time, no see."

"It has been a while. Why haven't you set up a broom display?"

"Haven't had time to get enough made. I did go to one festival earlier this year. But I ran out of broom corn and it came yesterday. They had it back-ordered."

Grandma started to leave—again.

"Wait, Grandma."

"I told you I need to go to the bathroom. I can't wait."

He'd ask Ansley to go with her, but she'd be likely to get sidetracked by a handsome man, then Grandma would be wandering around alone. "Ans, would you mind watching my booth a while? I'll be back as soon as I can."

"I don't need a babysitter, Andrew." Grandma tossed over her shoulder. "I've been going to the bathroom alone since before you were born."

Yes, but . . . Drew glanced around for Sara Jane again. Still no sign of her. Why did she go off and abandon her grandma at the craft festival? He didn't have her phone number or he'd call her. Would've called her, over an hour ago. "Ans, I'll be right back. Please stay here." He took off on a jog after Grandma. How could one elderly woman move so fast?

Brooms! Sara Jane made her way through the crowd, never so happy to see a display of straw tied on handles in her life. But it couldn't be the right one. There was no sign of Grandma or Drew, only a redheaded woman who talked—flirted—with a man across the table. Whatever her method for making a sale, it worked, because the man handed her money and walked off with a broom, a smile, and a phone number.

The pretty redhead turned to look at Sara Jane with a smile. "May I show you a specific broom? We have them for everything. Even pot scrubbers. Aren't they the cutest things?" She held up a tiny broom on a twine rope, probably for hanging in the kitchen. It was made in various colors of green, gold, white, red, and black.

"It is cute. But actually, I'm lost. I was looking for another broom display."

"Oh. Well, as far as I know, this is it, sweetie."

Sara Jane looked around in confusion. This was it? Had she wandered into another festival by mistake?

"If it isn't here, it can't be had." She waved a hand around like she was a model on a game show. "We have brooms of all shapes and sizes. Big ones, small ones, and in-between. Turkey wings, rooster tails, cobweb, hearth, whisk—"

The whisk broom was braided in the same odd color combination. Sara Jane wondered what it meant. She'd look it up online. "Yes, but I don't need a broom. I need a man."

The redhead laughed. "Then, sweetie, you're at the wrong place. Though, sometimes I get lucky. In case you haven't noticed, mostly women and couples are browsing."

Sara Jane's face heated. It didn't matter who shopped. What mattered was where Grandma had gone.

"You don't know Drew Stevenson, do you? He has a tent here, somewhere."

"Of course, I know Drew. Everyone who's anyone in the broom-making business knows Drew. But, sweetie, he doesn't go for the uptight, eat-prunes-for-breakfast type."

What! Sara Jane gawked at her a moment. How dare she? *An uptight, prune-eater?* She'd show her an uptight prune-eater. It stung to hear herself portrayed this way. But an element of truth was in the words. She wasn't Drew's type. . . . But she itched to set this flirty woman in her place.

Sara Jane pulled herself up to her full height. "I'll have you know Drew and I are seeing each other." In her dreams. And when he worked for Grandma.

Drew and Grandma entered into the tent. He walked past Sara Jane as if he didn't see her, kissed the redhead on the cheek, then gave her a hug. "Thanks. I owe you."

The redhead smirked at Sara Jane then wrapped her arms around Drew's neck. "And don't you forget it."

14

Drew gently disentangled himself from Ansley's arms. Someone made huffing sounds in the background. Probably Grandma. But Ansley always had been overly friendly, even the first time they'd met on the Appalachian Trial. She'd used the trail name "Foxy Lady." He'd been uncomfortable calling her by the nickname, so found out her real name. She'd hiked with him and Lion King for a few days, but couldn't keep up their pace, slowing them down. And she hadn't been a thru-hiker. She'd given up the first day they had to hike in the rain, complained her feet hurt and she was getting the flu. And at the next town they came to, she went home.

"Andrew! Are you two-timing Sara Jane? How dare you kiss another woman?" Grandma walloped him on the upper arm with her purse. He winced. She must've loaded it down with bricks. He backed away, holding his hands up in surrender.

"Easy there, Grandma."

Ansley pulled his sales money out of her purse and started to hand it to him. He reached for it and Grandma took aim again.

"And you, you little floozy, how dare you throw yourself at my future grandson-in-law?"

She swung her purse in Ansley's direction. Drew caught the handle, and looked around to see if Sara Jane might be anywhere in the vicinity yet. She'd returned sometime during the fray. She stood there, a clear plastic bag full of books by her side, her mouth parted, her eyes glittering with something resembling hurt. It couldn't be though. He must've imagined it and didn't care to further analyze it.

If this didn't get Grandma into a doctor . . .

"Future grandson-in-law?" Ansley blinked at her, then looked at Drew. "You're engaged?"

"No!" The words came out sharper than he intended.

Grandma smacked him with her purse again, then turned to Sara Jane.

"About time you got back here, girl." Grandma huffed. "Where did you get off to? Didn't I ever teach you it's rude to go off and leave someone at places like this?"

Never mind Grandma had left Sara Jane the last time. If only Drew could escape this current situation—except he had a tent full of brooms to sell.

"You got to keep your eyes on your man. Did you see him kiss the redheaded floozy?"

"Hey now." Ansley held the money out to Drew again.

He slid it into his pocket and steered her off to the side. "Thanks for watching the tent. Appreciate it."

"You're not engaged to her."

It wasn't a question. More of a statement. No need to confirm or deny.

"I work for her grandma."

"The one beating you up?" Ansley patted his arm. "You poor thing. I'll give you a call."

He managed a smile and turned to mind his wares. Sara Jane had pulled Grandma off to the side, but whatever her plan had been, it hadn't worked. Grandma laid into her about something. Probably their relationship.

Or lack thereof.

Sara Jane's foot tapped on the grass, jiggling her body. Her mouth was set in an angry line, and her brows furrowed.

It was almost enough to make him want to march over there, pull Sara Jane into his arms, kiss those soft-looking lips, and whisper they could pretend—at least until Grandma ended this matchmaking mindset. But it would be dishonest. He wouldn't feign a relationship, and he wouldn't subject Sara Jane to being kissed by a bristly backwoods mountaineer. Not to mention risk the rejection and humiliation when she laughed in his face.

But it didn't stop him from wishing he could.

Instead, he pulled a five-dollar bill out of his pocket and slid it into Sara Jane's clenched fist. "Go buy her some ice cream." *Please.*

Any potential customers had fled the tent when Grandma started slinging her purse around like a wild woman. They would most likely be warning other festival attendees about the armed and dangerous grandma.

Good thing Grandma padded the sales earlier since she drove customers away now.

Sara Jane gave him a surprised yet grateful look and took her grandma's arm. "Let's go get ice cream."

Grandma quieted right down. "Yes. Let's. Are you coming, Andrew?"

He moved his mouth, but wasn't quite sure it formed a smile. It might've been more of a grimace. "No. I need to stay with my brooms. You can bring me back a soda later if you want." He had a couple bottles of water in a cooler under the table. "No hurry. Take your time. Just as long as you're back here by closing time so we can go to my brother's house."

How would it work, with Grandma's current mental state?

Considering all the possible outcomes, tonight was enough to send him running back to the trail.

Sara Jane nodded and started to walk toward the sidewalk when Drew slipped something else into her hand. She glanced down at a key card for a local hotel. She looked up with a frown.

Ansley handed customers her phone number and Drew handed out his room key?

"My room number is 284 if Grandma wants to take a nap. There's an elevator near the lobby. Don't worry about bringing me a soda. I have water. If you don't come back by closing time, I'll meet you at the hotel."

"Thank you. It's so sweet of you." She sagged in relief. A safe place to take Grandma. Andrew Stevenson had to be the kindest man on the face of the earth. And the most considerate.

After the way Grandma had embarrassed him in front of his brother and wife, not to mention his girlfriend, he was nothing short of a saint.

Although, if he dated that redheaded floozy as Grandma called her . . . well, it proved he was human. She was beautiful. Outgoing. Friendly—up to the point when she called her "an uptight prune-eater." Seriously?

She probably had looked pretty pinched. Sara Jane didn't know how long she had wandered around after Grandma announced to the world Sara Jane and Drew were discussing a wedding date, then getting lost and not able to find her way back to them. The comment could be excused.

But—Sara Jane had seen the redhead enter digits into another man's cell phone. So it would indicate if she and Drew dated, it wasn't exclusive. He'd still be on the market. Besides, he deserved someone who wouldn't cheat on him.

She and Grandma stood in a long line for the small bowl of strawberry ice cream and a soda for herself. Grandma yawned, so they went to the car and drove to Drew's hotel.

Drew's room was a small area, with a king-sized bed and an easy chair, both facing the TV. Other than an overstuffed duffel bag, there was no sign anyone occupied the room. The bed was neatly made, as if the maid had been in and cleaned recently.

Sara Jane adjusted the room temperature, unfolded a blanket she found on a shelf, and, after Grandma crawled on the bed, covered her. When she was settled, Sara Jane pulled her smartphone out of her purse.

"You could practice your appliqué stitches," Grandma said.

"I could," Sara Jane agreed. She refrained from adding, "If I had a needle, thread, and material," because Grandma would probably pull them out of her purse. She'd rather not risk it.

Instead she accessed the trail journals.

Stalking Drew. A man she was quickly falling in love with.

She went to his very first post.

Arrived in Gainesville, Georgia. The shuttle driver waited for another man and me at the train station. His name is Wes King and he dubbed himself Lion King. Surprised to learn we came from the same town in West Virginia. We put together drop boxes the driver would leave at a hostel in Hiawassee. We arrived at Springer Mountain parking lot around nine a.m. The driver snapped a photo of us there. We hiked about a mile to Springer Mountain to get to the starting point, took some photos, and then took our first step in a 2,180-mile journey. Pine forest, rocky terrain, smooth wide paths, and some areas with mountain laurel growing over the trail. We crossed a lot of creeks and arrived at Hawk Mountain shelter around two-thirty p.m. I was met by a dog. Looked to be a Siberian husky. There were about fifty people sleeping in and around the shelter. I had no idea how many people would be out here. No one claimed the dog. I named her Wynter.

A light snore came from the bed.

Sara Jane smiled, clicked the "next" tab, and continued researching part of the history of one of the most fascinating men she'd ever met.

What would he look like without the bushy beard and long hair?

Drew's stomach churned as he pulled into the driveway at his brother's house. He hadn't seen Mom since a month after the funeral. It was a bad time to bring guests to dinner. First time he'd seen his family in four years, and he was going with strangers. Maybe it would eliminate questions. For now.

He'd have to face them sooner or later. He'd rather it be later. Much later.

How could he expect his family to forgive him, after abandoning them when they needed him most?

Though Joey hadn't seemed judgmental. He'd gone looking for him. Welcomed him back into his life with a hug, and indicated he wanted him in his child's life. And even the rare postcard he'd received since the wedding invitation—which Drew had ignored—had seemed friendly.

The fact Joey had gone to great lengths to locate him spoke volumes. Drew had rented a post office box, so they wouldn't have access to his home address. It said a lot they'd given him his privacy all these years.

He grabbed a broom and slid out of the pickup. A second later, the front door opened and Mom ran to him, arms outstretched, tears streaming down her cheeks.

"Andrew. Oh, Andrew."

Moisture dampened his cheeks as Mom pulled him into her arms. He hugged her back. "I missed you." He hadn't thought much about it, but it was true. He had.

"I brought you a broom."

Mom admired it. "Wow, it is beautiful. You always did such good work. Now, where's your girl?" Mom looked around. "Carly said you were engaged."

Drew pulled in a breath and stepped back. "Actually, Carly was wrong. I work for her grandmother and she's decided she wants me to marry Sara Jane." He gestured toward the road, at Sara Jane's car. "Sara Jane and her grandma are in the car, waiting to see if they're still welcome after you discovered the truth. I told them they would be, but . . . Grandma believes we are dating." He hesitated. "I think she is in the beginning stages of Alzheimer's. But it hasn't been verified."

"Poor thing." Mom made a sympathetic grimace, but then replaced it with a smile and handed Drew the broom. "Take this inside for me, please. Of course, they're still welcome. I'll go tell them while you tell Joey and Carly the truth."

Right.

The truth.

Because the truth was . . . what? He liked the idea of him and Sara Jane? Maybe too much?

He didn't stand a chance.

15

Sara Jane watched as a woman who could only be Drew's mom hurried toward the car. She was short and a bit round, with graying brown hair. She looked comfortable, soft. Cuddly.

What would it be like to have a mother hug her? She'd pushed Mama away the last time she'd tried. Twelve years ago. Now she'd give anything to tell Mama and Daddy she loved them and get another hug.

If only . . .

Mrs. Stevenson knocked on the car window.

Sara Jane swallowed. Would they be welcomed? If not, would Grandma understand why they left? She'd been insistent to get out of the car right away, but Sara Jane managed to restrain her by saying Drew needed to greet his mama first, without them. She rolled the window down, not sure what she hoped the answer would be.

Drew's mom greeted her with a warm smile. "Please, come in."

Sara Jane opened the door and got out and was instantly enveloped in a warm hug. She tried to let herself relax enough to return it.

"Drew told me. Don't worry a bit, Sara Jane."

How could she keep from worrying? Because it became increasingly clear Grandma's occasional memory lapses weren't normal. Something else was going on. It terrified her to find out what.

If she still talked to God, she'd pray about it. But God had abandoned her years ago. Even though she went to church Sunday mornings, Sunday nights, and Wednesday nights, she'd written off God. If it weren't for Grandma, she wouldn't pretend to have religion. Prayer didn't work. God didn't care.

Her lips twisted.

Mrs. Stevenson stepped back with a concerned frown, studying Sara Jane's expression. Sara Jane tried to find a smile.

"Nice to meet you, Mrs. Stevenson."

Drew's mom waved her hand. "Oh, call me Dottie." She leaned closer. "After all, we're already family in your grandmother's mind."

"Dottie." Her smile was real this time. "I can see where Drew got his wonderful personality."

Dottie's expression turned assessing as she studied Sara Jane. Then, without warning, she pulled her into another hug. "I'm going to love you."

Wow, his family was outgoing.

"I'm going to go around and help your grandma. Drew told me she possibly has the beginning stages of Alzheimer's."

Sara Jane sucked in a pained breath. It was what she was afraid of. The reason she needed to take her to a doctor, but the diagnosis she feared. Drew saw it. Recognized it.

No wonder he was so patient with her.

The man truly was a saint.

For a moment, she wanted to rush to the house and find Drew. Wanted to fall into his strong arms. Maybe he'd hold her, touch her. Perhaps she'd feel those sparks she'd felt the few times he'd briefly touched her. She wanted to kiss him, to wrap her arms around his neck and run her fingers through his hair and tell him he was the most wonderful man on earth.

She could only imagine how he'd react.

Especially with the beautiful Ansley in his life. Not to mention his terse warning to his mother that he was only her grandma's handyman.

Drew warned Joey and Carly, telling them essentially the same thing he'd told Mom. They were just as understanding, promising no matter what, it'd be okay. Carly had disappeared out into the kitchen to check the lasagna and to prepare a salad.

The table was already set. A fresh assortment of what might be dyed daisies sat in the middle of a white tablecloth. Carly had always liked flowers.

He was glad his family knew the truth. He didn't like being dishonest with them. Though he hadn't told them he was infatuated with Sara Jane.

And hopefully, they no longer knew him well enough to be able to see it.

The door opened, and Mom came in, followed by Grandma and Sara Jane.

"Your dad is going to be sorry he missed seeing you." Mom pulled him into her hug again.

He wrapped his arms around her. "Where is he?"

"Somewhere over the Atlantic Ocean, I would guess." Mom released him and turned to Sara Jane. "He's an international airline pilot. We'll have to get together again when he gets home."

How could his family be so welcoming to him? Abandoning them—his gaze darted to the hearth, and the pictures lined up there. Joey's house, but there were pictures of his family. Mom and Dad. Carly's parents and siblings. Their wedding pictures. Him—and Annie—oh, he missed her. Still. His eyes burned.

Grandma strode over to look at the photos, picking up the frame in the center first. The wedding photo.

Drew went to the kitchen to see if he could help before the questions started.

"How can I help?" Sara Jane's voice came from behind him.

He hadn't expected her to follow him.

Carly grinned. "I'm chopping up the vegetables for the salad. Grab a knife from the drawer. There are some fresh mushrooms in the fridge."

Sara Jane took a knife out of the open drawer and then retrieved the mushrooms.

He took a moment to enjoy the view. At least until Carly cleared her throat. Drew's face heated. He looked away from where Sara Jane worked at the counter, and focused on his sister-in-law. "What can I do?"

Carly shrugged. "Go in the other room with your brother and mother. They've missed you. I'm going to get to know my new best friend."

Yes, well. Just so long as she didn't spill any deep, dark secrets. Such as the way Drew watched her. . . . Or that he was obviously smitten.

He turned away and started down the hall. Carly said something. Probably about his roving eye. About him liking Sara Jane. Both women laughed.

His heart broke.

Sara Jane cleaned and chopped the mushrooms, a cucumber, and a green pepper for the salad as Carly commented about men being worthless in the kitchen, and talked about dating Joey since they were juniors in high school. Sara Jane hadn't dated anyone. She'd been known as somewhat of a control freak and no boy wanted to be bossed around by a woman—at least not by her.

She did wonder how Grandma had won Grandpa's heart. Grandma was as domineering as Sara Jane. More so. Grandma had bossed Grandpa around. He never said a word, either. Not when Grandma went out and did whatever she wanted and ruled him with an iron fist, even deciding what kind of vehicle he was allowed to drive—a beat-up, old pickup—and buying it for him.

Maybe it was why she was so infatuated with Drew. He hadn't let her boss him. He'd earned her respect.

She didn't feel the urge to try to control him now.

Just to discover everything about him.

Carly paused to take a breath and Sara Jane jumped into the sudden silence with a question. "I get the impression Drew hasn't been home in a while." She carried the vegetables over to the table and dumped them into the bowl with the lettuce, celery, carrots, onions, and whatever else Carly had added. It looked like purple cabbage, radishes, and bean sprouts.

Carly gave her a sober look. "It's his story to tell." She looked at the tomato she sliced. "But he took Annie's death hard."

"Annie was his . . . wife?"

Carly gave a sad-sounding laugh. "His twin sister. They were very close. He needs to tell you. Not me."

He probably wouldn't, given the superficial nature of their relationship. Honestly, it was amazing they were clicking as well as they were, considering they were mere acquaintances. And only because he worked for Grandma. Still . . . one could always hope.

After he finished working for Grandma, she'd probably never see him again.

If only she could pump Carly for information. She must be a well of information when it came to Drew.

But Carly had gone on to talk about their upcoming baby and the nursery they were planning.

Sara Jane tried to listen. But Drew kept intruding into her thoughts. Who was Ansley to him? They had some type of relationship. He'd kissed her cheek . . . but were they engaged? Dating?

Either way, it was clear her infatuation would lead nowhere.

Still, she couldn't wait to get home and read more trail journals. Or curl up on the couch with Drew and have him tell her his life story. And since it wasn't likely to happen, the trail journals were the next best thing.

She could feed her crush and he wouldn't know a thing.

It wasn't enough.

But, it was going to have to be. Unless . . . .

16

Monday morning, Drew parked in front of Mrs. Morgan's house with the load of shingles. The house was dark and quiet, as if she still slept. Sara Jane's car wasn't in the driveway. A good thing. It still grated hearing her and Carly laugh after his sister-in-law caught him ogling Sara Jane's backside. He'd hardly been able to look at her the rest of the evening and was relieved when Sara Jane and Grandma had left.

Grandma had been surprisingly good. She and Mom had a great conversation. Mom had carried most of it, asking Grandma about her life, which meant they talked about sewing and quilting.

The back shed was unlocked, so Drew took out the lawn equipment and went to work mowing the lawn. He hoped the sound didn't disturb Grandma. Sara Jane had said Grandma couldn't hear much when she took her hearing aids out.

He'd finished putting the edge trimmer in the shed when the back door opened. Grandma stood there in her housecoat, her hair in curlers, holding a cup of coffee.

"What are you doing here?" She came out on the deck.

Had she forgotten she'd hired him? He frowned, a sense of wariness creeping in. "Figured I'd start your roof. The shingles are in the truck."

"But Sara Jane won't be here today. She has some sort of teacher in-service type thing this week. School starts next Monday."

Drew frowned. "I don't need help with the shingles." She most likely would distract him to the point of personal injury. Like falling off the roof when he looked at her, or hitting his thumb with the hammer.

"No, but . . . how are you going to fall in love with her if you're not around each other?"

That was easy. They wouldn't. Well, he was halfway there now. He shrugged.

"You have to leave. Come back on Saturday. She'll be here then to help on the ballad quilt." Grandma smiled. "And since it's hot out, you can take your shirt off and she can admire your muscles as you haul those heavy bundles of shingles up to the roof."

Drew blinked. This was just plain foolishness. Sara Jane wasn't interested in him, and he wouldn't subject himself to ridicule by filling the role of a lovesick puppy. If Grandma wanted to play this way, she could hire a different handyman.

He shut the shed door. "I finished the yard work. And I have freed a few days this week to do your roof. I can't wait until Saturday on the off chance Sara Jane might admire my muscles. I have other plans for this weekend. If today doesn't work for you, I can recommend a few other men you can call."

Grandma studied him, her free hand balled on her hip.

He eyed her warily, uncertain what she'd come up with next. After another long moment, he shifted. The silence stretched too long. He didn't have time to worry about this. He had plenty of other work without this much of a headache. Though he actually liked Grandma and Sara Jane—and he'd always wonder how the ballad quilt turned out. "Okay. You can find someone else. Give me a few minutes to prepare your bill—"

"Fine. Have it your way." Grandma walked over and patted his hand, as if he were a small child. "Do you want breakfast?"

"No, ma'am. But I do have the lock for the bathroom door if you'd like it replaced first."

A sense of relief washed over him. He still had the job, not to mention the income, and could keep an eye on Grandma at the same time. He smiled. He'd stood his ground and now would be able to help her without the distractions.

"Okay. And no worries. You aren't the right type for Sara Jane. I'll find someone else to take the girl off my hands."

Drew nodded. "You do that."

But he'd rather be the one. Maybe he should rethink his weekend plans.

After Andrew had finished fixing the bathroom doorknob and started working on the roof, Sari went back to the bedroom and reached under the bed to pull out the wedding picture. She'd thought of it Saturday evening after dinner with Andrew's family when she looked at their photos.

She'd hoped her announcement, though it wasn't true, would push Andrew and Sara Jane together. Telling him she'd find someone else might work, if she could arrange for him to see Sara Jane out with another man. Sometimes, knowing someone was taken seemed to make others want them. She'd used the trick with Cade, after he left for California. He'd come home in a big hurry when she'd written she planned to marry Jimmy Bob in the fall. She had a twinge of guilt over her less than honest tactics. She brushed it aside. After all, the ends justify the means.

She needed to have Andrew and Sara Jane married off before she completely lost her mind to Alzheimer's. If the doctor's diagnosis was right. . . .

She hadn't told Sara Jane about her doctor's appointment. She didn't want to. But eventually she'd have to share the bad news with her. She ran her finger over her son's face, then got up and headed to the kitchen for a cup of coffee.

So far, her matchmaking attempts hadn't worked the way she'd hoped. Instead, she'd jinxed the whole thing. Andrew wasn't the type to be led around by a nose ring. With some men, you had to make things happen to open their eyes.

She poured herself a cup of coffee and warmed it in the microwave, then got out the liquid creamer. She wouldn't admit it to Sara Jane, but she loved the fancy stuff.

How could she fix the problem between Sara Jane and Andrew? One would have to be blind not to notice the way they looked at each other. Just like her son—Sara Jane's daddy . . . and mama.

Nathan and Jeannie had made goo-goo eyes for over a year at church, but were both so shy they didn't talk to each other. She'd managed to get them both lead roles in the church's Christmas play so they had to practice together. Soon the two of them were announcing their upcoming wedding date.

Sometimes children had to have a nudge in the right direction. Maybe it'd be true with Sara Jane and Andrew.

If she could find a way to get them together.

Sari went back to the bedroom and picked up the wedding picture. She'd put all her photos away several months after the horrible day when she got the news of the accident that took the lives of Nathan and Jeannie. It'd been a Tuesday. She'd never forget it as long as she lived. It had been a hard time. Her grief was surpassed only by the panic when she realized she didn't know where Sara Jane was. And then came her frustration with all the red tape to get Sara Jane out of foster care. It had taken months to get it all straightened out, plus a few calls by her lawyer, but finally she brought Sara Jane home to live with her. The poor child was so distraught. She wouldn't talk about it, but she seemed to have blamed herself for her parents' deaths. She'd awaken with night terrors, screaming, "I'm sorry, Daddy!"

After she'd found Sara Jane crying over her parents' picture, she had put the photos away. In hindsight, it might have been better to leave them out and let Sara Jane deal with her grief in her own way. Hiding the pictures hadn't helped.

Sari shook her head. She should've known avoiding grief wouldn't make it go away. After all, she'd struggled to forget when her baby boy, Travis, had died from whooping cough as a toddler.

And then a few years later when her middle son, Ethan, had gotten hit by a car when riding his bike to a friend's house.

Their deaths had nearly destroyed her marriage. It was rare for Cade to stand up to her, but he'd insisted it was time to wake up and start living again before they lost their remaining son—and each other. He should've stood up to her more often. The man was full of wisdom he rarely shared.

If Cade had still been alive, it would've killed him to learn of Nathan's death. It'd almost shattered her. A mama shouldn't have to bury any of her children, much less all of them.

She missed them all: Cade, Nathan, Jeannie, Ethan, and Travis. It'd been twelve years since Nathan passed and even longer for Cade and her other sons, but there were days it seemed like yesterday.

She ran her finger over the curve of Nathan's chin. The love he felt for Jeannie shown in his expression. He had a slight dimple in his cheek . . .

She'd never see it again.

Nathan would've approved of Andrew for Sara Jane. If only they were still here to help her get those two stubborn people together.

She collapsed beside her bed, holding the wedding picture of Nathan and Jeannie, tears dropping on the glass.

Sara Jane had just finished lunch when the school secretary handed her a note. She unfolded the slip of paper. "Andrew Stevenson called. He has some concerns about your grandmother. Come home as soon as possible."

She looked up. "Did he say what kind of concerns?"

The secretary nodded. "Something about her being inconsolable. He found her on the floor crying like her heart was breaking."

She'd have to miss the afternoon sessions, but Grandma had to be top priority. She could get the notes from Marci later. After making her excuses, Sara Jane quickly gathered her things and hurried out to her car.

She mulled over possibilities during the drive. Had Grandma been notified about the death of a close friend? Her typical response was usually a comment about it being a fact of life at her age. She read the obituaries in the paper on a daily basis.

An emotional breakdown was out of character. Serious to the point of worrying Drew enough to contact her at school.

Unless it was because he couldn't handle seeing a woman cry.

Somehow, Drew seemed made of stronger stuff. As if he'd seen his share of grief, cried his own tears, and then moved on.

After Carly had said something about his taking his twin sister's death hard, Sara Jane could almost imagine him by Annie's side, holding her hand—and himself—together until the end. Then hitting the hiking trail to grieve in private.

But she didn't know for sure.

She wouldn't, until she heard his story.

Sara Jane broke all the speed limits on the way from the school to Grandma's house. She parked behind Drew's truck, slid out of the driver's seat, and ran for the door. She flung it open and dashed inside. Drew met her in the hallway, holding his finger over his lips.

She skidded to a stop inches from him, trying not to notice how good he looked. A blue t-shirt stretched across his chest, tanned, muscular arms, and . . . had he trimmed his beard? Might be her imagination but it looked neater.

She needed to focus on Grandma. Not him. "What happened?"

He pulled in a breath. "I'm sorry for bothering you." He kept his voice barely above a whisper. "She didn't answer my knock, so I called out and entered. I looked for her in the sewing room, but she wasn't there. I found her on the floor beside her bed, wailing like her heart was broken."

He looked away, glancing over his shoulder toward the backroom. "I didn't know what to do. I worried she might be hurt, but she shook her head, so I picked her up and put her on the bed. That was when I noticed she was holding a wedding photo. I couldn't get her to stop crying. She was rambling about all these men: Cade, and Nathan, and I don't remember who else. Cade's name is on the mailbox so I figured out who he might be. But I panicked and called you."

Cade and Nathan? A wedding photo? Tears burned her eyes. She might get to see a picture of Mama and Daddy again?

He looked back at Sara Jane. "She just fell asleep. But it's good you're here, in case she starts again. Does she take any depression medicines? Or should you call her doctor?"

She wanted to run back to Grandma's room, find the picture, and cry, but she had to be strong and postpone her personal stuff in order to think logically about Grandma's medications.

"I don't know of any depression medicine. I'm not sure what all she has prescribed. She takes a whole collection every morning." She struggled to find her emotional footing.

She brushed past Drew, walked down the hall, and peeked in Grandma's room. Grandma was curled up on the bed, the living room afghan draped over her. She cradled a picture frame against her chest. She wanted to pull it from Grandma's arms and look at it. To see Daddy's face again. But . . .

Grandma slept peacefully. Thanks to Drew.

He was an amazing man. Strong and handy, yet gentle and compassionate. Exactly the right mixture for looking after Grandma—and herself. If only she could tell him how amazing he was.

Why couldn't she? He deserved to know.

Sara Jane turned, but Drew was gone. She hadn't heard him leave.

She found him in the kitchen, downing a glass of water. He put the empty glass in the sink, then turned to face her.

"Hope you don't mind. It's hot work out there. But I probably should go and finish the roof another day so I don't disturb your grandmother."

"No. Stay." Sara Jane pulled in a shaky breath and some courage to tell him—no, show him—what she felt. Took another tiny step forward. Then reached out and rested a hand against his firm chest.

He froze. Caught his breath.

"You are the most wonderful man ever, Drew Stevenson. And don't you ever forget it." She rose up on tiptoes and brushed her lips against his. His beard poked the skin around her mouth, but she didn't care so long as he kissed her back. Maybe even pull her closer.

He stiffened.

Please, don't reject me.

He didn't respond. At least not in the millisecond it took to brush her lips against his.

Should she go back for a second pass? Or accept it for what it was?

Rejection.

"What are you doing?" His voice was rough. He put his hands on her arms and started to push her away.

He'd be too nice to make fun of her.

But he had to be comparing her to the beautiful Ansley and finding Sara Jane wanting.

"I wanted to thank you for taking care of Grandma," she whispered. *Thank you for being such a wonderful man I could fall in love with.* Tears burned her eyes. "I'm sorry. I shouldn't have done that."

"No." His breathing was harsh. Ragged. "You shouldn't have."

She raised her chin to keep the tears burning her eyes at bay. "I guess you should go." Before she collapsed on the couch in tears.

"Yes." He studied her. The heat in his eyes almost made her want to risk his rejection again.

He pulled in a ragged breath. Then another. Turned away and walked toward the door.

Her shoulders slumped. A tear escaped. She took a couple steps after him before she caught herself.

Without warning, he swung around. His callused thumb grazed over her cheek, catching a drop of moisture. And he pulled her into his arms.

17

Drew trembled. He slid his hand to the back of Sara Jane's neck, tangling his fingers in her hair. Holding her still, so she couldn't pull away even if she wanted. She didn't appear to want to.

Her arms wrapped around his neck and she met his fumbling kiss with something akin to hunger. Her fingers ran through his hair, heating him to a fever pitch.

This was the stuff dreams were made of. Maybe he was actually dreaming, and would wake up to find himself alone in bed, having some wonderful fantasy about her.

He didn't want to ever wake up.

He kissed her with all the longing he possessed. His hands roamed down to the small of her back, and he pressed her tighter. Nearer.

He could've kissed her forever. She made a moaning sound, her hands running around to the front of his shirt, tugging at the hem, lifting it. Her fingers seared his skin.

His mouth hardened against hers. She whimpered.

But didn't pull away.

He wanted . . . He . . .

Reality crashed in.

What was he doing? He groaned and pushed her away. Her mouth looked tender, bruised, well kissed. Tiny scratches marred the skin around her lips. He hadn't meant to hurt her. He raised his hand and let his fingers run over the scratches, but then caught himself, jerking his hand back.

"Got a bit more than you asked for there, Miss Morgan. Hope you found kissing a caveman to your liking."

The caveman image was one he'd continued on his own. One he could change, if he wanted.

He hated himself for the hurtful things he said, especially when she winced.

"It'll never happen again. Tell your grandmother she'll get the bill in the mail. I quit."

He swung on his heel and stalked out the door, trembling from the assault on his senses. He'd be dreaming of this for weeks. Months. Years. The rest of his life.

He struggled for air, his hand running roughly over his whiskers, the pricks stabbing his callused hand.

He'd hurt her.

It was time to visit Chris.

Sara Jane's knees threatened to buckle under her. She slumped into a chair, unable to find the strength to continue standing. Rejecting her after he kissed her? Wow, that hurt.

More than she asked for? A caveman? She shook her head. "John the Baptist impersonator, maybe . . ." But his comment seemed to have come out of nowhere. Had Marci or Chris planted the suggestion?

Both were entirely possible. They spent every evening together—according to Marci. Chris could've called him, gushing about his relationship and spilled the beans about what Marci—and Sara Jane—felt about him. Or Marci had told him herself.

But wow. Who knew the man could kiss like that? Her toes still curled inside her shoes, and her knees couldn't support her weight. She could've kissed him forever . . .

At least she'd see him again when he came back to work for Grandma the next time. When Grandma wasn't looking they could sneak a quick kiss—and he'd ask her out and . . .

Wait.

Tell your grandmother she'll get the bill in the mail. I quit. Because they kissed?

She'd made herself into an idiot again. Kissing him. She'd only wanted to let him know she appreciated him. Liked him. More than liked him. Despite his appearance.

But . . . he'd come back to her. He'd initiated the second kiss. And the subsequent ones. It had to mean he'd wanted her as badly as she wanted him.

She stumbled to her feet, out the back door, and around the house. Stared at her car sitting alone in the driveway. Behind where his truck had sat. How had he gotten out without hitting her car? It was as if he'd pushed a button and vanished into thin air.

She hurried to the mailbox and peered down the street in both directions. He was gone.

And she had no way of contacting him, unless she somehow intercepted his bill.

Or found his business card. The one she'd scoffed at the day they'd met.

She swung around, hurried back into the house, and snuck into Grandma's room. Grandma's purse was on top of the dresser, where she always kept it. Grandma didn't stir as Sara Jane caught the purse up and carried it out to the kitchen. She'd had the card in her purse the day she'd called Drew at Pizza Hut. Maybe it still would be there.

Sara Jane opened the purse and eyed the clutter within. She started removing everything piece by piece. A slew of receipts, a checkbook. A pack of mint gum. Grandma didn't chew gum. Said it reminded her of a cow chewing its cud. Christmas candy canes. A package of Valentine conversation hearts. A cracked plastic Easter egg, filled with jelly beans. Sara Jane would've pilfered Grandma's purse sooner if she'd known they were there. She opened it up and took one. Mmm. Cherry.

But not as good as Drew's kisses.

She shoved another jelly bean in her mouth. Pineapple. It left a sour taste in her mouth. Kind of like when Drew said he'd quit.

Grandma's driver's license—Sara Jane squinted at it. Expired? Grandma probably shouldn't be driving anyway. Her Bible . . . the one she used at church on Sundays.

She finished sorting through all the miscellaneous objects in the bag and didn't see any sign of Drew's business card. She returned everything, except the broken plastic egg and the remaining jelly beans.

They were hers. Comfort food, after Drew.

Kissing her, and then quitting his job. Leaving her no way of getting in contact with him. No hopes of seeing him again.

Except—Marci and Chris. Marci would be able to put her in contact with Chris, and he could tell her how to find Drew. Or his family would help her.

Sara Jane bowed her head. If God listened—if He cared—she'd pray He'd bring Drew back or she'd be able to find him. To apologize for whatever she'd done to upset him.

But no. She was on her own.

Tears escaped and fell from her chin in rapid succession.

Drew didn't know how long he'd driven aimlessly around before he noticed the sign for Chris's Barber Shop. He parallel parked in front, pulled in a deep breath, and strode to the door.

He'd hurt her. Pain ripped through him anew.

He jerked the door open and stepped inside.

Chris's hand froze as he turned to stare at Drew. He held buzzing clippers in his hand. The old gentleman in the seat waved his arms. "You like this one? Let me tell you about the one that got away."

Drew glanced around the rest of the shop. The room smelled of strong coffee and peppermint, like the curiously strong mints Chris loved. There was also the hint of antiseptic cleaner and a musky aftershave scent.

He scanned the room again. It wasn't a good time. By the time he'd waited through one customer, he'd lose his nerve.

Besides, he'd never kiss her again anyway. Shouldn't have kissed her in the first place. Didn't matter if he remained shaggy. But he'd wanted the wisdom of his friend.

He turned toward the door.

"No, wait. Drew. What brought you here?" Chris abandoned the clippers and rushed over, blocking the door so Drew couldn't leave.

"I need a . . . hai . . . I need a drink."

A slight smirk. "Right. A drink. Have a seat, I'll be right with you. I have coffee." He gestured toward a dirty pot on the far side of the room. "But judging by the way your hands are shaking, you've either had enough caffeine or you came for a different reason."

Drew looked at his hands. They were trembling. Violently. "Do you have a root beer?" Maybe he should lay off the caffeine a while. At least until his jittery nerves calmed.

Chris nodded, disappeared into a back room, and returned a second later with a plastic bottle. "Have a seat, Drew. And tell us all about it."

"I quit my job." Drew took a long swig.

The old man in the chair guffawed. "Ain't nuttin', sonny. Let me tell you about the time I—."

"Now, Henry, let Drew continue." Chris ran a safety razor up the back of the man's neck. "We need to listen to him right now. Sharing our experiences comes later." He looked at Drew. "Which job did you quit? Broom-making or working as a private-hire contractor?" Chris leaned forward as if sharing a secret. "Best one in the area. Did you know all the building supply stores in town wanted to hire him on as their personal on-site contractor?"

"Oh, yeah?" The old man looked at him, brows raising. "He's good?"

"Yep." Chris finished up the old man. "Go on, Drew."

Drew shook his head. "Neither job. Just the one working for the grandma in Bruceton Mills."

"What made you decide to quit?" The man paid and made his way over to sit next to Drew. "Not paying enough? Trying to tell you how to do your job?"

Drew shifted. "Getting emotionally involved."

Silence fell. Chris's eyebrows hiked.

Drew squirmed. What if they took the comment about getting emotionally involved to mean he was falling for the grandma . . . or lacked basic compassion? If only the shop was empty, the other man gone.

But no. Two more customers wandered in and sat.

This was a bad idea all the way around. He should leave. He could shave his face himself if he decided he wanted to. And as for his hair . . .

"Emotionally involved. Care to elaborate? I don't see how it's a bad thing." The old man pushed up his glasses.

"I kissed her," Drew muttered.

Chris coughed.

"You kissed her." The old man chuckled. "Bet she enjoyed it. A young guy like you. How old is she, anyway?"

Chris cleaned up, then nodded at Drew. "Come over here for a bit. You'll feel more comfortable while you're in the hot seat."

Almost without thought, Drew pushed to his feet and moved to the barber chair. Chris snapped a cape loosely around Drew, then added some sort of paper resembling floater's tape normally used on drywall. Then he attached the cape in place.

"How do you want it?" Chris ran a comb through the length.

Drew shrugged. "I don't . . . I mean—I—well." He frowned. Shrugged again. "I don't know. I'm not sure I want it cut." He wasn't ready for a major step. Not as ready as he thought he might be. Except, he hurt her. "This is probably a bad idea. I mean, you have real customers you could see to." He motioned to the two men waiting. The door opened again and another man strode in.

"Trust me, this is not a bad idea." Chris swung the chair around so it faced away from the mirror. "Since you aren't sure, close your eyes. I'll clean you up some while you can tell us all about kissing Grandma. Must have been some kiss."

Drew pulled in a deep, shuddering breath. "It was amazing. But it wasn't Grandma. It was her granddaughter."

The old man whistled. "Yep, that'd do it. She'd probably fire you when she found out. Good thing you quit."

"Ah, the hottie at the fort. No worries, Broom-man. I saw how she looked at you."

Drew groaned. "Yeah, like I wandered out of some cave. I know. You told me."

Chris chuckled as he lathered up Drew's face and started shaving. "Marci said so. Not her. She looked at you like you were the most interesting man alive."

"Ha." If only she thought it. But . . .

Was there a chance Chris might be right? She did kiss him first . . .

"You kissed her?"

"I didn't mean to. It just . . . happened. It won't happen again, because I quit."

Chris finished shaving and then moved to start work on Drew's hair. "You need to quit running away. Face your problems head-on. I bet they wouldn't have fired you."

"Not if she looked at you like you're the most interesting man alive." Henry nodded. "Unless she meant, in a scientific way, meaning you're so weird, she—"

"Not helping, Henry." Chris waved something at the older man.

Drew glanced at Henry. "Yeah, it's exactly how she looks at me. Like I'm about the strangest thing alive." Although, the look in her eyes right before she kissed him sent a very different message. The way her hands tugged on his shirt hem wasn't exactly trying to explore scientifically. His face heated.

"Okay. I gave you a taper cut. It's buzzed short up the sides, left longer on top, so you can spike it if you like. Come see me again in about six weeks." Chris swung the chair around so it faced the mirror.

Drew blinked as he stared at the stranger reflected. Square jaw, bushy eyebrows. He remembered the eyebrows. Dark hair, dark eyes. He shook his head.

"It's a big difference from the wild man who barged in." Henry nodded. "Chris, you're a miracle worker."

"Yes. It'll take some getting used to." Drew ran his palm over his jaw. Smooth. Not a single poke.

"Probably no need to say this, but you'll need to shave every day to keep the look." Chris rested a hand on Drew's shoulder. "But women do like the five o'clock shadow, so you might want to leave it when you go on a date."

"Won't be going on a date."

"Sure you will. Because you're going to drive right back to Grandma's and apologize for quitting without warning and finish whatever job she hired you to do. And see what the hot granddaughter has to say about the man you were hiding under all the hair. Sorry. Can't remember her name."

"Sara Jane."

The phone rang and Chris moved away to answer it. "Chris's Barber Shop. Chris speaking. May I help you?" He fell silent, turning so his back faced the wall while he looked at Drew with a smirk. He pointed at the phone with a wink. "Yes, I believe I can find him. I'll send him right over."

18

Sara Jane stared out the window into the gathering dusk. Clouds obscured the moon and stars, and the scent of rain filled the air. Grandma went to bed for the evening after telling Sara Jane to go home. But still she waited. For Drew.

He didn't come.

Sara Jane hadn't told Grandma Drew quit. She'd hoped to find him and talk him into continuing to work for Grandma, but contacting Chris hadn't worked. At least not yet.

She might have to tell Grandma, after all.

With a sigh, Sara Jane grabbed her purse, locked up, and went out to her car. On her way home, she cruised down every street in Bruceton Mills, looking for Drew's truck, but with no luck. He might have it in a garage. Someplace. Of course, she didn't know where he lived, so it could be anywhere. His friend Chris lived in Morgantown. At least, it's where his barber shop was.

She parked outside her lonely apartment and headed to the front door, shoulders slumped. As she neared her door, her footsteps slowed. There, centered in front of it, was a clear glass vase filled with pink carnations and some greenery. She reached for the card tucked into the plastic fork. Who would send her flowers? Probably misdelivered.

The envelope clearly read Miss Sara Jane Morgan and her address. For her?

She opened it and slid out the small, white card. Plain white, except for the words "I'm sorry . . ." embossed on top.

Underneath it was printed in blue ink: *I didn't mean to hurt you. Drew.*

Wow. The flowers were actually for her. From *him*.

Hurt her? By walking out and quitting his job? It had stunned . . . shocked . . . hurt. Yeah. Or did he mean his comments after he kissed her senseless?

If he was sorry enough to send flowers, he cared . . . and he was the amazing guy she was falling in love with.

He didn't say whether or not he'd return to finish Grandma's house. And he didn't leave any way of contacting him.

But he'd known her address? He knew where she lived? She turned to scan the parking lot but didn't see his truck anywhere. Maybe he'd seen it in Grandma's contacts when he looked up the school phone number.

And cared enough to write it down or memorize it.

If only he'd stuck around, indicated he'd come back, or included a phone number.

Chris's barber shop would be closed for the night.

She'd talk to Marci during a break tomorrow.

With a sigh, she fingered the soft petals, then brought in the carnations and set them in the middle of the coffee table. Took a picture of them and uploaded it on Facebook. "*From the sweetest man ever.*" Wait. Was he on Facebook? If so, she could contact him. She typed in Andrew Stevenson and then tried Drew Stevenson. The ones she found didn't appear to be a hit. Disappointment ate at her. Then she accessed the trail journals. At least she could be close to him through them. The only way she had to learn more about him.

The second one was posted several days after the first.

We finally made it to North Carolina! Ansley, aka Foxy Lady, and a few of her friends joined Lion King and me. Wynter is still with us.

Ansley was with him on the trail? Sara Jane shut her eyes against the burning jealousy. After a moment, she opened them. Her eyes rested on the carnations. Ansley was in the past. He'd sent her flowers today. She continued reading.

It was overcast all day and still cold here in the mountains. The cliff faces were ice covered. Last night we camped in a clearing. We didn't want to deal with the crowds around the shelter. I woke to what sounded like a pack of monkeys. I realize it couldn't have been monkeys because they don't live in the mountains of Georgia. Whatever they were, they screamed, howled, and seemed very close to our campsite. In Ansley's words, creepy. Today began with a few smaller mountains, then we hiked up Standing Indian Mountain and found ourselves in North Carolina. Cell service is spotty. If anyone is actually reading this, I'll write when I can. Still having a hard time.

Still having a hard time with what? His sister's death?

She leaned back in the chair, staring at the screen. Annie's passing must've been what drove him out to the trail. The orange ribbons embossed on his phone flashed into her memory. Leukemia ribbons. His twin sister. The puzzle pieces fit.

But Ansley had hiked with him? He called her Foxy Lady?

Sara Jane shot up from her chair and paced around the apartment. No wonder Ansley knew he didn't go for the uptight, prune-eating type. She was the type he went for. Red hair and attitude.

Sara Jane wouldn't read anymore. She couldn't.

But wait. He'd said everyone had a trail name. Maybe Ansley's was Foxy Lady.

She swung around and went back to the computer to close the site. Instead she clicked on the "next" tab.

Curious about their relationship.

Or maybe she was a glutton for punishment.

Early the next morning, Drew jogged down the street, with Wynter at his heel. He was a coward was all. Responding to Sara Jane's phone call with a bouquet of carnations. He couldn't face her then. He still wasn't up to it.

Not after living up to his caveman reputation by kissing her like he had. He'd probably subjected her to questions from Grandma about having beard burn.

He wanted to pull her back in his arms and kiss her again.

Besides, how would she react to his new look? Would she like him more now? It would base everything on appearances, and not on his personality. He wanted to be liked for who he was, not what he looked like.

It was wise to keep his distance.

Permanently, if possible.

He hoped he hadn't come across as a stalker by having the flowers delivered to her home. Could he help it if her name and address had seared into his mind when he saw it taped next to her grandma's phone? He couldn't help noticing it. And it wasn't his fault it stuck in his mind. He couldn't forget it if he tried. But he hadn't tried very hard.

Drew scowled. Wynter whimpered as if she picked up on his foul mood. He stopped and bent down to rub her ears. "I'm sorry, girl. Another female has me all tied up in knots."

Wynter sat and looked up at him with her head tilted to the right.

"There's nothing to tell, okay? Chris is right. I need to face up to my responsibilities. Her grandmother hired me and I need to fulfill my obligations. Come on, let's go." He started jogging again, but Wynter stubbornly sat, not moving when he tugged.

After a sigh, Drew stopped and knelt in front of his dog. "I'm not replacing you with another woman, okay? I work for them."

Wynter wagged her tail and stood. A jealous pet. Who knew?

A job was all it would be. Could be.

Unless Sara Jane had already told Grandma he'd quit. And they'd found a replacement. It might have been the reason she called Chris, looking for him.

It was more likely she looked for him to make sure he understood what happened between them would never happen again.

She'd be right. It wouldn't. Shouldn't have happened in the first place.

Sara Jane had teacher's meetings all week, Grandma had said. If Grandma hired someone else, then she needed to be the one who let him know. And if she hadn't, he'd be sure he was long gone before Sara Jane arrived.

Drew and Wynter turned the way they came. Wynter dragged a little, as if he'd jogged farther than she was used to. But he had a bunch of issues to work through, and exercise helped.

He'd probably be in shape for a marathon if he kept working for the Morgans.

Drew showered, then waited until he was certain Sara Jane would be at work, since she checked on Grandma every morning. He parked in the driveway. He'd let Grandma know he was here. He knocked, but even though the blinds moved a smidgen, no one answered the door. It was locked when he tried it. Maybe she wasn't home. He set up the ladder and went to work. He'd keep an eye on the door and holler when he saw her.

Sara Jane glanced up at the speaker as he droned on and on about something she didn't care about. As long as she listened with half an ear she should be fine. Others in the room dozed; a few did something on their phones.

Which is what she planned to do.

She couldn't stay away from the trail journals. What would Drew say if he knew how she read—devoured—his entries? Had his parents and brother read them?

She needed to know more about him. About his relationship with Ansley. It was insane to be so jealous of the woman.

The journal page loaded and she found the next entry.

The terrain in North Carolina gently slopes and is gradual compared to the steep mountains in Georgia. I needed to be alone awhile, working through things. Wynter refused to leave me. We hiked seven and a half miles by noon. I found Ansley and Lion King at the Rock Gap Shelter. I thought I'd lost them. As we talked, someone said, "Hey, we've got dogs and beans." We looked over to see a kid pointing toward the parking lot. Sure enough there was a huge tent with a grill and the aroma of hot dogs. A man offered me a can of ice-cold Pepsi. I had two chili dogs with coleslaw, washed down with Pepsi. We all stood around chatting. I talked to the pastor some about my struggles. He encouraged me to take my eyes off my situation and see what God has given me today as he handed me a New Testament/Psalms.

A Bible. Well, it was good for some people. She wouldn't use it as a crutch. But it was okay advice for Drew.

The next entry was a few days later.

Left the shelter at nine a.m. The hiking trail conditions were much easier than yesterday. The climb up to the peak of the mountain was unbelievable and definitely a trip highlight. I wouldn't call it a trail up the mountain as it was more like a rock climb. Ansley refused to go up, so Lion King and Wynter went with her. Her friends have all quit already. Not sure why she keeps going. It took me a while to reach the fire tower, but once I did I figured I owned the mountain. Snow started falling, so I didn't spend too much time on top. The trail was downhill all the way to Long Branch Shelter. What a nice new shelter. It still had a new-wood scent. Only Lion King and Ansley were there when I arrived, so I made my bed inside. By nightfall the shelter was full of thru-hikers. Snow continued to fall but didn't accumulate. Lion King built a fire. Ansley complained about her ankle hurting and the weather. I read in the Psalms. "Lord, you have searched me and known me . . ."

The door clicked shut behind her. Sara Jane glanced over her shoulder as the secretary slipped into the room and laid a folded note beside her. She opened it with a flick of her finger.

"Your grandmother called about a strange man trying to break into her house through the roof. She's called the police."

Sara Jane sighed. Drew had hired a new roofer, without consulting Grandma? Or had Grandma's mind slipped to the point she didn't recognize Drew?

She picked up her pen and scribbled at the bottom, "Call Doctor." She'd put it off too long, despite all the worrisome signs she'd been seeing. Despite Drew noticing and telling his mother Grandma was in the beginning stages of Alzheimer's.

She'd call and make an appointment today—during her break. Then she'd call Grandma. Someone working on the roof was not cause for her to rush home, especially after leaving early yesterday. Her boss would definitely have something to say about it.

Though it tempted her to see if it was Drew. To give him a piece of her mind. To thank him for the beautiful flowers. And to ask why he'd left like he had—why he quit. Why hadn't he come after she called?

He'd gone to her apartment. When she wasn't there. When he should have known she'd be at Grandma's.

He might've gone to a florist in Morgantown, ordered flowers, and a more local florist had delivered them.

But even though Drew apparently knew her address, it didn't creep her out. Because maybe it meant he might—hopefully—be as infatuated with her as she was with him.

If only she'd known it when she'd first met him.

She would've asked for one of his business cards. Maybe two. One for her purse. And one for her bedside table.

She turned her attention back to the speaker. If Grandma called the police on a strange roofer they didn't know or hire, it'd serve him right. If it was Drew, he'd convince Grandma, and maybe he'd still be there when the meeting released. She checked her watch. If she held on for thirty more minutes, they'd break until afternoon . . .

On the other hand, he clearly didn't want to see her.

And it wasn't an option.

19

The strobing blue lights coming down the street caught Drew's attention. One of the neighbors had some sort of drama going on. He watched the police cars to see which house they went to. They pulled in behind his truck. He stood. Frowned. Had Grandma fallen? Did she have one of those push-button bracelets to notify first responders when she got hurt?

One of the officers grabbed a bullhorn. "Put down the weapon and put your hands up."

Drew blinked. The weapon? He laid down his hammer and the nail, then raised his hands. Another officer trained a gun on him.

"Is there a problem, officers?"

Neighbors began to appear on their front lawns. Great, an audience.

"Descend the ladder. Keep your hands where we can see them!"

He hitched an eyebrow, but did as the officers demanded.

"What were you doing up there?" an officer asked. Drew recognized him as the one who responded to the stolen car claim at the grocery store. Maybe he'd be sympathetic.

Drew glanced up at the roof. "Mrs. Morgan hired me to shingle the roof."

"Who are you?"

"Andrew Stevenson."

One of the policemen walked up to the house and knocked. A few minutes later the door opened. Grandma stepped out clutching a fireplace poker.

"Ma'am, he claims you hired him to work on your roof." The officer glanced at the metal stick and stepped back.

Grandma pointed the iron in Drew's direction. "I most certainly did not. I never saw this man in my entire life and he is clearly trying to break in to steal my silverware. He tried the door to see if it was locked. It was, so he climbed the roof. And you might want to check vehicle registration because he's driving a stolen truck."

The policeman looked back at him. "Any proof of who you are?"

"May I get my driver's license out of my wallet? It's in the glove compartment in the pickup. I have my business cards in there as well."

The officer gestured with his head to his partner. He went over to the truck, opened the passenger side door, and emerged with Drew's wallet.

"You don't appear to be the man in the picture."

Oh. He'd gone to Chris. Drew sighed. "I visited the barber."

"If this is you, it was long past time." He studied the photo again. "What is your address?"

Drew recited it. Along with his birthday.

A familiar silver car screeched to a stop on the road. Sara Jane jumped out, leaving the car idling, and raced up. "What's going on here? Who is this . . . I never saw . . . Drew? Oh, my word. Oh. My. Word." She came up to him and raised her hand, letting her fingers trail over his exposed skin, leaving fire in their wake. "What have you done?"

An officer cleared his throat. "Do you know him, miss?"

Sara Jane's attention shifted to the policeman. "Yes, sir. Grandma's handyman. Drew Stevenson. She hired him to do some home improvements." Her gaze darted back to Drew. "Wow." She cupped his cheek with her hand.

His face burned. He felt like a dolt, standing there with her soft hand touching him, but was unable to make his feet move. Somewhere between his head and his legs the command to change position had gotten lost. She pulled her hand back, but still stared at him.

The officers scribbled some notes, handed Drew his wallet, and left after saying a few more words. He wasn't sure what. His brain had turned to mush.

Grandma stormed down the steps, the fire poker in her left hand, and marched up to him, a finger wagging in his face. At least it wasn't the poker, but he eyed her warily.

"I don't know who you are and how you got off so easy, but just because you're easy on the eyes doesn't mean you're welcome around here. I have a perfectly good handyman. He may look like he got lost in the wilderness, but he is the absolute best. I had him checked out. You need to leave. *Now.* Before I run you off, and don't think I won't. As for you, Sara Jane. How dare you get so friendly with him? You're an engaged woman and you need to act like it. For shame! Touching another man's face."

Drew pulled in a shuddering breath and stepped back. "Yes, ma'am. It might be best if I go." In more ways than one. "Just let me get my tools."

"You're going nowhere." Sara Jane propped her fists on her hips. "You have some explaining to do, mister."

The scary Sara Jane had returned.

"And you." She swung around to face Grandma. "Why didn't you tell me you've been to the doctor?"

"Well, I . . ." Sari faltered a moment. How did Sara Jane know she'd been to the doctor? Did she know about her pesky diagnosis too? If she did, she'd completely take away her freedom, and she wasn't ready to give it up yet.

Though the memory slips were more than a little concerning. She didn't know how many combinations she dialed today to reach the police department, and it was a number she'd memorized. Only three little numbers. How hard would it be to recall them? She sighed. Harder than she thought.

She shook her head and glared at the good-looking young man who'd been on her roof, trying to break in. The police should've taken him away in chains, not left him here for Sara Jane to fawn all over. Andrew's heart would be broken.

Well, maybe. To be honest, she wasn't sure he was interested in Sara Jane. He needed to be, but she didn't see him making any effort whatsoever to ask her out, or be with her.

No, he was polite. Friendly. In a not-interested way. Which wasn't acceptable at all. He didn't make googly eyes at her. Like what this handsome stranger tried to do.

"Never mind me. Whether I go to the doctor is not any of your concern. They have these hippopotamus laws to respect a person's privacy. They aren't allowed to discuss something in the hallway, you know. Doors have to be shut. Stupid to name them after an animal in Africa, but no one asked me. What *is* your concern is who this man is and why you were touching him when you're engaged."

Sara Jane huffed. "Grandma, I am *not* engaged. I'm not seeing anyone. And for your information, this is Drew. Andrew. The guy you hired. Look in those eyes. Chocolate-colored. It is Drew. He went to the barber."

Sari peered closer. And a niggling of doubt appeared. Was it really Andrew?

"Yes, ma'am. If it's okay, I'll go."

"It is *not* okay." Sara Jane turned on him. "If you go anywhere, it will be on the roof, because I need to talk to you when I finish with her."

"You are finished with me. And if you're Andrew, prove it. What color are the mountains?"

The man blinked a moment. "On your song quilt? Or in real life?"

He knew about the quilt?

"In the quilt, you used a purple and a blue, if I remember right."

No way he could've known unless he'd been peeking in her window. Which would make him a pervert, spying on a grandma.

Where did the police go? She looked around, hoping one did a drive-by.

"What does Andrew sell in his tent?"

"Brooms?" He backed up another step, his brow furrowed. He looked uncertain.

"Brooms? It was ice cream." Sari distinctly remembered the ice cream. She lifted the fireplace poker in what she hoped was a threatening manner. It must've worked, because he backed up another step.

"No, ma'am. Brooms."

"Drew, you go up on the roof. Grandma, this is enough." Sara Jane turned. "You go inside. You're acting like a child. Besides, the nurse knows me. I have medical power of attorney. Remember? And she told me you have the beginning stages of—"

"You have no right to coddle me, young lady." Sari turned her attention to the man. "And if you are Andrew, you get busy on my roof right this instant. And do what I asked you to do, to impress Sara Jane." She swung around on her heel and marched toward the house. She locked the door behind her.

Sara Jane could yell at the imposter awhile. Though—maybe it was Andrew. He knew all the right answers. But if he were, whoo-wee he'd hidden a hunk under all the hair. If she were sixty years younger she'd give her granddaughter a run for the money.

She gazed at the man through the window. No. The cliché "run for the money" wasn't right. She'd give her granddaughter a run for the *honey.*

Sara Jane turned to Drew. He was absolutely gorgeous, though she wouldn't tell him. Who would've guessed the John the Baptist wannabe was so good looking under all his hair?

"I hate to ask, but what did she ask you to do to impress me?"

Red flooded his face and he looked away. "Uh, she asked me to take my shirt off. Don't worry, I won't do it. Don't want the sunburn."

Her face burned. If only she could blame it on the sun.

He glanced toward the roof, then the house. The blare of a full-blast television interrupted the peace. "But sounds like you'll have your hands full with her, so I'll get my things and go."

"Did you get my message yesterday? I called Chris, looking for you."

"Yep." He backed up a step. "If it's about quitting, I know. You need to fire me. I understand. I've been dismissed." He nodded toward the house.

Sara Jane slumped. "The nurse told me she has Alzheimer's. She'll have good days and bad days and it'll get to the point where she won't recognize me." Tears burned her eyes. "We only have each other. In less than ten years, I'll probably be all alone in the world."

He wiped his hand over his jaw. "Well, not to sound like I'm spouting platitudes, but you'll have God, and His grace is suff—"

That was so not true. "God. Who is God? Does He exist? If He does, then He doesn't care about me, and I care less about Him. If there is a God, He's punishing me for—"

"But you go to church . . . I thought . . ."

Sara Jane shook her head. "I go to church because Grandma tells me I have to. It's expected. Though, I think what was expected in her day and time isn't so common in mine. Not many of my friends nor their parents bother with it. It's the grandparents."

Something like disappointment crossed his face. He stared at his feet a long moment. "Yes. It's true. There was a time I felt the same way. I was encouraged to look past myself to see God."

"When your sister died." She waved her hand. "I'm reading your trail journals."

"You are?"

Her face warmed. Oops, she hadn't meant to tell him. Now he knew she'd been cyberstalking him. Nothing to do but admit it. "Yes. You're in North Carolina."

He nodded. "Keep reading. You might find something interesting." Uncertainty flashed across his eyes, and he shrugged. "I'm unclear about what I need to do here. Am I still working for your grandmother or not?"

She raised her chin. "You are. And you're engaged to me."

His eyes widened and he caught his breath. "In Grandma's eyes, but . . . No. I won't pretend something. We aren't. There's no hope of us ever being." Something buzzed. He pulled out his cell phone and glanced at it. "I need to take this, if you'll excuse me."

He walked away.

Disappointment ate at her. No hope. It sounded so . . . hopeless. She watched him go, then turned toward the house. She twisted the doorknob. Locked. She sighed and looked back at Drew as he strode toward his truck.

She'd forgotten to give him a piece of her mind and to thank him for the flowers. But somehow it didn't matter anymore.

Chasing the man until he caught her was all that mattered.

And she didn't have a clue how to proceed.

20

The next day, Sari stretched and rubbed her lower back. She'd spent the morning bent over the cutting board, cutting out quilt pieces. She lifted a black square and placed it off-center over a gold rectangle, to indicate a page in a poem book, depicting a line in the song, "If I were a poet and could write a fine hand." She would embroider the word *Poems* on the black square. The block would be fairly easy to make and should go fast.

She considered the layout, then shook her head. Something was missing. The quilt block needed something more . . .

It would look pretty to lay the book on a doily sewn to the background. A bit different. Hopefully, the overall effect would portray a beloved book of poetry. She used to love it when Cade read poetry to her when they courted, though she didn't think he enjoyed it so much. He'd discontinued it in a hurry after they married.

Sari had a stack of doilies in one of Cade's old shoeboxes in the closet. Used to be a time when doilies were a necessary part of setting up house. They went under lamps, on the arms and backs of chairs, and down the center of the table. One couldn't get married unless she had enough doilies.

People today didn't want the fuss and muss of them. Handwashing, ironing, and starching were things of the past. Or so Sara Jane said.

With a sigh, Sari went to the closet and lifted the box labeled "doilies." She picked out a plain, white one. A fancy one with multi-colored flowers wouldn't be needed for this project. She laid the doily against the dark fabric and redesigned the block. Much better.

She'd been working on the quilt all morning, and had cut out ocean waves from blues and greens as well as a winding road out of tans. The road was supposed to represent the line "I'm going to ramble this country all through." Which was exactly what Cade did for a while. The man had what used to be called an "itchy foot." Sari frowned.

Right now she didn't need to ramble, either mentally or physically. She needed to stretch her back.

She wandered over to the window and looked outside. The good-looking stranger who'd turned out to be Andrew had brought in a dumpster-type thing to pitch the old shingles into as he redid the roof. It wasn't industrial sized, but a mini one, with wheels on it, so it might be easy to roll. He'd wheeled it around to the back of the house easily enough.

Her yard was a mess, after the thunderstorms the night before. Twigs and leaves littered the lawn. Plus, Sara Jane had done more weeding in the flower beds, leaving the piles of weeds right where they were. She'd said she'd take care of them later, but who knew when later would be. School would be starting in a week. Sara Jane was busy with lesson plans, meetings, setting up her classroom, and whatever else teachers did when summer neared an end.

Sari sighed. She didn't know where the summer had gone. Her ballad quilt wasn't finished, although they had made progress getting the first six blocks laid out and appliquéd. They'd also made plans for what they'd do for the ship crossing the ocean and the road that takes the two lovers apart. Sara Jane wanted one of the old ships with lots of sails, but Sari thought it might be a little complicated. A single large triangle would work to portray a ship's sails.

She shook her head and stared at the little dumpster on wheels sitting there. Andrew hadn't told her to stay away from it. The yard did need work, and she needed the break. . . .

Since the thing took up space in her yard she might as well put it to good use. And since Sara Jane would be busy with school meetings all week. . . . Besides, Sari wanted her to help with the ballad quilt. The girl needed to learn some skills besides teaching. At least the child knew how to cook. Good thing or Sari might never get a home-cooked meal. Too much work to cook for one. Unless she made a pot of ham and beans or stew, and then ate on it all week.

Enough of the mental rambling.

She went out to grab a rake.

After finishing the work she wanted to do, she put all the loose yard waste in the dumpster. But then thought better of it. Was it illegal to use the dumpster for something other than shingles? Andrew might get upset with her. She wasn't sure what the policy would be with those rented dumpsters. She pushed it out to the curb and dumped the contents out. Andrew hadn't done much after the police came yesterday. He'd set up the dumpster, carried the shingles up to the roof, and started work, but then quit and went for more supplies after Sara Jane left. He said he'd be back later today.

It wasn't windy, so now probably would be a good time to burn this stuff. Besides, the trash company seemed to have issues with picking up bagged yard waste. Simply put, they wouldn't, unless it was city clean-up day. Twice a year. Not near enough, if anyone asked her. Which they didn't. Maybe she should run for mayor. Then they'd be forced to listen to her.

She pushed the trash bin back toward the backyard. What would she change if she were mayor? Maybe she'd start with . . . She tripped over the flopping dumpster lid or an uneven place on the ground and went flying.

She screamed as she hurtled into the container, crash landing headfirst on the bottom. For a long time she was still. Was she dead? She hesitantly opened one eye and then the other. She was upside down in this upright trash bin. Maybe. Perhaps it'd tipped over too, and she could back out. She kicked, but hit nothing except air.

Oh, wasn't this a sight. She couldn't help giggling. What would Sara Jane say if she saw her like this? Or Andrew? Or the neighbors who'd think someone had put her in the trash rather than believe she'd put herself there.

Andrew would be by today to work on the roof. Though he did say he'd be late, when he came. He'd had some other obligation.

She couldn't believe he went and shaved. He should've cleared it with her beforehand, so she would've been prepared.

Enough of the rabbit trail. He'd be along. And see her upside down in the dumpster with her feet kicking the air. At least she had the foresight to put shorts on. She didn't have the prettiest legs in town, not with her varicose veins, but at least her bloomers were covered.

She giggled, but then a belly laugh bubbled up and she started laughing so hard she was unable to do anything else for a bit. She finally settled down and tried to rock the thing over on its side so she could crawl out. After a few tries and fits of giggles, she managed to tip it.

"Hey. Easy there." A masculine voice broke in as the thing started to turn on its side. The dumpster stopped its fast flop, and instead eased down gently. "Are you okay, Grandma?"

"Nothing's broken," she choked out between giggles. She slid out and sat. "The next time you see me in the yard, bring your video camera. We could have made some serious money with this one."

Andrew didn't crack a smile. "Did you ever wonder why they tell you not to roll those big trash bins with the lid open? You could've been hurt."

Enough of his seriousness. Sari straightened her spine, but she couldn't quite find the strength to stand. Or the humility to ask for help. Instead she focused on his clean-shaven jaw. "You are a handsome hunk, Andrew Stevenson. If Sara Jane doesn't see it, the girl is blind."

Red flash-flooded his face. But he didn't acknowledge her comment. Instead he held out his hand toward her. "May I help you up?"

She took his hand. "I'm going to call the church and see about reserving a date. If Sara Jane won't marry you, then I will."

The empty classroom smelled of fresh paint. It was kind of a nondescript eggshell shade, the same color they'd used for years and years. But the hallway had some new spots of color. Vivid blues, greens, and yellows graced different walls. Gone were the boring rows of lockers attached to the wall. Now they had locker groupings, similar to the locker room at the fitness center.

Sara Jane dropped into the rolling chair behind her desk. Time for a break before she finished hanging the rest of the flyers and posters around the room. She picked up her smartphone, and almost without conscious thought, she went to Drew's trail journal site.

She could almost be a teenager in the throes of an unreturned crush. Had she ever felt this way about a man before? She couldn't remember ever liking anyone the way she liked Drew. Almost obsessed with him. But unrequited love—if it was love—didn't suit her. If he'd ask her out, let her get over her infatuation, it would be great. Unfortunately, her broad hints had gotten her nowhere.

In fact, he'd been blatant in his refusals. Stating in no uncertain terms any relationship between them was in Grandma's eyes only and nothing would happen in reality.

Which only made her more determined.

Even knowing he had Ansley in his life didn't deter her. Horrible. If she was Ansley, and another woman chased her man, she'd have serious issues. She'd confront the other woman. Hearing a footstep, she glanced toward the doorway, almost expecting to see the redhead materialize there. She quickly closed down the trail journal site and looked up.

The doorway was empty.

Silence reigned. She must have imagined the noise. Her guilty conscience worked overtime.

Sometimes she hated herself.

She stood and went to look in both directions down the hall. Nothing moved. She crossed it to stare out the window. The bright sun lit the streets, flashing blindingly off the passing cars. But there were no answers.

She should take Drew's firm refusal as fact.

Should. Would. Well, maybe. Probably not.

"Give up" wasn't in her vocabulary. Grandma taught her "Quitters never win and winners never quit." She could be ruthless when she went after something she wanted.

Sara Jane wanted Drew. At least some positive attention from him, if not the man himself. She moved back to her desk, plopped back in the chair, and keyed in "how to get his attention when he doesn't notice you," but lost her nerve before she clicked enter. Deleted it. Keyed "I like him but he doesn't like me."

Ugh! She was a twenty-four-year-old woman. She should be far beyond this adolescent behavior. As Grandma often reminded her, she'd been married and had a couple of babies by the time she was Sara Jane's age.

She sighed. Maybe Marci would have some good advice. She caught men easily enough.

Drew was a catch Sara Jane wanted to land.

She clicked on the saved link to his trail journals, but couldn't stop another guilty look aimed at the doorway. Nothing moved.

I have been without good cell service a while. The views during the day are great, especially of the sun setting over the Smokies. It was cold and windy last night, about twenty degrees. Word is the mountains had significant snow and the road from Gatlinburg to Newfound Gap splitting them into north/south sections was closed. Lion King, Ansley, Wynter, and I hiked together. We're heading into the Smokies tomorrow and will be out of cell service for as many as four days.

Sara Jane stared at the screen a moment, a moment of panic filling her. Four days? How would she feed her crush? Her heart stopped a moment.

Wait. This was his history. Not current events.

She had it bad. She glanced at the clock above the door. Would Marci be in her classroom? Hopefully she wouldn't be meeting Chris for lunch. She needed advice.

But first, she clicked "next."

Slept okay last night, though there was a trio of snorers going before I put my earplugs in. After that, I didn't know it poured during the night. Lion King suggested it might be wise to get to Newfound Gap as early on Sunday as possible since more bad weather is coming in. It meant some pretty big miles today over harsh terrain. The trail was slippery. Sometime around noon we crossed the point where we have less than 2000 miles to go. For most of the rest of the way in the Smokies, we'll be on the border of Tennessee and North Carolina. Does it mean our left foot will be in Tennessee and our right foot in North Carolina? Ansley says she'll take a zero day when she gets to Newfound Gap. She needs to rest her sore ankle/foot. She said she'd catch up with us later if we don't take a zero day. I was wet and muddy by the time we reached the shelter.

Sara Jane stood and slid her phone in her pocket. Lunchtime, either with or without Marci. She went down the hallway to Marci's room and peeked in.

Marci dropped her phone in her purse as Sara Jane entered. "Chris and I are meeting for lunch at the burger place next to his barber shop."

"I hoped you were free. I need to talk to you."

Marci glanced at the wall clock. "I have a moment. What's up?"

Sara Jane swallowed. Maybe she shouldn't ask about getting a man's attention. If he were interested, she would know it, right? But, Marci did something right. Or maybe men went for redheads over brunettes, no matter the shade of red. After all, Drew seemed to prefer Ansley. Chris snagged Marci in a hurry. She sighed.

"I don't have all day." Marci shifted her weight.

"Oh. Sorry." Sara Jane groaned. "I'm discouraged. There's this man I like, and he doesn't seem to notice me. I'm wondering how do I get him to notice me?"

Marci laughed. "Don't you pay any attention to the girls between classes and after school? Watch them sometime. They have it down."

So much for Marci being helpful.

Marci straightened her posture, and strutted in front of Sara Jane. "Girls walk in front of guys they like all the time. They pretend they don't see them. The guy is forced to notice her, so he doesn't mow her over. Plus, she's got the swing going so they look."

Big help. Not.

"The most important thing is to be his friend. Flirt, but don't be too flirty. Talk to him. Try to find things of interest to you both and talk about them. Hang around him, but don't stalk."

Oops. She'd been cyberstalking Drew. And confessed it to him. She'd also probably been too flirty. Touching his face. She cringed.

"Another thing they do is hang around the guy's friends. He's forced to talk to her." Marci giggled. "I want to hear about this mystery man, sometime, but I've got to go. Good luck."

"Yeah. I'll need it." Sara Jane turned away. What did she have in common with Drew? She liked his personality. He was gorgeous without all the facial hair. She loved his eyes. . . . But nothing was common ground. She'd never gone hiking. He'd thru-hiked the Appalachian Trail. She loved history. . . . Did he? He *had* gone to Fort Necessity. He was artistic. She was a bookworm. She slept under a quilt and used a broom to sweep up dirt. He helped Grandma design her quilt and made brooms.

They had nothing in common.

At least nothing she could see.

But she wasn't ready to give up.

Drew looked down from his perch on the roof when Sara Jane's car pulled into the drive. She emerged looking cool and comfortable in a pair of white pants ending about halfway between the ankle and the knee, and a pink shirt with a v-neck. Some sort of strappy shoes matching the shirt revealed her feet. He swallowed and looked at his watch. Noon. She'd blocked him in so he couldn't beat a hasty retreat. Did she do it on purpose?

He reached for the bottle of water and took a swig. It was hot. He should've put the roofing job off for cooler weather—or worked evenings. He put the lid on and set it down.

Drew couldn't resist another peek. He watched as she bumped her car door shut with a swing of her hip, held up a takeout bag from a taco place, and waved it at him. "I brought sustenance."

His stomach rumbled in response. Being in close quarters with Sara Jane would be a mistake.

His gaze dropped toward her lips. They formed a smile.

She probably wouldn't wear a pleasant expression if she knew how often he'd relived their kiss. How he wanted to do it again . . . and again . . . and again. He'd considered submitting to Grandma's matchmaking schemes and marrying Sara Jane. His blood heated as his thoughts drifted toward the honeymoon.

Though Sara Jane would have a say in a relationship. And she wasn't interested. Well, she *had* initiated the kiss, but only because she wanted to see what it was like to kiss a caveman. Research for her history class, probably. Though it didn't explain why she'd continued the kiss, touched his face, or refused to let him quit. Asking him to pretend to be in a relationship was simply for Grandma's sake.

He'd bitten off more than he could chew with this family. She wasn't interested. Couldn't be interested. It was the nuances of her female mind confusing him to make him think she might be.

He wouldn't risk the hurt, the sarcasm, the ultimate rejection if he bared his heart. "Thanks, but I'll eat later." He ignored the rebellious rumble his stomach made in response.

Her smile faltered, but she kept it in place. "Then come down off the roof and sit with us while we eat. You need a break."

He slid a glance at the cardboard drink carrier by her side, holding three large cups of something cold . . . then glared at his bottle half full of hot water. He swallowed and tried to search for a refusal that wouldn't be a lie.

"I won't take no for an answer. If you won't come down, Grandma and I will come up there." It would be something to see. But he wasn't sure he wanted to risk it by calling her bluff. Judging by the way her hand holding the plastic carryout bag balled on her hip, she probably was serious. She seemed to have taken up the fist-on-hip move from Grandma.

"A cold drink would be good." He put down his tools and stood. Maybe Grandma would let him refrigerate his water so it'd cool. He bent to retrieve it, then descended the ladder.

Sara Jane approached, stopping too close as he reached the bottom. He caught her lilac scent. She was near enough he could lean forward and touch her mouth with his, without worries of toppling over. And he couldn't step back. Not with the ladder behind him. Sidling sideways might cause him to brush up against her. Not knowing what to do, he froze.

What Sara Jane did to his senses should be illegal. He frowned, trying to keep his gaze focused on her face instead of following the trail of the sparkly gold chain around her neck to where something dangled tantalizingly.

"Can I carry something for you?" Did she hear the huskiness in his voice?

"Sure." She moved the cardboard carrier his way. But there was no way for him to take it by the handle without his hand brushing against hers. He gulped, then reached with both hands, and took it by the bottom.

"It'd be easier to carry it by the handle." She had a knowing sound in her voice, as if she realized the power she held over him and relished it.

Right. He waited until she released it, then balanced it on one hand, and moved his other to the handle. Mission accomplished, without skin contact.

She brushed against him as she turned away. He watched her go.

Pathetic.

Especially when she glanced over her shoulder and caught him staring at her. Unable to look away.

It would be a long lunch hour. With no way of escape.

21

Sara Jane's face heated as she headed toward the house. She wished she'd had a few minutes to collect herself before facing Grandma. She'd probably notice the strain between Sara Jane and Drew—since she'd attempted to flirt with him again, and it'd fallen flat. As usual. Why did she try?

If what Marci said was true, then "the strut" should have worked like a charm. Sara Jane must have done it wrong. Didn't Marci say he'd follow?

She glanced back. Drew apparently didn't know he was supposed to follow her. He stood there with a strange expression on his face as he watched her.

No, Marci had said it'd catch his attention.

She'd gotten his attention. But the wrong kind.

She wanted to ask him why he didn't like her. Was she too flirty? Not flirty enough?

Or did Ansley have such a hold on him that he couldn't see any other woman?

His devotion to Ansley was impressive. Sara Jane shouldn't be chasing after a man who wasn't available.

She held her head high as she arrived at the door. Behind her, ice sloshed in a cup. A masculine hand touched hers when she reached for the knob. "Let me."

She pulled away. "Thank you." Ugh, she sounded formally polite to her own ears.

His hand closed around the knob. But instead of turning it, he held it. His arm extended there, without so much as a muscle twinge.

She was afraid to move. His breath tickled her neck as he expelled a forceful breath of air.

"I'm sorry." His voice was low. Rumbly.

He didn't say for what. But she could figure it out. He knew her interest and didn't have any desire to pursue her, despite their moments of weakness spent in each other's arms, kissing. She stared at his hand on the knob. If only she were brave enough to turn and face him. She didn't want to see the pity in his eyes.

Her heart ached. "I understand. It's wrong of me to chase you anyway. She's a lucky woman." She forced the words past the lump in her throat. Great. Now Grandma would notice the tears burning her eyes.

He stood still another moment, then his hand released the knob. "Hold on. What? I mean, who?" He sounded a bit confused.

The door swung open.

Sara Jane sucked in air, then expelled it. "Hi, Grandma. I brought lunch." She hoped no one noticed the tremble in her voice.

"What are you doing here?" Grandma had a fake smile on her face. "I wasn't expecting you today." She glanced at Drew and aimed her "keep your mouth shut and don't you dare say a word" look at him. "I'll never get used to you being clean-shaven. But I like it." She turned her attention back to Sara Jane. "You're joining us for lunch?"

Sara Jane laughed. "If it's okay." She held out the carryout bag. "What's going on? What are you keeping from me?" She looked from Grandma to Drew.

"Nothing. Don't know where you got such an idea." Grandma's fake smile didn't waver.

"Grandma . . ."

"You hush. You have no business going around questioning me. And what is this Grandma business?" Grandma took the carryout bag from her. "Hamburgers. I hope you got onion rings instead of fries. Although, on second thought, they aren't good for courting couples. Come along, honey." She glanced at Drew before she turned away and started down the hall.

The "honey" was clearly meant for Drew. Sara Jane's stomach churned in discomfort. What was going on? Besides, it wasn't hamburgers. It was tacos and burritos.

"Grandma?"

The older woman ignored her.

Sara Jane swung to face Drew. He sidestepped and placed the drink carrier on the entryway table, then grasped her arm and pulled her outside, shutting the door behind him.

"She fell headfirst into the trash bin when she was doing yard work. At the time, she didn't seem to be hurt, except for her pride. She didn't want you to know."

"But . . ." Sara Jane pulled in a strangled breath when his finger rested against her lips.

"I think she's fine. I talked to her awhile. The only concerning thing was she decided she'd marry me if you won't." He chuckled. "I have no intentions of marrying her."

Or you. The words dangled unsaid between them.

Sara Jane moved back a step, dislodging his finger. "Speaking of which, I'm sorry. I shouldn't have been chasing you. I should've honored your previous commitment to Ansley."

He frowned. "I have no commitment to Ansley. She's a friend—and a fellow artisan. That's it."

"But you hugged her . . . and kissed her . . . and . . ." Her face heated. "Sorry, your relationship is not any of my business."

One corner of his mouth flexed, forming a dimple. "No, it's not. But to rest your mind, I'm not seeing anyone."

"Why not?" She tilted her head. Why would such a hunk be without a girlfriend? Oh, wait. He'd been so rough-looking, he probably scared girls away. "Will you go out with me?" Almost immediately, she wished she could snatch the words back.

His mouth worked. She closed her eyes, dreading his response. Before sound emerged the door opened.

"Why are you two back outside? Those burgers are getting cold." Grandma planted her fists on her hips. "Were you out here smooching where the neighbors can see you?"

Drew coughed. The pretty blush staining Sara Jane's cheeks morphed into a vivid red shade. He was sure his skin tone matched, judging by the heat searing it. He forced his attention to her grandmother. "No, ma'am. We're on our way in."

"Good. Because kissing is private and the neighbors don't need to be seeing. Now, get in here. I'm hungry."

Sara Jane glanced at her watch. "I need to be back at school in ten minutes. My lunch break will be over."

"Nice of you to stop. Take your lunch and go. You'll stay for supper, right, honey?" Grandma looked back at Drew.

Drew smiled. "Thanks, but no thanks. I need to work on some broom orders." He couldn't decipher Grandma's mood. It seemed to have swung from the fun and laughter of the morning to more gruff and angry, though maybe it was a show for Sara Jane. He didn't understand the nuances of their relationship, but Grandma seemed more angry and bossy when Sara Jane was with them. He wasn't a psychologist, but it was almost as if she fought to keep control of her granddaughter. Or blamed her for some events of the past.

Sara Jane pulled in an audible breath. "I won't be over tonight, Grandma. I have plans. I'll take my *tacos* since I need to get back. Before I leave, Drew, could I have your business card?"

He glanced at her as his hand moved to his pocket. He pulled out his wallet and removed a card. His eyes held hers as he handed it to her.

"I . . . Uh . . ." Her gaze shot to her grandmother and then back. "I might have a project. I'll call you."

A project? She lived in an apartment, owned by a landlord. He couldn't think what type of job she'd have. But he nodded. Then it dawned. She'd asked him out.

Sara Jane glanced at Grandma. "I can work on your quilt some tomorrow night, or over the weekend, if you like." She entered the house and moved down the hall, then emerged with a couple of tacos. She grabbed a drink from the carrier sitting on the table.

Drew reached to take the drink from her. "I'll carry this out for you. Grandma, I'll be right in, okay?"

"You don't need to call me Grandma. I'm not much older than you. Call me Sari." She smiled. "Hurry back, honey." She shot a baleful glance toward Sara Jane.

Not much older? He blinked. She had to be in her late seventies or early eighties compared to his mid-twenties. Not to mention, it was kind of weird, hearing the flirty, possessive sounds in Grandma's voice. He nodded, his brow furrowing. Had the fall affected her more than he'd thought? He wasn't sure what to do, except nod and go along with whatever she wanted him to do.

Sara Jane shot him a confused look, then glanced back at her grandmother. "Grandma?"

"Don't you start with me, you floozy. Trying to steal my man. There's a name for girls like you." Grandma's eyes flashed. "Get on out of here, and don't come back."

Drew's mouth parted and he sucked in a breath.

Sara Jane backed up and pulled her cell phone from her pocket. "Maybe I need to . . ."

"Yes." Drew steered her out of the house, shut the door, and led her out to the car. "Call her doctor. He probably won't be able to do anything, though, if the fall affected her memory. This is none of my business, but you should talk to your parents about some sort of supervision. Someone needs to be with her."

"I'll call the pastor's wife." Sara Jane looked up. "My parents are gone. I'm all she has. And she doesn't know me." Her voice broke. Tears filled her eyes. For a second, he wanted to pull her into his arms and try to comfort her.

"I'm sure it's temporary." He hoped.

"I have to go to work. But I'll make the calls. Will you be here?"

"I'll keep an eye on her until the pastor's wife comes."

She nodded. "Thanks. I appreciate it." She slid into the car, and accepted her drink when he held it out. His fingers brushed against hers. He wished he could grab them and hold on.

"Call me," he said. And backed away.

Sara Jane had wanted an excuse to call him, but not like this. She half considered asking him about her clogged sink in her apartment, wishing he was the maintenance man. But he wasn't. In truth, she'd rather hoped he'd call her and ask her out. Or had accepted her when she asked. Neither seemed likely to happen. Even if it did, if Grandma was worse. . . . She didn't want to face it.

Grandma would be at the doctor's office, right now. The pastor's wife took her in, since Sara Jane couldn't get off work. It was nice the doctor had an opening at three o'clock and they took her. She'd need to stop by on her way home from work tomorrow to get Grandma's diagnosis, because Grandma wouldn't tell her. Thinking of the possibilities made her stomach churn and hurt. At least the pastor's wife agreed to stay until Sara Jane arrived.

Sara Jane prowled around her classroom, trying to see it from the eyes of students and parents. Open house would be later in the evening, with parents coming in to meet the staff, help students find their classrooms, and tour the facilities. She *had* to be present.

She pushed a chair in under a table and straightened a timeline, then retrieved a dry-erase marker at the white board. She scrawled her name across it, in black. "Miss Morgan."

Sara Jane stepped back, observing it. Miss Morgan reminded her of what Drew called her, before he switched, at her insistence, to Sara Jane.

She needed to call him. Though he probably was back on the roof, because Grandma was still at the doctor's.

She didn't know what to say to him. She hadn't heard anything about Grandma. She couldn't ask him out again with this uncertainty over her head, though she could invite him to the open house . . .

He'd refuse. He had broom orders to fill. He'd already said so.

Sara Jane sighed. She'd call him when she knew something. When she had some idea what job she could ask him to do, to have him around her.

He wasn't seeing Ansley. Or anyone.

Nothing stood in the way of him asking her out.

Unless he simply wasn't interested. She really should catch a clue.

Right now, nothing mattered except Grandma. What was going on? She couldn't lose her—the only surviving member of her family. She'd be all alone.

If she thought for a half-second God listened, she'd pray. He didn't. She wouldn't waste her time.

She pulled out her chair and dropped, fighting the tears again over losing her parents. She'd hoped Grandma would leave the pictures out, but she hadn't. They'd vanished before Grandma emerged from her room. At least Sara Jane knew where they were now. Someday she would get into the pictures.

She'd take a few minutes' break, before finishing her preparations. And she wouldn't cry.

She glanced at the clock, then accessed the trail journals. It'd keep her mind off Grandma . . . off her parents . . . and on Drew. Someone she needed to keep her mind off of. At least thinking of him wouldn't make her cry.

Wow, it poured last night. I wished I'd left out an empty water bottle as a rain gauge. Lion King said we got five inches, easy. I love the sound of rain hitting the roof of the shelter, but this much might be an issue.

The weather is turning sour again. Forecasts are up to a foot of snow and wind chills to drop below zero.

Sat by the fire to read in Psalms.

The next entry was several days later.

What a crazy day of hiking. It stayed slightly above freezing all night. The snow got soft and slushy in places. With the melt starting at above 6,000 feet, the trail turned into a river, with knee-deep ice-cold water flowing in our direction. Hiking in icy water made me concerned about frostbite. Where the snow wasn't slush, we post-holed, making travel slow. It was so bad we considered heading back to the shelter we'd slept in last night.

Post-holed? What did that mean? Sara Jane looked up the word. "The hole left behind when your foot sinks into deep snow." It made sense.

When the trail lost elevation, conditions started to improve. We passed Cosby Shelter and decided we wanted to get out of the Smokies. This meant a high-mileage day. Big miles and wet feet are a bad combination. I have a couple blisters forming. Made me think of Annie and how she'd gotten bruises everywhere. Will I ever work through this? I did what I could. I donated my stem cells! Why wasn't it enough? Or I wasn't good enough?

We went under our first interstate. Someone was there with "trail magic." We scored the last of his hot chicken noodle soup. Annie's favorite. . . . I hiked alone the rest of the day. Glad Lion King is willing to give me space.

Sara Jane looked away from the phone's screen. Tears burned her eyes. So much for not crying! Drew worked through a lot losing his twin sister. His pain radiated off the screen.

She'd been totally engrossed in the journals. It was as spellbinding as reading the diaries of a famous historical person. Maybe she'd read one more before she got to work.

It was cold and windy last night. I huddled in my sleeping bag with a flashlight to read the Bible.

Coming down off the mountain into Hot Springs, I stared at the Monopoly houses and Matchbox cars until I accidentally kicked a rock off the trail. I watched it roll and fall for several hundred feet, and realized if I didn't start watching my footing closer it could be me.

Spring might be coming. I saw a butterfly on the trail today. I thought of how excited Annie would've been. Hard to keep from crying. God, why did you take her? Why not me?

Almost without thought, she clicked next. Two days later.

Yesterday was a mistake. We were comfortable with the knowledge it was going to rain all day. We planned to hike ten miles. We didn't have cell signals, so relied on others for weather reports. They made it sound like rain. We hiked into a Winter Storm Advisory. Above 3,000 feet it was all freezing rain and gale force winds. Ice fell from the trees, hitting us in the head. The trail was ice-covered on steep downhill areas. Falls were common.

Today, we broke camp late. When we arrived at the opening at the gap, there was a car with the trunk open. "Trail magic." They had ham/egg/cheese sandwiches, donuts, and orange juice. I think I drank a half gallon. If only I could've convinced the couple to follow me to Maine.

Sara Jane straightened her aching back and forced herself to put the phone down. She was eager to get to the part where Drew had his revelation. He'd said, "Keep reading."

But she had things to do tonight. Starting with the open house, and ending with spending the night with Grandma, depending on how she was when Sara Jane went over after work.

She swung around and picked up the phone, and pulled Drew's business card out of her pocket. After a moment of hesitation, she dialed the number. She'd ask him to let her know how Grandma acted when she got home.

"Drew."

Her mind went blank. She couldn't think of what to say. She pulled in a shaky breath, a whole bunch of nonsensical things coming to mind. Such as, "I think I love you."

But she couldn't say it. She didn't know him. Maybe she did. Those trail journals were a glimpse into his heart, his life. His compassion, patience, and kindness spoke volumes. He was someone she wanted to spend her life with.

Or asking again, "Will you go out with me?" But would she be able to access the heart of this man in person the way he was on the screen? When she was nothing more to him than a cyberstalker?

Besides, when could they go out? How could she consider it with Grandma the way she was? Maybe, if her memory loss were temporary.

"Hello?" He sounded a bit annoyed. As if he'd said it more than once.

A movement at the door caught her attention. She disconnected. And forced a smile when the principal appeared.

22

Fifteen minutes later, Drew's phone rang. Again. He laid down his tools, pulled the phone out of his pocket, and glanced at it. Same unknown number as the previous call. He frowned, but accepted the call. "Drew."

"Hi. It's Sara Jane. The doctor's office called. They're admitting Grandma to the hospital. She has a concussion. Quite a bad one, I guess, which caused her confusion. But they aren't eliminating the possibility of a mini-stroke."

Sara Jane had been his hang-up call? Maybe she'd lost coverage. He knew the spotty service here in the mountains.

How had he missed a concussion? She'd seemed coherent. At least until Sara Jane arrived and Grandma got all possessive and flirty. Though a mini-stroke could explain it as well. He hesitated before answering. Maybe a beat too long. She'd think he didn't care. "I'm sorry. Is there anything I can do?"

"I'm not sure how long she'll be in the hospital. I have open house at the school tonight at seven, but the principal told me as soon as everything's finished in my classroom I can go to the hospital until time for the open house. It'll probably take a while to have her settled in a room anyway. Will you . . . meet me there? In case she's still confused and doesn't know me?"

More than a little awkward, with Grandma thinking he was her man.

Besides, he hadn't darkened the doorway of any hospital since Annie.

How could he refuse Sara Jane this? She needed him.

"Which hospital?"

"The one in Morgantown."

Drew was afraid of that. He raked his hand through his sweaty hair, still not used to the short length. The lack of tangles. He should go home and shower before going to the hospital.

"I need to clean up first. I can meet you there. What time?"

"By the time I finish here and drive out to Morgantown . . . Let's make it five. This way we can visit Grandma, grab a quick supper, and I'll be back at the school by seven. Give me your address and I'll swing by and pick you up."

He rattled it off.

"Great. I'll find it. Thanks, Drew."

He disconnected, saved her number, and then slid his phone back into his pocket.

He wished he dared ask Sara Jane out. Dared accept her offer to take him out. But he still feared rejection. She'd seen him at his worst. Though, he supposed he'd seen her at her worst too. Frazzled, a bit controlling at times . . . would it come out if they started dating? Would she try to micromanage him? He didn't think he'd do so well if she did. He was a free spirit, used to working at his own pace, not answering to anyone, and if he wanted time off to go hiking, canoeing, or to a broom festival, taking the time and going.

Sara Jane, on the other hand, thrived on organization. Minute details would drive him nuts, if he considered them.

There were things he liked about her. She seemed to enjoy history and the museum they visited. She got along with his family. She was patient with her grandma under extreme pressure.

He brushed those thoughts away. Even if she were interested, they were incompatible. A relationship between them would never work.

He wanted someone who'd accept him as he was.

Footloose and fancy-free. Sort of. Maybe not totally.

He did try to be there when needed. And Sara Jane needed him.

Sara Jane pulled up in front of a modest white house in Morgantown's suburbs. Drew's truck sat in the driveway. She got out of her car, strode to the front door, and rang the bell. A dog started half-barking, half-howling inside.

"Shush, Wynter. It's okay." Drew opened the door. Sara Jane glanced at the Siberian husky standing beside him.

"Pretty dog." She'd always wanted a pet, but Grandma said they were too much bother.

One side of Drew's mouth lifted. "This is Wynter. I found her on the trail. She was a thru-hiker too. She's my better half."

Wynter's tail swished back and forth.

Sara Jane laughed, though she hoped Drew didn't mean it the way it sounded. The way married men talked about their wives.

"Are you ready?"

"Yes." Drew stepped out. The dog made a move to follow. "Wynter, stay."

Wynter dropped to her haunches with a whine.

"Are you okay?" Drew glanced at Sara Jane.

She nodded. "The pastor's wife stayed with her until they admitted her to a room. I'm glad it was confusion from her fall and not from the Alzheimer's. I need to make an appointment with the doctor and ask about this disease, but I didn't think it could progress this fast—fine one day, and not the next."

"I doubt if the doctor could give you a timetable." He shrugged. "I don't know."

She slid into her car and waited while Drew folded himself into the seat beside her. She never realized how small her car was until Drew squeezed in. His shoulders brushed hers. The close confines were invigorating. And helped to ease her worry. She drove the short distance to the hospital, relieved to have his strong shoulders to "lean" on.

A tension headache began. After Grandma didn't recognize her this afternoon, what would she be walking into? Would Grandma still not know her? If only she could grab onto Drew's hand for support. It was a blessing he agreed to help her through this. Giving up his broom time to visit Grandma. Such a wonderful man.

She'd have to reward him with a kiss—if he'd accept it—when she took him home. And if he wouldn't . . . How would a bouquet of flowers go over? Did men like flowers?

They walked into the hospital and rode the elevator to the floor the pastor's wife had mentioned Grandma was on. And found the room.

Both beds were occupied, with dueling TVs sounding in the room. Both played the news, but different channels. Drew and Sara Jane walked around the curtain to the bed nearer the window. Grandma half-sat, the head of the bed raised, an IV attached to her left hand, glowering at the TV.

She reached for the remote as Drew neared the bed. "Oh, good. You came. You can take me home now. I am *not* staying here."

Sara Jane frowned. "How are you, Grandma?"

The glare moved to Sara Jane. "I am *not* your grandma, you floozy. And how do you think I'm doing? I have a massive headache. They are giving me all kinds of tests for a brain injury, which I don't have, hooked me up to some needle, claiming nonsense about dehydration, and they didn't feed me lunch! My hamburger is still sitting on the kitchen table, half eaten. By the way, were you trying to poison me? The hamburger was unlike any I've ever had in my life. Rolled up in some flat bread. And it tasted wrong. You're to blame for me being here, so you could steal my man."

"It was a burrito." Sara Jane pulled in a shuddering breath, tears burning her eyes. She turned on her heel and left the room. She needed to find a nurse and insist on information as to what was going on with Grandma. Was it a mild stroke? Did concussions do this?

She glanced behind her as she reached the nurses' station. Drew hadn't followed, instead staying with Grandma. He was a good man.

Grandma liked him.

Whereas she didn't know her granddaughter.

Sara Jane caught back a sob as the nurse looked up.

"May I help you?"

"Yes. I have medical power of attorney for Sari Morgan. I'd like to talk to someone about her condition." She hoped her voice didn't wobble, and sounded firm and in control.

The nurse nodded. "Follow me." She led her back to a small conference room. "Have a seat. I'll send her doctor or the charge nurse back to talk to you."

Fifteen minutes later, the door opened and shut. A woman wearing pig-patterned scrubs came in carrying a folder. "I'm the charge nurse. May I help you?"

Sara Jane straightened. "I need to know what is going on with my grandmother, Sari Morgan. I have medical power of attorney."

The nurse opened the folder and perused it. "She was admitted for observation for a severe concussion after a bad fall. She is dehydrated, greatly aggravated, and confused. Depending on how she's doing in the morning, she may be released. But sometimes symptoms can linger longer for older adults."

"So this is temporary? She doesn't recognize me, but does know her handyman."

The nurse nodded. "She has no recollection of the fall either. She failed the memory test the doctor administered and is very argumentative. She's on a blood thinner, which gave us some concerns about her having a brain bleed, but nothing showed up on the MRI."

Sara Jane stared at her hands. If only she understood what the nurse said. The words were plain enough, but the underlying meaning eluded her. She struggled to find the words to ask.

They grabbed a quick dinner of hamburgers at Drew's favorite drive-thru and drove to his house. "Thanks for supper." He opened the car door and slid out, holding his meal in a paper bag and a soda. "Hope your open house goes well."

"Thanks for coming with me. I appreciate it." Sara Jane turned the engine off and got out, leaving her food in the car.

She trailed him up to the door. He'd expected her to drop him off and leave, not follow him. Should he invite her in? He lifted a shoulder. He'd offer, but she'd need to leave. He was sure of it. After all, she had the open house tonight. Thus, grabbing supper to go. "Do you want to come in?"

"I could, for a few minutes."

He glanced at his watch. What time did she say the open house started? She still needed to drive back to Bruceton Mills. She wouldn't stay long. He held the door for her. Wynter rose, stretching, from a pillow bed in the corner of the room.

He watched as Sara Jane glanced at the dog, and then around the room. He followed her gaze. Sparse. Plain. Empty. No decorations, unless you counted his brooms, in various finished and unfinished forms. "Would you like something to drink?" Stupid of him to ask. Her drink still waited in her car.

"No. I need to go."

"Okay." Why had she followed him in? Just to see where and how he lived? "I'll be praying for your grandmother."

"Thank you." She walked over to a whisk broom he'd started last night. Picked it up and fingered the colors in the braiding. "Why do you use colors here? I've never seen it done before. It's kind of your broom signature."

Drew shifted. "Have you ever heard of the wordless book?"

Sara Jane shook her head. "No. What is it?"

He hesitated a moment, then set his dinner on the table, came over, and picked up the unfinished broom. He pointed to the black straw. "It's a test . . ." He almost said testimony, but knowing how she felt about God . . . would she care to hear?

He'd determined to share the gospel with all who asked. "I don't want to assume you know things if you don't, so forgive me if I seem repetitive. Black is for sin. In Romans 3:23 the Bible says all have sinned and come short of the glory of God. And in Isaiah 64:6, it says all our good works are like filthy rags. We can't ever be good enough for God."

Sara Jane blinked at him. Almost as if she didn't understand. Or if his sharing a salvation testimony had been the last thing she expected. But she needed to know where he stood on these matters.

"Red is for the blood Jesus shed, because He loves us. If we believe, trusting in His name, He will wash us whiter than snow." His fingers moved from the red to the white. "I'm sure you know John 3:16. 'God so loved the world that he gave his only Son, so that everyone who believes in him won't perish but will have eternal life.' And in Isaiah 1:18, it says, 'Though your sins are like scarlet, they will be white as snow.' "

Should he get his Bible and show her the actual verses? Or maybe give her the business card he passed out with the brooms, explaining the meanings. They had the biblical references so she could look them up. He sat on the couch, next to the end table holding his Bible.

"What is the yellow for?" She walked nearer and sat next to him, leaning closer to touch the colored broom straw.

He swallowed. His focus shifted from the broom to the lilac-scented, beguiling female sitting next to him. Too close. Why had she followed him in? She should go. . . . He needed to finish the testimony, so she could. "Gold is for heaven where we'll live someday, if we believe. And green is for growing in Christ through prayer and Bible study."

"Why do you weave it into your brooms? Is it your testimony?"

Drew nodded. "My pastor calls them my witnessing brooms. Most people who see them ask. I promised God I'd serve Him how He wants. This is one of the ways He called me."

"One of the ways?" She shifted nearer. His stomach clenched as she lifted the unfinished whisk broom from his hands. She studied it a moment, then laid it on the coffee table.

He started to get up. He didn't need to be so close to her.

"Someday I'd like to hear more about the other ways."

He dropped back down.

"When I have more time." She glanced at her watch. "I do need to go. But before I do, I need to thank you for everything."

He shook his head. "No thanks are needed . . ." His breath caught as her gaze shifted to his mouth. His heart rate kicked up.

Before he was quite sure what happened, her arms were around his neck, her lips on his.

And he was in heaven.

23

Sara Jane shifted closer, wishing he'd wrap his arms around her. Take a cue from her and kiss her back with some semblance of passion.

At least he returned her kiss—after the initial moment of shocked stillness. His hand moved to loosely grasp her waist as he took control of their closeness. Leading. She willingly followed.

The dog bumped against her, whining. She ignored it, squirming closer to Drew.

He groaned, his hands moving slightly, before they froze.

The dog barked.

If only she could get up, put the dog out, and then return to Drew.

She wove her fingers through his short hair as his kisses changed. Deepened.

The dog barked again, this time jumping up on them.

Drew broke off the kiss, releasing her. "You're going to be late." He didn't correct the dog.

"I don't care." It should tell him volumes. "Put her out and come back to me."

His breath hitched. Then he gently pulled her arms from around his neck. "You need to go." He eased her away and stood. "Let me see you to your car."

Somehow, she found herself sitting alone in the darkness of her car, driving toward Bruceton Mills. Her mind scrambled to make sense of it.

She must've been too forward. Or did his God keep him from taking advantage of the situation?

He shooed her out when she as good as admitted she wanted him. When she *needed* him. At least needed his comfort to deal with Grandma's rejection.

After she listened to him get all religious.

A witnessing broom . . .

All have sinned . . .

Yeah, she was a sinner. Big time. She murdered her parents. Fighting with Daddy about something—she couldn't remember what anymore—right before he and Mama walked out the door. Daddy had left angry. She was furious and crying over their unfairness. And then they were dead . . . and she was in foster care.

God couldn't forgive her. How could He, when she couldn't forgive herself?

Tears escaped, tracking down her cheeks. She'd be a mess when she got to the open house. She needed to get herself under control before she faced her peers, her future students, their parents, her boss. She couldn't have anyone doubting her ability to cope.

He'd rejected her. Again. After they kissed. The ultimate rejection.

Maybe not. It would've been worse if she'd succeeded in her half-formed plans to seduce him, give herself to him completely as Marci had suggested, and then been rejected.

She was despicable.

And it was all God's fault for not forgiving her. For hating her.

God loved the world . . .

It was clear He excluded Sara Jane Morgan.

A day later, Drew still mentally kicked himself. He never should have invited her in. Hadn't anyone ever told her men like to do the pursuing?

But if he hadn't asked her in, he never would've shared the witnessing broom with her . . . and she needed to hear it. Needed to listen.

She still needed to hear. What would it take for God to get her attention? It was fairly obvious to him, an innocent bystander, God pursued her. After all, Drew had been there.

Sometimes it was hard to sit back and wait for God to act. His family had probably felt the same way about him when he angrily—and publicly—rejected God after Annie's funeral. A month later, he'd disappeared into the wilderness, never to be seen or heard from again. At least not until Joey found him at a festival.

Now he tried to see his family at least once a week. Mom had shared with him they'd followed his trail journals too, when he'd mentioned Sara Jane read them.

And she gave her approval of the "nice Sara Jane."

Drew hadn't had the heart to tell her their relationship was. . . . He didn't even know how to explain it.

He didn't fear Sara Jane rejecting him anymore. He was certain he could ask her out and she'd accept without laughing in his face. She'd made it clear. She'd asked him out. First. And initiated both kissing sessions.

What about their differences in values? He was a red-blooded male. It'd be so easy to give in. They weren't married. Weren't engaged. Weren't dating. Yet. They probably would go out, sometime. Were they friends?

Definitely more than acquaintances.

He sighed.

He parked his truck outside the hospital and headed upstairs to check on Grandma. He needed to finish her roof, which would be the next stop, if she was okay with it. He hoped, for Sara Jane's sake, Grandma was in her right mind today. For his sake too. It was uncomfortable having her hit on him.

The room was quiet this morning. No dueling TVs. The first bed was empty, freshly made, though personal items still waited on the bedside table. He made his way around the curtain. Grandma lay in bed, staring out the window.

He cleared his throat.

She glanced at him. He was surprised at the tears in her eyes.

"Are you okay?" He touched her hand.

"They want to keep me until later this afternoon. My headache isn't all the way gone. But I think my mental faculties are working now. The nurse told me I was hateful to Sara Jane."

He wouldn't have told her. He hoped she didn't ask what she'd said. After all, she'd been out of her mind. She seemed to be better now. Greatly subdued, but better.

He looked down. "I plan to finish your roof this morning, if it's okay."

Grandma winced. "The way my head aches, you'd best do it while I'm not home. I want you to sharpen my sewing scissors, if you know how. They're dull and I need to finish up the quilt. Sara Jane said she'd be over . . . I think she said she'd be over on Saturday to help me."

"Yes, she'll be coming over Saturday to work on the quilt." He backed up, ready to leave.

"I told you?"

"Yeah. I should finish up the roof today. Hopefully before you get home. I'll plan on coming by on Saturday to sharpen your scissors."

Grandma sighed. "You're a good man, Andrew. A good man. Some woman will be lucky to land you someday."

He waited for her to add "like Sara Jane."

Instead she turned toward the window.

"I'll be going now." He walked toward the door.

"Sara Jane talks about your trail journals. Do you think I should read them? Are they in a book?"

He glanced over his shoulder and chuckled. "No, ma'am. And they aren't likely to be. I honestly don't know what all the fuss is about."

"You, Andrew Stevenson. The fuss is about you. The thing is everyone's mantra is 'It's all about me.' And with you, it isn't. I don't understand your humbleness."

Sara Jane found a business card on her seat when she went out to her car the next morning. She picked it up and glanced at it. It appeared to be the biblical references for the witnessing broom.

Had he dropped it in when he escorted her out of his house and to her car?

He was serious about the witnessing stuff.

If God was what made Drew who he was, then maybe she should pay some attention . . .

No. She wouldn't pay homage to some God who was either too small or too uninterested. If He were truly all-powerful, He would have saved her parents from the awful accident. If He could have and didn't, then He wasn't the loving God Drew talked about. If He cared, if He really cared, He'd have to show her beyond a shadow of a doubt He was the one who sent the sign. Maybe return her parents.

That'd be the day.

She stuffed the card in her purse. She'd throw it away at school.

24

Drew finished the roof, then made sure Grandma's yard was mowed and raked, the bushes trimmed, the flower garden weeded and watered. He climbed into his truck to leave for the day as Sara Jane's car pulled up beside his. Not behind, this time.

Grandma sat next to her, looking a little pale and drawn. He got out of the truck and came around to help Grandma inside the house.

"I'm going straight to bed." Grandma took his arm and shuffled up to the front door. "The doctor says it'll take a day or two for my head to stop aching. Might stop a bit sooner if I take a strong pain pill, I'm thinking. But would he give me any? No. He muttered something about addictions and conflicts of medications." She huffed. "What does he know?"

Probably wiser not to answer. Drew managed a sympathetic nod.

Sara Jane followed them with the plastic bag full of supplies the hospital sent home with Grandma. "I'll get her to bed. Thanks, Drew."

"Do you want me to sharpen the scissors today, since I'm here?" He opened the door.

"Saturday is fine. I might need your help with other things, too," Grandma said.

"Write them down." Drew closed the door.

"Are you busy this evening?" Sara Jane glanced back.

"Visiting my family."

She nodded. "I'll be staying with Grandma."

"Stuff and nonsense. I'm fine. I want to sleep off this headache and don't need a babysitter. You can always call and check on me or ask a neighbor to. I look in on Mary Brown all the time. She's a widow-lady like me. I bet she'd be glad to come over and have dinner. She buys these little premade potpies, and they aren't too bad. I keep meaning to get some, but I never remember when I go to the store. I'll give her a call as soon as I get settled."

"I'll get you some, Grandma." Sara Jane shrugged, then glanced at Drew. "I guess I'm not spending the evening here."

Drew nodded and stepped back. He should go. But he was half-tempted to see if Sara Jane wanted to join him at his parents.

He waited while Sara Jane got Grandma settled, then she came out with a check.

"Grandma said to give this to you." She avoided his eyes.

He took the payment, folded it, and slid it into his wallet.

"Would you like to come with me to my parents'? Meet my dad?"

She shook her head. "Not tonight. I don't think I'd be very good company. Besides, I'm suffering from an acute amount of embarrassment from my actions last night." She gave him a shy look, peeking up at him through her lashes. "And I think I'd rather cyberstalk a certain somebody."

Cyberstalk? Him? "That so?" He half-smiled. Touched her cheek. "No need to be embarrassed. I seem to remember being involved with the kissing." He liked this shyer version of Sara Jane.

"Besides, your parents won't be expecting me, and I'd rather be close, in case Grandma needs me."

He nodded. "I understand."

"I'm reading about this guy who is walking through an ice storm and I want to know how it turns out." She smiled.

His trail journals. She was getting close. . . . He pulled in a deep breath. Then leaned forward and brushed his lips against hers.

"I hope you find what you're looking for, Sara Jane."

Sara Jane stopped in front of the manager's desk. "Do you know when someone will come by to fix my clogged sink?"

The woman frowned. "Our old maintenance man quit, and I haven't hired a new one. I don't know how long it'll be before someone gets to it. I hope this doesn't affect you signing a new lease." She shoved a stapled collection of papers toward Sara Jane.

She glanced at them. A copy of the lease agreement. The manager handed her a pen. Sara Jane poised it to add her signature on the indicated line. But then hesitated. How could she renew her contract on the apartment for another year? She couldn't. Not with Grandma's recent diagnosis, and the uncertainty facing them. The doctor seemed so noncommittal about what she could expect. Saying things like, "Everyone's different." And, "There's no way to tell."

She'd start preparations to move in with Grandma, ending the nonsense about putting the cabin Grandpa built on the market. Sara Jane didn't understand why Grandma wanted to sell her home anyway. Or in light of the Alzheimer's diagnosis, maybe she wanted to wrap things up—moving to an assisted living apartment instead of leaving Sara Jane to deal with her house.

Her heart deflated. It was hard to think about losing Grandma. How would she survive? She and Grandma might not see eye-to-eye about everything, but they loved each other.

Grandma might have several good years left. Would they survive being so close after both being alone and independent for so long? They had their own ways of doing things. It might be hard to get used to obeying Grandma's orders again. Being bossed around like she was a twelve-year-old orphan. "Put this here. Make your bed. Didn't your mother teach you anything?" It'd be difficult.

Would she eventually end up having to quit her job to take care of Grandma full-time?

She wouldn't go there. When Grandma got so bad, she'd worry about it. Not now. She could rent another apartment later.

She wouldn't sign. She laid the pen on the desk and shoved the unsigned lease agreement toward the manager. "I'll be moving out at the end of the month."

Oh, it hurt to say it.

She blinked back tears as she walked out of the office, around the side of the building, and upstairs to her apartment. She stepped inside, gazing around her space. Drew's flowers—they were wilted. She hated the thought of throwing them out. She firmed her shoulders.

What would she do with her furniture?

Would Grandma give up her sewing room—Sara Jane's old bedroom—and allow her to take it over again? She'd complained when Sara Jane had moved in the first time, acting as if it was a major inconvenience for her to lose her sewing room for something as insignificant as an orphaned granddaughter.

Though Sara Jane had been told by Grandma's pastor and friends she'd about ripped the state apart looking for her. Fighting to get custody. Hiring a lawyer.

She could sleep in the loft. Grandma never used it. The room had stood empty since Grandma cleared out all her sons' and husband's things. She could move her furniture up there, and have a semi-private efficiency apartment in Grandma's loft. It was open to the living room, but it included a bathroom and a bedroom.

She'd plan on it.

She could ask Drew if he'd help her move. Maybe he'd do it for free, if she threw in dinner.

She picked up the phone to call and ask him, but then remembered he was with his family. She'd call him later. Grandma might pitch a fit about Sara Jane moving into the loft—but she could counter with the point that she'd get to keep her sewing room.

Perfect.

Sara Jane moved over to the computer and sat. She opened up the trail journals.

We've had a lot of rain the last several days. Starting out yesterday seemed like it'd be drier. Little did I know.

I looked up at Lion King's shout. A wall of mud raced toward us, like an avalanche. I scrambled to get out of the way, but as I struggled to climb on a boulder, I lost my grip and was swept away.

Sara Jane gasped and gripped the computer mouse.

I was going to die. I threw an arm up over my head, like I'd heard should be done in avalanches, so rescuers could find me easier. But then I worried about breaking my arm.

My mouth, nose, and ears filled with mud, and my life flashed before my eyes.

I tried to pray. I couldn't die without being right with God. I couldn't. "Lord. . . . Oh, Lord. . . ." Words wouldn't come. Would God understand the refrain scrolling through my head, nothing more than a heart cry?

If I lived I'd . . . Never make promises to God. He is the only one who is perfect, who can keep His promises without fail.

Would it be too late to be made right with God when I crawled into heaven, covered in mud, broken and battered, and fell before Him?

All those things flashed through my mind like a runaway train, mixed in with the cries to God.

And the next thing I knew I was lifted up as if I weighed nothing and set on a boulder.

As I fought to keep my footing with my mud-covered shoes, I looked at my rescuer. He held on to me, helping me hold my balance. It was a man who called himself X-Amish. I'd met him at a few shelters and hostels along the trail. X-Amish hiked alone. Angry. Sullen. Silent.

I owed him my life.

I stood there, wobbling, gasping for breath and coherent thought, while he supported me with one arm, dragging my mud-soaked backpack off my shoulders and flinging it behind us with his other.

The second he released me, I fell to my knees.

X-Amish muttered something and reached as if to pick me up again, but I shook my head. God saved me. He'd rescued me out of the miry clay and stood me on a solid rock.

I owed Him my life, my heart, my soul, my all.

I don't know why He saved me and not Annie, but He did. He has a purpose for me yet. And I will spend the rest of my days worshipping Him. Serving Him.

Forever, these will be my life verses—Psalm 40:1-3. "I put all my hope in the Lord. He leaned down to me; he listened to my cry for help. He lifted me out of the pit of death, out of the mud and filth, and set my feet on solid rock. He steadied my legs. He put a new song in my mouth, a song of praise for our God. Many people will learn of this and be amazed; they will trust the Lord."

I don't know what I said. I remember crying. Praying. Begging for forgiveness. Praising. I finally silenced, sobs still wracking my body, when I realized I wasn't alone. Two people had witnessed my complete surrender to God. Lion King stood behind us, silently crying, and X-Amish knelt beside me, tears streaming down his own face.

Sara Jane stared at the entry. Went back and reread it. Tears burned her eyes.

Drew had almost died on the trail. Was it what caused his ultimate surrender? She never would have guessed.

Something about this pulled her in. She wished she could somehow appear on the trail, behind Lion King and see what he saw. Hear what he heard. What had Drew said? Whatever it was had been powerful enough to bring a sullen man to his knees beside him. Just reading about it . . . well . . . almost made her want to fall to hers.

Not quite though.

What was it about God that called her? Was it Drew and his testimony? Or was it something more?

"Why didn't you bring Sara Jane?"

Drew popped open his soda can and looked over at Carly, his eyebrows rising. His mom had been asking about Sara Jane—and Grandma—a lot, but he hadn't expected his sister-in-law to take up the questioning.

He shrugged. "Why would I?"

A faint pink colored Carly's cheeks. "I thought with her grandma thinking you were a couple, you and . . . you aren't dating?"

"Nope." He kicked his legs out straight and leaned back, folding his arms over his stomach, still holding his soda can. He hoped the casual, there's-nothing-to-tell pose would cause her to back off the questioning.

"But I saw how you . . . and she . . . how you looked at each other. And . . ." She lowered her head, twirling a lock of hair. "Well, Joey and I—"

"Hey, leave me out of this." Joey took a swallow of his soda. "I'm going to go out and check on the grill. See if Dad needs any help."

"Good idea. I'll join you." Drew straightened.

"Running away?" Carly quipped as she got to her feet as well. She ran a hand over her pregnant belly. "Your mom and I think . . . you know what? How about if I give her a call? As a friend? See how she's doing. I did tell her we were going to be the best of friends. And I haven't talked to her, no thanks to you."

Drew hiked an eyebrow up further. "Go ahead." He started to leave the room.

A pillow hit him in the back of the head. He looked over his shoulder at Carly.

"I need her phone number, you . . . you . . . meanie."

He chuckled.

Carly stomped her foot on the floor as if she were a little girl, then noticed his cell phone on the end table. She snagged it.

"Oh, no." He made a grab for it.

She giggled and darted out the front door.

He didn't chase after her. He wouldn't wrestle his brother's wife to get his phone back. And the chances of her actually calling Sara Jane?

Nah, he was safe.

25

Sara Jane read over the journal entry a third time. This one stirred her. Moved her. She reached for the phone, half-tempted to call Drew. To ask for more details. Did he remember what he'd said?

He was still with his family. She shouldn't bother him.

The phone rang in her hand. She jumped. Her pulse pounded when she recognized Drew's number.

She answered the call. "Hey, Drew, I was reading your journal entries. I think I got to the place you meant when you said, 'Keep reading.' And I have some questions."

Silence.

"Drew?" Was he paying her back for hanging up on him the other day? He didn't seem the type.

Still no answer.

She pulled the phone away and looked at it. Was the call dropped? She put it back to her ear. "Hello?"

Someone pulled in a breath. "Sara Jane? This is Carly. Drew's sister-in-law?"

Sara Jane caught her breath. "Carly . . . Oh! Is something wrong with Drew?"

"No, it's just that he's here, and you aren't. We're all wondering why not. I mean I know you aren't dating or anything, but it seems as if. . . ." Carly laughed. "I guess I'm sticking my foot in it. But we'd love to have you join us if you aren't busy."

"Not busy. Drew did ask me to join you—"

"He did, did he? Hmmm." Carly giggled. "He doesn't tell me anything."

"I needed to sign a new lease agreement and Grandma just got out of the hospital, so I wanted to stay close."

"Oh, I understand. But it would be nice to see you."

"I know. I would've liked to have come. But now I'll have even less free time. School's starting and I have a month to get out of my apartment. I decided not to sign the lease."

"Oh, you're moving? Joey and I can come help you Saturday. We'll talk to Drew about it too. Or did you ask him already?"

"No, not yet." Wow. This weekend. It'd be nice to have help. "I'm supposed to help Grandma with the ballad quilt on Saturday. She's anxious to get it finished." So was she, but for a different reason. An idea for a story quilt of a different sort slowly formed.

"Not a problem. We'll tell him. I'll have him call you to set up the details. Let me write down your phone number. I'm using Drew's phone." Papers rustled. "Okay, I'm ready."

Sara Jane recited her cell phone number.

"You were reading Drew's trail journals? They're engaging, aren't they? Joey and I checked every day for an update once we figured out what he was going by. It was a hard time. Joey lost his sister, and for all intents and purposes, his brother at the same time. Andy—I mean Drew—had donated stem cells to save Annie's life. When it failed, he fell apart. Literally. Emotionally, I mean. Poor guy."

Andy. It explained why he hadn't wanted Sara Jane to call him Andy. It was his family's name for him—as part of a twin. Annie and Andy. She winced. She'd been so unkind to him. But then again, she hadn't known. Which made his continued kindness more remarkable. No wonder she'd fallen in love with him.

"I love him." She said the words out loud. Trying the sound out. Testing the truth of them. Then said it again. "I love him."

"Of course you do. It's so evident. I can't believe you two aren't dating yet."

Sara Jane's face heated. How had she forgotten she was on the phone, with his sister-in-law, no less? Drew would know her feelings by the time Carly disconnected the call. She shook her head. "This weekend won't work to move. I have to work on Grandma's quilt."

But then, if she did move on Saturday, she would be there evenings to help. Every evening. She was glad they'd have the quilt to work on as they eased back into living in the same house. It'd be something to serve as common ground. Something to build those last good memories around.

"We have plans with my parents the following weekend. And the weekend after—."

"You know what? Maybe it will work. I'm moving in with Grandma because of her health. We can move Saturday."

"Great! I'm looking forward to seeing you. I guess Drew knows your address?"

He did, didn't he? He'd sent the flowers to her apartment. He must. "Yes."

"Talk to you Saturday morning then! Bye."

Carly came around the back of her house, waving a slip of paper. "I have her phone number!"

Drew nodded, but otherwise ignored her. Of course. All she had to do was look up the number on his phone, write it down, and taunt him. He flipped a burger, resisting the urge to demand she hand over his phone so he could check the calls. She'd expect him to and it would give away more than he'd like. Best to pretend he didn't care.

"We're helping her move on Saturday."

Okay, this was unexpected. He looked up.

She smirked and held out his phone. "I volunteered the three of us."

He pocketed his phone. He wouldn't ask. He turned away from the grill, walked over to the picnic table, picked up his pop, and took a swallow.

Carly waited a beat. Then her impish smile lit up her face. "Oh, and she loves you. She said so. Twice. 'I love him.'"

Coke spewed from his mouth and he started coughing.

Mom jumped up—on the receiving end of his impromptu spit. "Andrew Craig Stevenson!" She grabbed a napkin and mopped her face, then disappeared inside the house.

Laughing, Carly followed her.

Joey and Dad both looked at him. "Something you want to tell us, son?" Dad broke the silence.

Drew shook his head. "Nothing to tell. I'm working for her grandmother. She's a friend." Though he'd like to be more. Someday. Maybe.

"Sounds like there's more to the story, if she's telling Carly she loves you." Dad raised a brow.

Drew sighed. "It does sound like it. But there isn't."

"Yet." Joey grinned at him.

"The potential is there," Drew conceded.

He'd call her to check on the details of Carly's claims since she'd been rather blatant in her "pushing Sara Jane" campaign. He wouldn't put it past her to say something untrue—such as Sara Jane's move and the love stuff—to get Drew to visit her apartment bright and early. If she was moving, she would've mentioned it to him. Right?

He replayed their conversation in his memory. She definitely hadn't said anything about it.

He shook his head. Chances were Carly hadn't called and made up a conversation to see how he'd react. As soon as he was alone, he'd check the call log.

Still, maybe he would give her a call—under the guise of checking on Grandma.

Sara Jane filled another box with books, folded the top shut, then looked up when someone knocked. She sidestepped the empty boxes she'd gotten from the grocery store and peered out the little peek-hole in the apartment door.

A pink rose surrounded by baby's breath met her one-eyed gaze.

Flowers? She looked over her shoulder at the wilted bouquet on her coffee table. Smiled. And opened the door.

Drew carried the flowers. Her heart pounded in overdrive. He held them out. "I thought you might enjoy these. Grandma doing okay?"

Sara Jane nodded. "Thanks. They're beautiful. Grandma's fine. I talked with her neighbor a few minutes ago. How's your family?"

"Good . . . Are you busy?" He shifted and looked downstairs at something or someone. A door slammed on the first floor.

"Not really. Do you want to come in?" She stepped aside.

He looked at the boxes as he came in. Then glanced at her, his eyebrows rising. "Moving?"

Sara Jane's shoulders slumped. She despised her selfishness in wanting to keep her space. Her privacy. No one telling her what to do or how to do it. This wouldn't be easy. "In with Grandma. She needs me. Didn't Carly tell you? She said she'd ask you about helping me move."

He opened his mouth, shut it, then set the vase on the table. She closed the door, turned, and almost ran into his chest. She blinked.

"Anything else I should know?" He almost growled the words.

She hesitated. "Such as?" Did she look guilty? Had Carly told him she loved him?

"Why didn't you mention it to me when we were at Grandma's? Why did I find out from Carly?"

"I didn't know. I had a lease renewal waiting when I got home. When I went to sign it I remembered what you said about getting more care for Grandma by talking to my parents and other relatives. I'm all she has. And you're right. I need to be there. I told them I was moving out at the end of the month."

He nodded, but then raised his hand and caught a tear she hadn't realized had escaped. "I understand. It's a difficult decision to make, and everyone has to follow their heart."

She bit back her whimpers and whines about her unwillingness. What was giving up a little bit of her freedom to make sure Grandma was safe? Grandma had done the same for her all those years before. Even if it had seemed like Grandma wasn't thrilled about the arrangement back then.

Besides, this was so minuscule compared to what Drew had gone through with his sister.

"I'll come by to help you move. What time would be good?"

"Maybe eight or so." She hesitated. "I'd say seven, but I don't want to wake anyone sleeping in around here by tromping up and down stairs too early."

"We'll make it seven. I'll bring breakfast."

She smiled. "I'll provide lunch."

Drew chuckled. "It's a deal." He backed away. "Joey and I will both have pickups and plenty of stuff to tie down with. See you the day after tomorrow." He shut the door behind him.

Sara Jane returned to her packing. Finding help was easy enough. Now, she had nothing to worry about except how Grandma would react. It wouldn't go well at all.

Would it be better to upset Grandma this late at night, ruin her day tomorrow, or not tell her at all and present her with fait accompli?

26

Saturday morning, Drew carried two boxes of doughnuts and a large plastic bottle filled with his favorite pomegranate-blueberry fruit juice up to Sara Jane's apartment. He glanced around the parking lot. Joey's truck wasn't there, so Drew must be the first to arrive. He looked forward to the opportunity to steal a private kiss. But then . . . maybe being alone wasn't a good idea. Too much temptation.

Sara Jane answered the door on the first ring. "Hey."

He caught his breath. She wore beige shorts hitting mid-thigh, and an orangeish-red tank top. Why did she have to wear necklaces that dangled in . . .? He forced his gaze up as she took the food items.

He stepped into the apartment and was greeted by a maze of boxes piled as high as Sara Jane could safely lift. "Wow. You worked hard. Were you up all night?"

"I couldn't sleep. So yeah. Decided to pack and clean. I hauled everything out of the bedroom." She motioned toward the mattresses leaning against the hallway wall. The bed frames were taken apart and standing beside them. Wow. All by herself? He glanced at her muscles. He should've been there to do the heavy lifting for her. "I'm nervous about moving in with Grandma. I haven't . . . She might not be happy about it."

He blinked. Grandma didn't know? From what he knew of her, she wouldn't like it one bit. Maybe he misunderstood. "You didn't ask if it was okay?"

"I . . . I haven't talked to her. The decision was made spur of the moment and I thought it might be better to show up and not give her a chance to refuse. I could tell her I was evicted or something."

"You'd . . ." Drew frowned. He wouldn't get judgmental about her lying to Grandma. It was best for Sara Jane move in. He shook his head. "If she asks why you were evicted? What would your reason be? Nonpayment of rent? I know it wouldn't happen. Or wild partying and disrupting the peace, damaging property, and all that? Why can't you tell her the truth?"

"If I tell her I'm moving in to 'babysit' her, and keep her from selling Grandpa's cabin, she . . . well, let's just say it'll get ugly fast."

If she used those words, it would be bad. Drew winced. He could imagine Grandma's screech of protest like the time Sara Jane had accidentally dropped quilt pieces. "You could find a more tactful way of saying it."

Sara Jane looked away. "Tact isn't in my vocabulary."

He chuckled. "Sure it is. Did you call me a caveman to my face?"

Her eyes widened and her gaze rose to meet his. "I never called you a caveman. A 'John-the-Baptist-wannabe.' I'm sorry. I never should've. You are so much more than you appeared."

Yeah, since he shaved and got his haircut. Drew managed a half-smile and moved past her, cautious not to bump any of the leaning towers of boxes. He wanted to suggest she call Grandma. But it might be wiser to tell her in person. Sara Jane knew her better than he did. He pulled in a breath. "Let's put breakfast on the table and get started." He moved through the small apartment to the kitchen. "I know this isn't as good as the oatmeal you made the first time I went to Grandma's, but I'm not much of a cook."

Sara Jane followed him. "Do you think I need a small moving van? Or will all this stuff fit in your truck?"

"And Joey's. Might have to make a couple trips each, but we'll be fine. We'll load up your car the first trip and leave you at Grandma's to direct where you want things." He opened the box and took out a chocolate-covered doughnut with sprinkles. "Hold it. Grandma's house is pretty cluttered. Will she have room for all your stuff? Or will we need to divide what goes to a storage unit and what goes to Grandma's house?"

"The loft is empty. I'm moving up there."

The loft? He pictured Grandma's house. A rough set of log-hewed stairs led from one side of the living room, to the loft—which was little more than a balcony over the living room, as far as he knew. "Will it be big enough?" He took a bite, then looked for a cup. She must've packed them already. The juice would have to wait.

She reached into an unsealed box and pulled out a coffee mug. She set it on the table. "There's a bathroom, and a bedroom, and the main area of the loft, which is open over the living room. It'd be my living area."

So bigger than he expected. He glanced around the cluttered apartment. Probably would have more room than she did here. What was her decorating style prior to boxing everything up? Fancy and frilly? Charming and comfortable? Utilitarian without a personality?

He lifted the mug and rotated it enough to see the motto. "Old hikers never die, they just trail away." His type of mug. Surprising. He imagined her owning fancier matching dishes. "I didn't know you hiked."

Her face flamed red. "Um, I don't. I saw it at a gift shop and thought of you."

Ah. He tried to think of something to say in response. His face heated to the point it probably matched hers. His heart skipped. Did it mean she thought about him as much as he thought about her?

She pulled out another mug. This one was from a library reading program. She opened the juice, poured some into his mug, and then filled the library mug.

A knock sounded on the door. Sara Jane swung on her heel and went to the door.

A moment later Drew heard Carly's voice. He chugged his juice. They could start loading now that Joey was here.

"I'm so glad to see you! How's my future sister-in-law?"

Sari heard the rumble of a truck. It sounded similar to Andrew's. She put down the fabric she handled. She'd tried to design the next quilt block, one of a girl, but she couldn't decide if she wanted to use an angel pattern, minus the wings, or a sideways bonnet-girl in a long dress. Sara Jane wanted the latter, but she had next to zero creativity. It'd be nice to get Andrew's opinion. He could advise while he sharpened her scissors.

Sari hurried from the room and flung open the front door. "Sara Jane isn't here yet, but . . ." She frowned. Andrew had backed the truck into the driveway, and another unfamiliar truck waited on the side of the road, both loaded with boxes and furniture. Andrew opened the tailgate.

She put her hands on her hips. "What's all this? Are you moving in with me? I hired you as a caretaker, not a caregiver." Her face warmed as she recalled her ramblings and flirting about marrying Andrew herself. "Even if I was out of my mind talking about marrying you, I'm not that kind of girl."

Andrew opened his mouth, but before he answered, Sara Jane rushed over. "I'm moving into the loft. My lease came due, and I didn't want to renew. I'm not overly fond of those apartments, and since we want to finish the quilt, I thought it'd be better to live here, so we can work on it evenings."

"You thought *what*?" Sari shifted. Two months ago she would've railed at Sara Jane for making such a fool decision. But now—with the pesky diagnosis staring her in the face, and her declining health—it wasn't a bad idea. She'd spend time with her granddaughter, get the family pictures out, and have someone to share memories with. Sara Jane needed to remember her parents. Still, she couldn't give in so easy. The girl didn't ask! She firmed her shoulders. "What makes you think I want a roommate? I'm not giving up my sewing room or any other room for you again." She planted her hands on her hips and pursed her lips. She'd fight for this until the bitter end.

"I didn't ask for it. The loft is empty. I'm moving up there." There was a patient note in Sara Jane's voice.

Oh. She'd said it already, didn't she?

Sara Jane's voice sounded firm too. As if she'd thought of the objections and had steeled herself for them. Sari fought a smile. Her granddaughter had a hint of her personality.

Sari considered her options. Then nodded. She did want her granddaughter near. She should be more agreeable. Especially after being so unkind the day she was hospitalized. "Plenty of room for you and Andrew when you get married."

Andrew coughed. The unknown, but somehow familiar man standing near Andrew frowned and looked at her as if she were certifiably insane. The girl who approached the front porch laughed. Grandma remembered her from the festival they'd gone to. Her mind whirled as she tried to recognize her. Andrew's sister-in-law. What was her name? Charlie? Must be short for Charlotte.

Sara Jane's face had turned a bright pink. "Just me, Grandma. Drew and I aren't getting married."

Sari opened her mouth, but then shut it. Might be best not to push the issue. She might drive them apart. But even her old eyes could see when two people belonged together.

Sara Jane couldn't believe how quickly Grandma relented—nor how fast she was moved in. Two trips with both pickups and all her earthly belongings were upstairs. Not where she wanted them, and not unpacked, but there would be plenty of time for arranging.

Carly put clean sheets on her bed, while Sara Jane called the local pizza restaurant to place an order. Cash in hand, from Sara Jane's wallet, Joey went to pick up lunch while Drew retreated with Grandma into the sewing room to sharpen the scissors she'd mentioned.

Sara Jane wandered into her old bedroom, though she didn't want to be drawn into quilting right now. Grandma still seemed like she'd expected Sara Jane to embrace the process, and she didn't. Well, maybe a little. After all, she had visions of making an Appalachian quilt for Drew. If their relationship ever got to that point. She'd sketched out a few rough drawings of what she might use in the quilt. She thought a wall hanging would look nice in their future home.

What was she doing, day-dreaming like this? Thankfully, Drew didn't seem to notice her staring at him as if he were a movie star and she a starstruck worshiper. Instead, he focused on the scissors he sharpened, while Grandma rambled about the girl she wanted on the quilt. Something about Sunbonnet Sue and an angel without wings.

Drew tested the scissors, then laid them on the sewing table. "Why don't you cut them both out and see which you like better? I'm not sure what Sunbonnet Sue is. You would need to embroider eyes and a mouth either way."

"No, the one is a front view and the other a side view. I want the front view. Sara Jane wants the other."

Drew shrugged. "It's your quilt." He didn't look at Sara Jane.

Grandma sighed. "But she's the one who's going to inherit it."

They acted as if Sara Jane wasn't in the room. She cleared her throat. "I'll cherish it either way, Grandma." And she would, if for no other reason than it was Grandma's dream—and apparently, her love story.

Grandma huffed. "You have a better eye than I do, so I want to know what you'd choose." She kept her attention on Drew, ignoring Sara Jane.

Drew picked up another pair of scissors. "What does the girl stand for in the ballad?"

Another huff. "Me." Grandma hesitated a second. "Not me, but rather Pretty Saro, but the story is about me. Except for crossing the ocean, but it's part of the song. Can't have one without the other."

That made almost no sense. Sara Jane shook her head.

"If it's all about you, we should use the girl you want. The angel," Drew said.

Grandma nodded.

If Drew conceded on the point of the angel, it must be the better choice. She smiled, glad to see Grandma calm and happy.

Drew picked out some material, Grandma's favorite color, a pretty shade of blue. "We'll use this for her dress. What color was your hair when you were younger?"

"Red. Of course. Anybody who's anybody has red hair. Not a boring shade of brown." She cast what seemed a disparaging glance toward Sara Jane.

Sara Jane shrugged and kept the hurt at bay. Grandma had hurled insults about her unfortunate hair color all her life. Nevertheless, she'd keep it, unaltered. It reminded her of Daddy and his dark brown hair. And she could be as stubborn as Grandma.

Drew reached for more material. "Okay. Red hair it is. However, there's not a thing wrong with brown hair. I like it."

He didn't glance toward Sara Jane. If only he would've. And added a wink. But he didn't.

"I'm not so good at portraits, but I can do caricatures." He grinned.

"Andrew, I don't want any carrot-captures in my quilt. I have no idea what they are."

Sara Jane backed toward the door. She wasn't needed, and she should help Carly with unpacking. Guilt ate at Sara Jane as she moved away. She should've been working with her anyway, instead of following Drew around like a lovesick puppy.

Which was exactly what she was. Lovesick.

He looked up as she backed out of the room and gave her the wink she'd longed for. Her knees weakened and she tried not to melt into a puddle on the floor.

Instead, she smiled.

And fled.

27

Drew finished sharpening the last pair of scissors and handed them back to Grandma as loud bangs and bumps came from the loft. "I'm going to see if Sara Jane and Carly need any help."

Both women were on the outside of the bedroom door shoving Sara Jane's dresser over the uneven carpet. He hurried over. "Let me." He lifted it over the threshold. "Where do you want it?"

"By the window." Sara Jane pointed to the window on the side of the room. She'd already hung curtains, some frilly sheer things that touched the floor. Ultrafeminine. As tantalizing as the necklace.

Drew hauled the dresser to where she indicated, then scanned the room. Joey had put the bed frame together before he left to pick up the pizza, and now the bed was in position, freshly made. The yellow gingham coverlet made the room bright and cheery.

"I want my computer desk in the open part of the loft. . . . Oh. Shoot." Sara Jane slapped her hands against her thighs, drawing his attention to her tanned, toned, shapely legs. "I forgot Grandma doesn't have internet. I'll have to get it connected." Her gaze skittered to Drew, then away, her face reddening.

"Yeah. Won't be able to cyberstalk anyone without internet." Drew grinned.

Carly giggled. Whether at him, for ogling Sara Jane, or her for cyberstalking, he didn't know. Sara Jane's face flamed brighter. She tugged at the necklace and fingered the dangly thing drawing his attention to her curves. He swallowed hard and looked away.

Sara Jane Morgan was one *hot* lady.

And he was in hot water.

If only . . .

The front door slammed. “Pizza delivery!”

His brother’s arrival was a welcome intrusion. He hurried downstairs, breathing in the rich tomato-basil scent. He couldn’t allow himself to daydream about things he shouldn’t.

Even if Grandma’s suggestion earlier made him wish things could be different.

Sara Jane forced her attention on the quilt blocks Grandma had brought into the kitchen. For some reason. She couldn’t think why she’d want to talk quilting over lunch. Unless she felt more urgency to get this project done and stories told before it was too late. Sara Jane cringed with the pang of coming loss.

At least it’d help to keep her attention off Drew. Maybe.

Grandma waved the pinned block in the air, catching everyone’s attention. “This is the ocean scene. Cade and I went there on our honeymoon. Sara Jane’s daddy was conceived there.” The square had variegated blues cut in wavy lines with a tan fabric below it to represent the beach. “Any suggestions on what I can do to improve this, Andrew?”

“What does it mean in the ballad?” Drew took a bite of supreme pizza. It seemed to be his standard answer to the quilt inquisitions. Maybe it bought him time to think. It also gave Grandma time to tell another story showing glimpses into her life, telling the history she might forget and need repeated back to her.

Grandma pulled in a breath and quoted, “On the banks of the ocean or the mountains’ sad brow.”

Sara Jane frowned. She’d heard the line before. “Didn’t the mountain scene have the same line?”

Grandma pursed her lips. "Yes, but I needed twelve quilt blocks. And since I went on my honeymoon to the ocean, I wanted it represented. I also wanted the mountains because I live there."

Drew swallowed. "Could you find a more glittery piece of tan? Possibly a shiny gold? Sand sparkles in the sunshine."

Grandma considered the material. "I'll have Sara Jane take me to the fabric shop, and I'll look." She glanced at Carly. "I love his artistic eye."

Carly nodded. "Yes, both Drew and Joey—"

"This one is supposed to be a farm scene." Grandma picked up another square as Sara Jane smiled apologetically at Carly and Joey. "All I can think of is a red barn on a hillside or a field. How are you at animals?" She turned her attention to Drew. "Before you ask, in the ballad it means, 'She wants some freeholder and I have no land.'"

Drew frowned. "Not very good at real-life drawing. Joey is better at animals. He's a graphic artist."

Joey swallowed. "I can design a decent horse or cow if you don't need them today. I'll work on it."

"Good. I'll plan on it. The ladies in my quilting group at church agreed to do the quilting when Sara Jane and I finish with the design and appliqué work. It'll be finished soon." Grandma slumped and put the quilt blocks on the counter. "All that's left is the letter block. Honestly, I'm stumped." She put a slice of pizza on her plate and started picking off the green peppers, mushrooms, and onions. "In the song it stands for 'I'd write my true love a letter she might understand.' Since Cade and I wrote letters when he went out west, I want to include it."

Sara Jane took a swallow of her soda, then put the can down. "Have you considered using one of Grandpa's letters? You could use a piece of white fabric and embroider words on it." She'd thought about something similar with the Appalachian quilt she wanted to make Drew for Christmas.

Grandma blinked. "Sara Jane, I think it's the best idea you've had. I like it." She directed a rare smile at her. "I'm impressed."

Sara Jane looked down. Grandma's smile seemed almost as rewarding as when she had gotten A's on her papers in school. She yearned for them. The only bright spot in her life. Maybe there was hope of winning Grandma's approval for something other than her cooking skills. She'd aim for it. She'd love a close, friendship-type relationship with Grandma.

If only God didn't hate her. But then, she wanted nothing to do with Him. Or—at least she hadn't. Now, she couldn't explain the strange longing . . .

She glanced toward Drew and thought again of the journal entry where he shared his testimony. He'd been mad at God too. And God had met Drew. Why couldn't He meet her?

Sara Jane took a big bite of her pizza. If only she was as valued by God as she'd been by her professors.

She wished she knew what Drew had said. Whatever it was had been powerful enough to bring another man to his knees. Drew's story had made her cry.

She wanted what Drew had. His peacefulness. His kindness. His self-control. His gentleness. She wanted his God.

She bowed her head. She didn't know how to pray or how to approach Him. Besides, would He listen?

Drew would know. His witnessing broom flashed through her mind. She shouldn't have thrown away the card he'd given her. He'd said it explained the colors on the broom.

Sara Jane finished her slice of pizza. Drew and Joey both reached for another one. Grandma rambled on about the quilt and appliquéing and her quilting group. . . . Whatever it was could wait.

"Drew?" Did she sound as desperate as she felt?

He glanced at her and a slow smile formed. Her heart did a slow roll as warmth spread through her. It'd be so nice to see his smile every day for the rest of her life.

She almost lost her train of thought. But then something reminded her. *God* . . .

"Do . . . do you have another one of those cards about your brooms? I . . . I lost the first one."

Drew reached into his pocket, pulled out his billfold, and removed one of his witnessing broom cards. His hand shook. Was it too much to hope Sara Jane's heart was changing?

Grandma's hand snaked across the table, palm up, as if she wanted one too. He pulled out another. Gave one to Sara Jane, and placed the other in Grandma's hand.

She squinted at it. "What's this? Witnessing? Why would you want this, Sara Jane? I raised you in church. You don't need this." She shoved the card at Drew. "Give it back to him. Let him give it to someone who needs it." Grandma's voice was cold, chilly, sucking all the warmth from the air.

He took the card. Put it in his wallet and searched for the right words. Confrontation wouldn't be a good approach. Sara Jane had asked for it. . . . She should have the right to choose.

"You're wrong, Grandma. I do need it." Sara Jane raised her head in a slight challenge. But instead of starting a discussion about the card, she slipped it into her pocket. Maybe she felt the change in the atmosphere too.

Drew frowned. He'd hoped the card would generate some conversation about his beliefs, especially with Joey and Carly there to help answer her questions. But he needed to let the Spirit move how He willed and not force the topic. Drew took a bite of pizza instead. Could he take Sara Jane on a walk in the neighborhood or get her alone for follow-up later? And what about Grandma's reaction? Was it an indication of the condition of her heart or an outburst based on her diagnosis?

When lunch was over, Grandma wrote out a check as he took out the trash and checked to see how the move was coming. All of Sara Jane's furniture was in place. There was nothing to do but unpack, then finish cleaning her old apartment. She could do that without help.

Drew needed to work on his brooms anyway. Though he'd hoped—planned—to spend the evening with Sara Jane, Joey, and Carly.

Grandma handed him a check. "Thanks for all your help. I'll call you if I need you for anything else. I have your card. Somewhere."

It sounded like a dismissal. He nodded. "I'll be back to pick up the dumpster on Monday."

Grandma frowned. "I won't be home. I'll be at the church, giving the quilting group instructions on how I want my quilt sewed together."

"I won't be here either." Sara Jane came into the room.

Fine. He didn't need either of them around in order to pick up his dumpster. He nodded again. He had Sara Jane's number. He'd wait a couple of days and then call to see if she had any questions.

"Thanks for your help." Sara Jane hugged him. He pulled her closer, wishing for the hundredth time they were alone. But Grandma's stare pierced through him. He needed to step away. He turned to face her as Sara Jane hugged Joey, then Carly. "Maybe we can get together sometime."

"It'll be fun." Carly smiled. "Next time Drew visits, you'll have to come."

Drew winked at Sara Jane. "See ya."

She brushed what could have been a tear from her eye.

Grandma followed him out and cornered him as he climbed into his truck. "I thought you were the right one for Sara Jane, but you're not. I don't want you coming around here anymore."

Drew frowned. "But—"

"I raised the girl in church, Andrew Stevenson. How dare you imply it's not good enough?"

He didn't say any such thing. But then, being in church didn't guarantee she had saving knowledge. He hadn't made a commitment until he was on the trail. And Sara Jane had readily admitted to him she had no relationship with God. She went to church only because Grandma insisted.

Grandma turned and stalked inside. Drew glanced toward the second-floor windows. Sara Jane stood framed in one. Her hand rose in a silent farewell.

He formed an L shape with his thumb and pinkie finger and raised it to his ear, to indicate "Call me."

She nodded.

A forbidden princess in a castle tower.

28

Three months later

Sara Jane opened the front door and almost stumbled over a box on the floor. Grandma dozed on the recliner, TV blaring, as she so often had the past three months.

Sara Jane clicked off the TV.

Grandma stirred, then opened her eyes. "Is it you, Sara Jane?" She reached for her glasses and hearing aids lying on the end table beside her. "Mary Brown took me to the ladies' group at church today. We finished my ballad quilt. It's in the box there. I waited for you so we could get it hung and take a picture."

"Where do you want it?"

Grandma frowned. "I don't know. I wish Andrew still came around. He might have some ideas."

"You fired him." Sara Jane turned and put her purse and briefcase on the bottom step to the loft. She hoped the warmth in her face wouldn't give anything away. Especially since she'd still been in phone and personal contact with Drew over the last three months, questioning him about his witnessing brooms and the Scriptures, then having general "getting-to-know-each-other" type conversations.

It had not been easy, but they had both been determined. They'd met daily after she got off work for a snack and communication, plus every night, Drew called her after Grandma went to bed, and they talked for hours.

She'd asked him for his pastor's name and phone number, figuring she'd give him a call and visit with him. She wanted to make the official decision to get right with God. It probably needed to be done with a pastor. His pastor seemed the logical choice since, well, she didn't want Grandma's pastor to know how much she'd pretended.

Maybe she could do it this week, since she needed to go to Morgantown every afternoon to walk Drew's dog. He was going to a broom makers' event in Arkansas and said something about needing to find someone to take care of Wynter. Sara Jane volunteered for an evening shift. She'd always wanted a pet—and she didn't think Grandma would allow Drew's dog to live with them for a week.

Grandma pursed her lips. "Maybe we could spread the quilt out on the sofa and take a picture."

"We can try." She lifted it from the box and carefully draped it on the sofa.

Grandma sat beside it and beamed.

As Sara Jane lowered the camera, Grandma frowned. "I hate those newfangled cameras. Back in my day, you could take the film into the store and they'd develop it and you'd get pictures you can actually see and enjoy. Now they're stuck on the camera."

"I can print them off." She viewed the picture. It wasn't the best. Maybe she should've waited for the quilt to be hung before she photographed it. She snapped a couple more from different angles. "I'll take another one when it's hung up. It'll probably turn out better."

Grandma folded the quilt. "I need to find someone to hang it." She issued a heavy sigh. "If only Andrew hadn't quit."

Sara Jane sighed. Grandma apparently didn't remember saying the same thing a few moments ago.

"Wait right here." Grandma took off down the hallway, carrying the box.

Sara Jane's phone buzzed. She peeked at it. A text from Drew. *"Leaving 4 AR. Key under lilac bush. LK doing it 2nt."*

Lion King would walk Wynter tonight. "*K. Miss u.*"

"*U 2.*"

She slid the phone into her pocket as Grandma returned to the living room lugging another box. Sara Jane hurried forward. "Let me help."

Grandma relinquished it, then went back down the hall again. "Don't open it. Be right back."

Sara Jane put the box on the dining room table. She heard a thud and a grunt. She started down the hall. Grandma emerged from her room lugging another box.

"Are you moving out?" Sara Jane teased.

Grandma shook her head. "I promised you something. And I had a long talk with Pastor when I was out. I needed to do something else as well."

Stranger and stranger. Sara Jane shifted the box, then set it beside the first. "What's going on?"

"I promised you when we finished the ballad quilt I'd show you the one Sarah Morgan made."

Sara Jane caught her breath. She'd get to see the one Daniel Boone's mama had made? Her ancestor?

Grandma removed the lid and started lifting out quilts. "Your mama made this one. Not a song quilt. Couldn't talk her into it. Figured we did well to get her to do a simple patchwork one."

Sara Jane smiled. Mama made this? She must've inherited her lack of sewing skills from Mama.

Grandma lifted another quilt. "My mama made this one for Cade and me when we married. It's the wedding ring pattern." She set it on the table.

She lifted the bottom quilt out.

"It needs to be restored. Suppose someplace in Morgantown might do it, but this is the one Daniel Boone's mama made."

It was a simple patchwork quilt too, in grays and blues. Nothing fancy. Something even Sara Jane could do. Nothing identifying it as something a historical person might've made except for the *SJM* embroidered on the bottom of one block and an index card attached to it with a straight pin reading *Sarah Jarman Morgan made this.*

Sweet.

Sara Jane could hardly breathe. She reached out a shaky hand and trailed it over a dark blue print. "Wow." Tears burned her eyes. It made Grandma's wild story about being related to Daniel Boone through his mother, and one of his other siblings, more believable.

It was too bad Grandma didn't have her diaries, if she'd kept any. But having a quilt—even if it wasn't museum quality—was enough.

Grandma fingered the wedding ring quilt. "Cade and I never used this. I always wanted to, but . . . thought I'd save it for one of my sons. When they married. Then, I—for whatever reason—never gave it to Nathan."

Sara Jane caught her breath and shot a glance at Grandma. She brought up Daddy? Would she say any more about him? She stiffened, hoping Grandma wouldn't blame her for the loss. After all, she blamed herself enough for it.

"Seems only right I should give it to you and Andrew when you marry." She shoved it into Sara Jane's arms. "Take it."

"But Drew and I aren't marrying . . ." Even if they were getting closer and she dared to dream. The topic hadn't even come up between them.

Why did she bother trying to talk reason to Grandma? She believed what she wanted. And conveniently forgot information.

Sara Jane rubbed her thumb over the quilt. "Thank you."

Grandma pushed the quilt box aside and opened the lid of the other box. It was filled to the top with pictures and photo albums. She pulled out the first one and set a picture of her and Grandpa on the table. Then a picture of Mama and Daddy.

"I was wrong. I shouldn't have hidden the pictures. You needed to see your family. To grieve their loss in your own way instead of with me trying to make you forget they existed. How could you forget? You lost the most important people in your world."

The trembling in Sara Jane's hands increased. She gently laid the quilt on the table and reached for the photo of Mama and Daddy. She pulled it to her chest, tears streaming down her face.

Her phone buzzed again, but she ignored it. She cast a blurry look at Grandma, then turned and ran for the stairs.

And privacy.

Even though it was November, Arkansas was hot and sticky. Drew would be glad to get home to West Virginia. Might still be warm, but . . . there was a distinct difference in the feel. He couldn't explain what.

People walked around in shorts and tank tops. Ansley had packed a bright red string bikini for the hotel pool. "Come on. Go swimming with me." She leaned against his doorframe while he blocked the opening and tried to avoid looking at her. He squirmed in discomfort. "We have an hour before we go to supper."

Drew glanced over his shoulder. He'd wanted to talk to Sara Jane, but she hadn't answered his last call. It'd gone straight to voice mail. Other than a rather cryptic voice mail message several days ago, he hadn't heard from her. Instead they'd played phone tag.

She'd said Grandma missed him and something he couldn't quite make out about quilts and pictures. Then added she would meet with his pastor on Friday. Today.

She hadn't said what time, but since she taught school all day and drove into Morgantown in the evening to walk Wynter, he imagined she'd arranged for a late meeting with Pastor Hannon.

If it was an hour before supper here—then it would be suppertime there. He'd call her later.

Unless she called him first. He'd take his phone to the pool with him. Just in case.

He looked at Ansley. "Sure. I'll get changed and meet you there." He shut the door.

Fifteen minutes later, Drew laid his phone on a poolside table, put the hotel keycard beside it, and dropped his towel on the chair. He slipped off his shoes, headed for the deep end, and dived in.

His eyes widened and his breath left his body in a whoosh. The water was cold. Too cold. He swam to the surface and gasped for air.

Ansley stood on the edge of the pool. "They do have a hot tub." She pointed to the side.

"Is it hot?" His teeth chattered as he swam for the ladder.

"No. Warmer than the melted ice cubes you're in."

He hoisted himself out and followed her to the hot tub.

Ah, heaven. He lowered himself with a sigh.

Ansley sat beside him. Too close.

Maybe she hoped for romance between them. He shook his head and slid away. He wasn't interested. Hadn't been—even when he only knew her as Foxy Lady.

No. He only had eyes for Sara Jane.

He stretched out his legs and closed his eyes. "Wake me when it's time to get ready for dinner."

The sun was beginning to set when Sara Jane left Pastor Hannon's house. She wanted to believe. The pastor made a lot of sense. She'd been tempted to do as he suggested—what she'd planned—and ask the Lord to be her Savior before she left. But one thing stopped her.

Did God *really* care for her?

She didn't want to hike the Appalachian Trail, but it'd be so nice if God would meet her where she was. Some dramatic story of her own, so she would know beyond a shadow of a doubt He existed. He cared, really cared, for her.

Too bad Drew had no recollection of what he'd said on the trail.

Tears burned her eyes.

She'd lose cell service soon, but she wanted to try to touch base with Drew before she did. Hopefully, she'd get him, rather than voice mail this time. She reached for her phone and pushed her speed dial.

The phone rang three times. "Hello?" A woman answered. She blinked. Who was he with?

"Is Drew there? This is Sara Jane."

"He's sleeping. Can I take a message?"

Sleeping! With her? "No. Thanks anyway." She disconnected, her eyes blurring.

Guess Drew wasn't as perfect as he pretended to be. Was he even in Arkansas for a broom-thing? She pressed her lips together to keep from howling her outrage. Her jealousy. The pain.

She threw the cell phone on the seat beside her.

She pushed a disco CD into the player and turned it on loud. *I will survive. . . . I hold my head up high . . .*

She was midway between Morgantown and Bruceton Mills when she noticed a deer jump out ahead of her. She slowed, and it ran safely across the road. She sped up, then a second deer ran in front of her. *Thud.* His head, with a great rack of antlers, came through the window, tangling with the steering wheel. She screamed—unable to see the curvy road, unable to steer.

God, if You're real . . . If You love me . . . Really love me . . . How could she pray?

How could she not?

The pastor's words replayed. "If you were to die tonight, do you know where you'd go?"

No. She didn't. Or maybe she did, if heaven and hell were real. She wanted it to be heaven.

She fought with the steering wheel as the deer thrashed. Would his antlers pierce her arms?

"Oh, God, forgive me!" Her voice echoed around her. The deer stared into her eyes with fear. Pain. An echo of her own emotions at facing the end.

"I'm sorry. So sorry. Please forgive me for all my sins." She struggled to remember the words the pastor had said.

The car left the road and went airborne.

"For by grace are ye saved, through faith and that not of yourselves. It is the gift of God, not of works, lest any man should boast." The pastor's words replayed.

"Please save me. For eternity." Peace washed through her.

The car crashed into a tree.

The world went black.

29

Sari stirred. She'd heard something, but nothing had changed since she dozed off. Sara Jane lay unresponsive in the hospital bed, the machine hooked up to her beeping. The IV dripped into her bruised arm.

Sari pushed to her feet. Her granddaughter looked so pale. She smoothed a lock of hair off Sara Jane's face.

She dug in her purse for Drew's business card. She'd found it in the cookie jar when she reached for one of the shortbread cookies Sara Jane brought home from the grocery store. She picked up the hospital phone, asked for an outside line, and dialed Andrew's number.

"Drew."

Her throat clogged. She started to talk, but instead it came out as a wail. She tried to control herself. "Andrew, this is Grandma. Sari Morgan. Sara Jane is in the hospital, and they don't know if she'll live. She was in a car accident."

There was a moment of silence. "I'm on my way home from Arkansas. I'll come as soon as I get back in town."

"Hurry back." Sari scowled. Arkansas! What on earth was her handyman doing in Arkansas? He might as well be in a foreign country, for all the use he was.

Sari spent the night at the hospital. Alone, except for the nurses popping in and out of the room. If only she hadn't sent her driver home. She didn't want to sit alone when she was about to lose her last relative.

Sometime in the early morning, a man and the nurse strode into the room. The doctor checked over Sara Jane, made some noises to his nurse, and then looked at Sari. "I'm cautiously optimistic."

Whatever it meant.

He turned and strode out, the nurse following before Sari found the strength to demand answers.

A short time later, rattling sounded in the hall and paused outside the door. A white-haired lady came in, carrying a bouquet of pink rosebuds and baby's breath. "Sara Jane Morgan?"

Sari pointed to the bed and the woman placed the clear vase on the rolling table. She patted Sari's shoulder on the way out. She frowned. She didn't want pity. She wanted reassurance Sara Jane would survive.

Sari rose and pulled the card from the plastic fork stuck in with the flowers. A pink heart graced the right corner. "Praying for you. Love, Drew" was printed on the thick paper.

Love, Drew. Love . . .

Quick steps sounded behind her. Sari turned. Andrew stopped beside the bed.

With a sob, she ran around the bed and threw herself in his arms. "You came."

"Of course. I drove all night." He returned her hug then leaned down to brush his finger over Sara Jane's cheek. "How is she?"

"I don't know." Sari couldn't stop the tears. "I don't understand anything they said. Something about a medically induced coma and cautiously optimistic."

Andrew pulled in a long breath. Nodded. "Do you mind if I pray for her?"

Sari mopped her face. "Andrew, I changed my mind. You can marry her."

He glanced at her, his lips pressed together.

Sari sighed. "Please pray for her."

He nodded, pulled up a chair, sat, then grasped Sara Jane's hand and reached for Sari's.

"Dear Heavenly Father . . ."

Seven days later

Sara Jane's head hurt. Annoying beeps filled the air. Her hand shifted—but not because she moved it. She forced her eyes open. Where was she? The light hurt her eyes.

"Sara Jane? How are you feeling?" A woman leaned over her.

Was she kidding? It hurt to breathe, her head throbbed, and tears burned her eyes. "Been . . . better."

"Do you know what happened?"

The question brought back the last images before the world went black. She must be in a hospital. Still alive. Because God saved her. Her own personal private meeting with God, like she'd wanted. Did He have to be so dramatic? Tears sprung to her eyes even as a fresh wave of peace washed over her.

"I hit a deer and a tree. Was anyone injured?" She didn't remember seeing any other cars.

"No. A one-vehicle accident."

"How . . . long have . . . I been . . . here?"

"A week."

A blood pressure cuff on her arm tightened, and the nurse reached for her wrist.

Someone squeezed her other hand. She painfully turned her head. Drew sat beside her, head bowed as if he was praying.

If she could move, she'd run her fingers through his hair. Touch his face. Kiss him.

The blood pressure cuff released. The nurse straightened. "I'll notify the doctor you're awake." She left the room.

Drew raised his head. His brown eyes met hers. She gazed into them, not wanting to look away. He was there . . . with her. . . . A sharp pain in her chest reminded her of the pain she felt on the phone when . . .

Ansley.

It had to be Ansley. Who else could it have been?

She pulled in a pain-filled breath. Jerked her hand from his.

"Go. Away."

"What?"

"Ansley . . . was with . . . you . . . in Arkansas. She said . . . you were . . . sleeping. Sleeping . . . with her." Tears burned her eyes.

He blinked. "You think I . . ."

She turned her head. "Go. Away."

Chair legs scraped the floor.

"Don't. Come. Back."

"Sara Jane, I'll leave. But yes, Ansley was with me. She told me you called. I called back and got voice mail. It must've been right around the time of your accident. Ansley went as a fellow artisan. Not my lover. It's you I love. You. Never has been her."

His words didn't register at first. By the time they clicked, he had disappeared. But she had to try.

He told the truth. She heard it in his voice. Remembered his touches, his kisses. The way he'd apparently stayed by her side the whole week she'd been in the hospital.

"Drew!" Her throat hurt. Her voice didn't reach farther than a whisper. She tried again. A little better. Not much. She pulled in a deep breath and put everything she had into his name. If only she had her cell phone. It probably was still in her car.

A nurse hurried into the room, followed by the doctor.

She shook her head and kept screaming for Drew. The doctor said something, then the nurse left and came back with a new IV bag. Without a word she attached it.

The world faded.

Drew haunted the hospital for the next week Sara Jane remained in there. Grandma kept him updated, and he peeked in on Sara Jane as long as he dared. He didn't want to upset her further by overstaying his welcome.

Grandma and a nurse both told him she asked for him, but . . . He didn't know for sure. Not without hearing it directly from her. She certainly hadn't called.

Now, Sara Jane was home. Back at work even. Fast, in his opinion, but God was a God of miracles.

Drew tugged on the hem of his shirt as he approached the log cabin. Christmas lights sparkled in the window.

Another job for the Morgan women.

He still wasn't ready to face Sara Jane. She should know him better than to automatically assume the worst. She never called to apologize. He hoped she'd be willing to listen. If not today, then someday.

He knocked on the door and shoved his hands in his pockets.

A moment later, the door opened.

Grandma gazed at him, then frowned, staring past him to his truck.

"No. You can't park there. Park at the church down the road and walk back."

He frowned. "What did you need me to do?"

Grandma's lips tightened and she moved her hands to her hips. "I need you to move your truck. Now. Before it's too late."

Drew backed away. Maybe she expected a delivery and needed to be sure the truck could park and unload.

He complied, returning a short while later.

Grandma waited at the door. "Oh, good, you're back. Let me take your coat."

He shrugged it off and handed it to her. She hung it in the coat closet.

"What do you need me to do, Grandma?"

She turned. "Not there." She grabbed his arm and pulled him to the Christmas tree. "Stand here. We'll have a quick practice run. Do you have a ring?"

A ring?

"Never mind. I can tell you don't. *Men!* Never prepared. Wait here." Grandma disappeared down the hall.

Drew frowned. Grandma's erratic behavior must've gotten worse. What exactly had she asked him to do on the phone? She'd scolded him for quitting, mentioned she had odd jobs for him, and . . .

Grandma reappeared. "Okay, here. I know you love her. You came to the hospital every day to check on her." She held out a diamond ring. It glittered in the tree lights. "This belonged to Sara Jane's mama. She'd want her to have it."

"Hold it—" He and Sara Jane were hardly at the proposing stage. Not with this huge disagreement between them.

"Don't argue with me. Down on one knee."

"This is ridiculous. I'm not—"

A car door slammed.

"We're out of time. I hope you have enough intelligence to figure out what to do with it. Put it in your pocket. Nooooow."

Drew obeyed. "Just what do you have planned?"

Grandma smiled. "I need you to hang my ballad quilt. And I have dinner prepared in the kitchen. I won't take no for an answer. You're eating with us."

Right.

"First things first, though. Ballad quilt, dinner, then proposal. Got it?"

"Seriously?"

Grandma glared, spun on one foot, and went to open the door for her granddaughter.

Nothing to do but go along with the ballad quilt and dinner.

A proposal wouldn't be happening. But his heart clenched at the loss of this dream.

If only she believed as he believed. If only she trusted him.

He still didn't know what he could've said or done to make things right.

30

Sara Jane opened the door. Her gaze lit on Drew standing beside the tree. His eyes brightened, then they shuttered. A shadow crossed his jaw. He nodded his greeting, as if he didn't trust himself enough to speak.

She wanted to run to him, throw herself in his arms, and never let him go. But she still moved slowly, painfully, from the accident. She still used a cane for support. And her face still held ugly yellow from the bruising. She hardly wanted him to see her like this.

Not to mention there was her embarrassing behavior. She didn't want witnesses to the inevitable I-was-a-jerk and can-we-still-be-friends conversation.

He wouldn't be here unless Grandma called—because Sara Jane hadn't. Wouldn't have, until she'd been prepared emotionally and healed physically.

It hurt to see him. He'd left—and hadn't come back.

Which was exactly what she'd asked him to do.

He shouldn't have obeyed her.

Grandma's hands went to her hips. "About time you got here. I asked Andrew to come out and hang my ballad quilt. Told him he was staying for dinner. And speaking of which, dinner's ready. If you'll get it on the table, I'll show Andrew where I want the quilt."

Sara Jane put her purse and briefcase on the bottom step and limped toward the kitchen. Grandma had gone all out for supper. Country-fried steak with white gravy, mashed potatoes, and green beans. She'd made a Jell-O cheesecake too.

Muted conversation came from the other room as she placed three plates and silverware on the table. She filled drinking glasses with ice and water. She put the food in serving dishes, and remembered other meals around this table earlier in the summer when they met.

Grandma and Drew entered the room together. His brow furrowed, and he shifted, avoiding her gaze.

No matter. She could give him the silent treatment too. But she didn't want to. She wanted . . . *God, how can I fix this?*

Grandma sat between them and bowed her head. For the first time Sara Jane could remember, Grandma prayed.

As they ate, Grandma talked about her ballad quilt and how nice it looked hung over the sofa.

Sara Jane thought about the Appalachian wall-hanging quilt she made for Drew for Christmas during those three months they talked to each other but hid it from Grandma. She'd helped her with the quilt, never asking Sara Jane why she was making it.

Maybe Grandma was just plain thrilled Sara Jane got a creative idea.

Would she have a chance to give it to him? Or was their relationship too shattered?

She half-listened as Grandma rambled on about odd jobs she wanted to hire Drew to do after Christmas, while Sara Jane picked at her food in silence. She couldn't keep from stealing peeks in his direction. She caught his gaze on her a couple of times. They both looked away shyly.

Grandma ate about half her dinner, took a sip of water, and stood.

"I have an awful headache and need to lie down. Leave me be. I'll eat later."

She left. The bedroom door clicked.

Drew lowered his fork. A muscle ticked in his jaw. "Thanks for dinner. Before I go, though, I'm sorry. I never meant to hurt you. I didn't go *with* Ansley to Arkansas—we both went separately. We stayed in separate rooms."

Sara Jane bit her tongue. So many things she wanted to say. Starting with "I'm sorry." She expelled the words on a breath. "I shouldn't have accused you of having an affair."

"No. You shouldn't have." He held her gaze. "You should've known better. But . . . I forgive you."

"And I forgive you for not visiting me in the hospital after I told you not to."

He frowned. "But I did. Every day. Grandma gave me updates. Seriously, Sara Jane, do you think I'd be able to stay away?"

"You were? You did?" Hope flared in her heart. Tears sprang to her eyes as she recalled the precious words on the flower card hanging on her bathroom mirror. *Love, Drew . . .*

"Every day."

She swallowed. "Please stay long enough to finish your dinner. Grandma will be disappointed." And so would she.

Drew hesitated then lifted his fork.

"I talked to your pastor the day I had the accident." Sara Jane studied her plate.

"And?" Hope lifted his voice.

"He made sense. But it wasn't until I headed home, and the deer was tangled in the steering wheel, that I cried out to God. I was going to die. But like you said, I couldn't without being right with Him. He forgave me. I felt . . . peace." The peace stayed with her. A longing to know more about this God. All her free reading moments were spent studying God. Stalking him, the way she had Drew.

He nodded. "I'm glad." His mouth quirked. "Listen, Sara Jane, I have to be honest—"

"Drew . . . I'm sorry. I never meant to destroy our friendship. I want to be friends again. But I don't know if I can." She swallowed, her face heating. "I love you."

"And I . . ." He stilled. A strange look crossed his face. He rose and shoved his hand into his pocket. "I want to show you something. Come with me."

Sara Jane winced as she stood. He tucked her hand around his elbow and slowly led her from the room.

He stopped where he'd been standing when she came in. In front of the Christmas tree. "Maybe I should've practiced."

She tilted her head.

"I wanted to wait a while. But I can't. I know it hasn't been long, but I've never been more sure of anything." He faced her, pulled in a shuddering breath, then dropped to one knee. "Sara Jane, I . . . I . . ." He wiped his hand over his jaw. He stuffed his hand in his pocket again, then pulled something out and held it up.

A diamond ring? It looked like Mama's. She caught her breath.

"I love you. Will you marry me?" His words rushed out.

She released a strangled cry. "Yes!" Her knees weakened. She'd dreamed of this moment—but never thought it'd happen. Not with Drew.

He slid the ring on her finger as he stood.

A moment later, he pulled her close.

She threw her arms around his neck and met his kiss with abandon.

A chuckle came from behind them. "About time."

Group Discussion Guide

1. In *Swept Away*, Sara Jane plays the blame game. She blames herself for her parents' death. Are there times when you find you blame yourself for things that aren't your fault? How do you move past it?
2. Drew lived out Psalm 40:2 during his thru hike on the Appalachian Trail. Do you have a verse you lived out literally?
3. Grandma Sari was determined to accomplish two things: finish her ballad quilt and marry off Sara Jane. Why do you think those things were so important to her? How do you think the story would have ended if she hadn't accomplished her goals?
4. Drew was estranged from his family at the beginning of the story. He turned away from them during a crisis. How do you handle crisis? Do you turn away from friends and family or to them?
5. Grandma Sari has what looks like the onset of Alzheimer's disease. Have you had to deal with a long-term illness of a loved one? What verses did you lean on to give you strength to make it?
6. Sara Jane goes to church to appease her grandmother, and she has heard the gospel message before in church. Why do you think she was closed to the gospel when Drew initially showed her the witnessing broom? Do you think this is something that is prevalent in churches today: some people attend who don't know the Lord?
7. What is something in your state or area that is a passed-down tradition? In *Swept Away*, we learned it is an Appalachian tradition to make ballad quilts. Discuss traditions for your area. If you don't know what they are, take time to find out.

8. Both Sara Jane and Drew find their way back to God. Do you enjoy stories that add romance to an issue or theme in the book? Why or why not?
9. Sara Jane had a hard time trusting Drew since she believed he had a fling with Ansley. Is trust an issue for you? How do you think people can overcome trust issues?
10. In the story, there is a hiker called X-Amish. This character makes appearance in another book series authored by Laura. Do you like meeting familiar characters in other books? Why or why not?
11. Sara Jane was raised by her grandmother. Have you had to raise your grandchildren because their parents were unable? Or have you taken in foster children to raise? Did you find this hard or easy?

And now for a sneak peak at

Masterpiece Marriage

by Gina Welborn

New from the Quilts of Love Series

1

Spring 1891

In all his thirty-one years, Zenus Dane had never expected to see seven inches of rainfall during a six-hour period.

He trudged through the flooded floor of the textile mill he was able to inspect since the fire marshal had declared it safe. Still, the water reached the third metal clasp of his vulcanized rubber boots, a product he wished he had invented, but was thankful Charles Goodyear did. Although, at the moment, he felt more nauseated than thankful. Through the hole in the roof, the morning sun revealed the full extent of the destruction caused by Friday afternoon's deluge setting a record for one-day rainfall in Philadelphia.

April was the month for deluges. Not May.

His mouth sour over the damage, Zenus looked to his foreman on the other end of the mill. The man didn't have to speak for Zenus to know he shared his grim thoughts.

Zenus stopped at the loom farthest from the collapsed roof. A floral cotton print lay half-woven in the machine. Unlike the bolts of textiles in the storage room, the print was as dry as his gabardine suit. It was also water-stained on the bottom portion of the roll. As he had with the other machines, he examined the loom's frame, the crankshaft, tight-and-loose pulleys, picker stick, shuttle, and race plate. All damp. He knelt. Oxidation here, too, on the bolts where the floodwater reached its highest level. The looms hadn't even had a month of usage, and now rust?

As if his flooded warehouse of raw cotton bales wasn't a torturous enough loss.

A fitting *why God?* moment if there ever was one.

Zenus whipped his newsboy's cap off his head, ran his hands through his hair, then put the cap back on. Living by faith could be hazardous.

With a shake of his head, he released a breath.

No sense bemoaning fate. Count it all joy—it was the only contingency he had. And he *would* count it all joy he'd fallen into this trial, because the testing of his faith was producing patience in him. He didn't consider himself an impatient man. His well-planned schedules allotted time for the unexpected and diversions; they resulted in maximum efficiency. Everything would work out, in time. Optimism: the first necessary ingredient for success. Don't lament the obstacles was the second. A few days were all he needed to solve this setback.

He could—no, he would—do it.

After a slap to the loom beam, Zenus stood.

"Cousin Zenus!"

He looked across the mill's vast floor to the entrance. His ten-year-old goddaughter Aimee stood with her father, waving frantically, while wearing her perpetual smile. The parts of her blue dress not stuck in her rubber boots grazed the surface of the floodwater.

He waved back with a silly expression, knowing it'd make her giggle.

And she did.

"Morning," his cousin Sean Gallagher called out, his voice echoing in the practically empty mill.

Sean said something to the fire marshal then touched Aimee's head. The fire marshal, nodding, motioned Sean to enter. As they did, he resumed pointing to the second-story rafters and speaking to three other firemen, likely, about the hole in the flat roof.

Sean gripped Aimee's hand. He slogged forward with the pants of his gray suit tucked inside his own pair of shin-high galoshes, his arm and Aimee's swinging between them, their legs creating ripples in the water.

"I should've insisted you buy flood insurance," Sean said.

Zenus's lips twitched with amusement. Typical of Sean to cut to the *should've*. "Buying flood insurance wasn't logical. When was the last time this part of Philly flooded?"

Sean gave a yeah-you're-right shrug as he waded through the water.

"I'm sorry about your mill," Aimee said in almost a whisper.

"It'll be all right, sweetheart." He gave her a gentle smile. "Did Noah have flood insurance?"

She shook her head, her dark corkscrew curls swaying.

"Did he survive?"

She nodded.

"Then things will work out for me as well."

"Sometimes your optimism annoys me." Sean stopped with Aimee one loom from where Zenus was. He rubbed the back of his neck as he glanced about the mill, his blue eyes even lighter in the morning sun. "You'll need a new roof before production can resume. Insurance will cover it. Unfortunately, it won't cover damage caused by rising water."

Zenus motioned to the looms around the mill floor. "Is any of this fabric covered by insurance because the damage was caused by the collapsed roof brought on by an act of God, not by flooding?"

"Yes, but" —Sean removed folded papers from his suit coat's inner pocket—"let me see what your policy says."

Zenus blinked, stunned his cousin actually remembered to bring the policy. Details, Sean never forgot. Items—always. If the man ever married again, his wife would have to accept Sean would remember their anniversary, but wouldn't remember to get a gift. Or if he did remember to buy a gift, he would leave it at his law office or in the cab or at the café where he always had a coffee after leaving work.

Good man. Honorable. Just forgetful.

"What isn't excluded," Sean said, "is included, so it's covered. But from what I can tell, none of the fabric on the looms looks damaged."

Aimee ran her hands across the orange-and-brown plaid, one of his new textile designs. "It's not wet."

"Because it dried overnight." Zenus trudged to the loom where Sean and Aimee were. He looked to his cousin. "Even if the textiles don't have stains, I have to declare they were exposed to water and sell them at a drastic discount, which means no profit. I lost all the raw cotton bales in the warehouse too."

Sean repocketed the policy. "You'll get insurance money to help you equal out. Why are you shaking your head?"

Zenus leaned back against the loom. "I have forty-seven bolts in the storage room"—Aimee touched his hand, and his fingers immediately curled around hers—"all damaged or partially damaged by the flooding."

"How much fabric is it?"

"A hundred yards per bolt. Each bolt, fifty-four inches wide."

Sean opened his mouth then paused, clearly thinking, running numbers through his head. "Were those bolts already paid for?"

"Almost all. They were scheduled for cutting and delivery this Monday. Forty-five days of weaving will go to fulfilling those orders." Zenus loosened his tie. "Insurance money will go to repairing the roof and making my loan payment. I have enough left in savings to make payroll for a month."

"Maybe this is God's way of telling you to sell the business and do something different."

Zenus nodded thoughtfully. Maybe this was God at work. He'd go to his grave believing God worked in mysterious ways. He also knew God generally did not cause a field of wheat to grow unless a farmer sowed said grain. Made no sense for God to tell him to expand his business, if God wanted him to sell the business. The loan he took out to buy the looms—to "grow his flock"—could now cause him to lose everything.

He needed guidance. Heavenly guidance. Jesus-inspired guidance.

"Maybe," he answered.

Sean stared at him in shock. "Maybe?"

"I should consider all my options."

"How adventurous of you, Queen Victoria."

Sean's face shared how much he believed Zenus was capable of doing something different. It pricked. Court a mail-order bride. Take out a loan. What else did he need to do to prove to Sean he was open to change? And he *had* changed.

Zenus withdrew his pocket watch, holding it in his palm. "The problem is the MacKenzie brothers' offer was made before rain created a hole in my roof," he said calmly, restraining the twinges of irritation from growing into a roar. "Would be foolish to presume their offer stands as-is."

"Then take a lesser offer and be done with—"

"Boss," his foreman called from the exit doors, "I'll get some millhands to start cleanup here and at the warehouse."

Zenus nodded and hollered back, "I'll lock up." He looked to Sean.

"No. I can't risk my employees losing their jobs. A quarter are unmarried women—" His gaze shifted to Aimee long enough for Sean to understand his silent *with children.*

Sean leaned against the loom, his shoulder slightly touching Zenus's. "All right, Coz, selling isn't an option then. Insurance will help you through a month, maybe two. Then what?"

"You could ask Great-Aunt Priscilla," Aimee cheerfully offered. "She likes helping people."

If his eyes rolled, Zenus would not admit to it. His aunt was the last person he'd go to for aid.

"Thank you for the suggestion, sweetheart." Zenus gave her hand a little squeeze. "But I can't ask her."

"Why not?" she asked.

"I'm not allowed back into her home."

"Until he apologizes," Sean tacked on.

Aimee's confused gaze shifted between them. "For?"

"Being me," Zenus answered.

Sean, to his credit, did not snicker.

Aimee looked at Zenus with some surprise. "I don't understand. What's wrong with you?"

Sean chuckled. "His sentiments exactly."

Zenus quirked a brow. "Flaws, I have, as everyone does, and I can admit—"

"Confession is good for the soul." An unusual edge tinged Sean's words. His gaze never wavered from Zenus, never flickered, never stopped hammering nails right there in the center of Zenus's chest. He couldn't know. Couldn't.

Zenus looked away. Not everything needed to be confessed.

"The problem is," he said to Aimee, "Aunt Priscilla sees flaws that do not exist. She is quite secure in her opinions, thus she and I are at an impasse."

"Impasse?"

"It means when neither person can win," Sean answered. "What about the girl from Boston you've proposed to? Maybe her family could loan—"

"No." Zenus's response sounded a little tight, which betrayed a lot of emotion to anyone who knew him well, and Sean did. Fact was, being emotional about another failed courtship would not do, considering Zenus had not yet formed an attachment to the lady in question. "No," he repeated this time in a lackadaisical tone. "My courtship of Miss Boesch has reached a mutual conclusion."

"You proposed in your last letter." While Sean didn't add a *didn't you*? the implication was clear.

Zenus checked his pocketwatch. He needed to get to the next item on today's agenda. "Yes," he answered, pocketing his watch again. He began the slow walk back through the mid-calf-deep floodwater to the mill's entrance, Aimee clinging to his hand.

Aimee looked over her shoulder. "Papa, can we have ice cream for lunch?"

"Certainly. Your mother would have insisted," Sean said, the water sloshing against his boots as he caught up to them. "I'm confused. The time line doesn't make sense. You mailed the letter on Wednesday, three days ago. Mail doesn't travel overnight even to Boston."

Moments like this were when Zenus wished his cousin was less tenacious. He gave Sean a bored look. "She mailed her proposal acceptance before I mailed my proposal offer."

Sean's frown deepened with his continued confusion. He grabbed Zenus's arm, halting him. "Explain."

"The proposal she accepted was from a Wyoming rancher to be *his* mail-order bride."

"Ouch."

Ouch, indeed.

"Do you mean you aren't getting married?" Aimee asked, brow furrowing.

Zenus shook his head.

"Are you sad?"

He ignored the interest on Sean's face from Aimee's innocent question. Irritation, not sadness, was his more prevailing emotion.

"Things always work for our good." Believing it didn't ease his sour mood. He resumed their trek, the water splashing and rippling, Aimee singing, "Row, row, row your boat."

Five months of courting Miss Boesch through letters. Five months of weekly correspondence. Five months of examining his schedule for the next year and finding the best date for a wedding and honeymoon to Niagara Falls so he wouldn't miss a Thursday Canoe Club meeting or a Friday symphony attendance (both had free nights on the fifth Thursday/Friday of a month), or a Saturday hunting trip (off-season), and he would have been home in time for Sunday morning worship. Five months wasted. Why? Because even when he'd had hours—days even—to plan what to say in his letters, she chose another man over him.

He was cursed to remain a bachelor.

And someone with his qualities and assets shouldn't remain a bachelor. Women should be fighting with each other to marry him. It was a logical and self-possessed—not vain—assessment.

His current financial quandary aside, he was well-to-do; owned his own business, house, two canoes, and a box at the opera house; faithfully attended church, where he taught a Sunday school class for boys; and dutifully gave to charities. Yet upon at least two occasions, he'd overheard women describe him as "a Gothic rogue, so aloof and cold." Even though he and Sean had the same dark-hair-with-blue-eyes coloring—not surprising considering their mothers had been identical twins—Sean always earned a sigh and a "he's *so* charming."

A man's appearance should not define him as a rogue.

Nor should his past forever delineate him as one.

He should count it joy God spared him from the wrong match with Miss Boesch because there was a better-suited woman for him. If only he could find a way to convince the lovely and vivacious Arel Dewey to see him for the charming, devoted man he truly was.

"Too bad you couldn't figure out a way to repurpose the damaged fabric," Sean said, breaking into Zenus's thoughts.

"What?"

His voice raised an octave. "I said it's too bad—"

"No, I heard you." Zenus stopped at the opened double-door entrance and met his cousin's gaze. Repurposing the fabric? He should have thought of it on his own. "I could cut up the fabric to sell as packaged scraps and then I could charge at least the minimum market price. Or . . ." Think. He closed his eyes and pinched the skin between his brows.

Aimee kissed the back of his other hand, then let go. Sloshing. Humming.

There had to be some way he could repurpose the fabric and get a better return.

"I should introduce you to Miss Corcoran," said Sean.

"Uh-huh," Zenus muttered.

What if he added something to the fabric? Like a bonus. The prime buyers of his textiles were women who purchased them at the mercantile, who bought them from the distributor. He needed to become the distributor himself to increase his profits. He needed something to entice his prime buyers to buy small pieces of fabric instead of yard sections.

"You aren't such a bad catch," Sean continued.

"Uh-huh."

With his eyes closed, Zenus could hear the fire marshal yelling to his men to leave. Could smell the dirt in the floodwater. Both distracted him from focusing. Think. Ignore Aimee's humming too. Find something to lure buyers. Who wants fabric even if it's water stained? With a little washing, the fabric would look like new anyway. He needed a woman who would settle—no, who actually desired something less than perfect. A cast-off. Leftover.

". . . my new transcriptionist."

Zenus opened his eyes, absently noted the pirouette Aimee performed with all the grace her mother used to have. "What?"

Sean was grinning. "I said I am going to introduce you to my new transcriptionist."

Aimee didn't stop pirouetting to say, "She's nice."

Zenus kept his grimace internal. The dozen secretaries and transcriptionists Sean had hired in the five years since his wife's death all looked the same: lackluster black hair and unmemorable faces that had forgotten how to smile. "Does she look like your last one?"

"She's not married, knows how to read and write, and is still within childbearing age," Sean said in a most pitying tone, "and it makes her the prime matrimonial catch for you."

Aimee nodded. "And she's nice."

Zenus let out a low growl. "Having Aunt Priscilla fail to matchmake me last Christmas with the niece of her quilting friend was humiliating enough. You were there. You saw how—Wait! This is it." He held his hand up, stilling his cousin from speaking. "Quilters use every textile known to man. They love scraps." He snapped his fingers and pointed at Sean. "They're what I need."

Sean's brow furrowed. "A quilter?"

"Quilters. Plural."

"Trust me, you don't want more than one wife."

"I'm not talking for marriage, Sean. I'm talking about buying my textiles."

"Miss Corcoran doesn't look like the sewing type."

Aimee stopped pirouetting. "What's a sewing type?"

Sean scratched his dark, bristled jawline, having clearly not taken time to shave this morning like Zenus did. He didn't appear to have any more of an idea of what the sewing type looked like than Zenus did, beyond being the female sort and domesticated.

Zenus stepped to the threshold. He patted the top of Aimee's head, murmured, "Keep dancing, sweetheart," and then reached in his suit pocket for his set of keys. "Sean, I need you to hire a couple of guards today to watch over the mill during the night, while I go arrange for the roof repair." He withdrew the keys, finding the one for the lock. "Offer a week's pay, although I doubt I'll need them so long. Hopefully when I return, the mill can resume operations."

"Return from where?"

"Belle Haven. I'm leaving early Monday morning. Return Wednesday."

"Why not leave today?" True to lawyer form, Sean focused on the least significant detail in what Zenus had said.

"Why doesn't matter." Zenus snapped.

"I think it does." A knowing smirk on his face—

With a growl under his breath, Zenus grabbed the left door's iron handle and drew it closed.

Sean let out a bark of laughter. "Church is tomorrow, and you don't want to lose out on another perfect attendance pin. Aren't eight enough?"

Zenus gritted his teeth. "It's not about the pin." He drew the right door closed then threaded the chain through the handles. "As a Sunday school teacher, my responsibility is to model faithfulness to those boys."

"You have a point there."

For as many years as they'd known each other, Zenus couldn't consistently tell when his cousin was being sarcastic or not. It was disturbing.

Zenus knelt down and kissed Aimee's cheek. "See you tomorrow, sunshine."

Her curly hair and bubbly effervescence were all her mother's. Aimee should have been his daughter, not Sean's. Clara Reade should have been his wife, not Sean's.

She kissed him back. "I love you, Cousin Zenus."

"I love you too."

Sean held out his hand and Aimee took it. "So you are actually going to your Aunt Priscilla for help?" was what he asked. Unstated was *Have you forgotten what she said to you last Christmas?* and *I'm glad I have no blood relation to her.*

Zenus stood and gripped the iron lock, cold against his palm. He hadn't forgotten. In fact, what Aunt Priscilla had said spurred him into deciding to stop playing life safe. The next day he'd filled out a loan application and begun the courtship of Miss Boesch, the niece of a deacon in his church. He'd been determined to disprove Aunt Priscilla's assessment of him and his apathetic (pathetic, according to her) approach to finding a wife. His first two risk-taking attempts both ended in setbacks, which he wouldn't bemoan. Every failure brought him one attempt closer to success.

Despite his optimism, Zenus did nothing more than nod his response to Sean. The thought of having to grovel before his aunt soured his mouth, churned his stomach, and warmed his cheeks with embarrassment. Her last lecture included "mule," "pig-headed," and "scaredy-cat." Nothing like being viewed by a woman as a barnyard animal.

But she was his best hope. No one knew quilts like Priscilla Dane Osbourne.

No quilter had national name recognition like her either.

To save his business, home, livelihood, and future, all he had to do was the impossible: convince a fiercely protective quilter to give him one of her precious patterns. This was one wooing at which he could not—would not—fail.

Want to learn more about authors
Laura and Cindy?
Want to know more about out other great
fiction from Abingdon Press?

Sign up for our fiction newsletter at
www.abingdonfiction.com
to read interviews with your favorite authors, find tips
for starting a reading group, and stay posted on what
new titles are on the horizon. It's a place to connect
with other fiction readers or post a comment about this book.

Be sure to visit Laura and Cindy online!

http://lauravhilton.blogspot.com/
http://cindylovenwrites.blogspot.com/